LIVING THE FALL

Patrick G. Heaney

tapiola
publishing

tapiola
publishing

2697 1½ Street
Cumberland, WI 54829
tapiolapublishing.com

Manufactured in the United States of America

ISBN 0-9768635-0-2

To my mother, Mary B. Heaney

Acknowledgments

This story would never have seen publication without the assistance and support of many people. I would like to acknowledge Joseph and Mary Heaney, Kristina Zengaffinen, Sharon Miller, Scott Edelstein, Peter Doughty and Kevin Theese for all their hard work and advise. You made this possible. Thank you.

Patrick G. Heaney

Show me a story about the end of the world.

All right, how about I tell you a story about the end of the world. How about I tell you what is worth knowing and teach how to live the hero's path. Only then will you understand.

Will you not tell of the pestilence, plagues, disasters and judgment that will befall our world?

No. I will show you the intention of such things. I will show what must befall your soul. For in your end is your beginning.

Chapter 1
A Seed Planted

The two cities, with unlimited optimism, were marching eastward, westward and expanding in all directions from their twin epicenters. People below scurried about and conducted their daily business, writing new chapters in their full lives. The freeways teemed, yet the traffic continued to crawl forward. EPA approved emissions drifted effortlessly from cool-gray power plant smokestacks toward the heavens. For the most part, all of those individuals in that great metropolis were content on this early June morning. At least that was the impression.

In the office spaces, faxes and e-mails arrived promptly. Devoted employees logged onto their computers while sipping coffee, or, perhaps, they had the pleasure of sitting through another corporate workshop. At the shopping complexes, urgent mothers in newly waxed mini-vans and SUVs decorated with soccer league stickers vied for parking space. That entire complex hummed as one organism, expanding and creating. It was the necessity of growth. And each person played a part in the social machine. They may have been unaware of their roles, but they played them nonetheless.

The Twin Cities of Minnesota were not the most prominent metro area in the popular American consciousness. Rarely did a movie take place there, more rare for a Thursday night sitcom to feature its environs. Yet, in most respects, the Twin Cites were the same as New York, Los Angeles or any other American metropolis. The skyscrapers were positioned in the twin centers of the organism, the great centers of economic activity and entertainment vitality. The ever-expanding suburbs, enclaves of well-fed, upper-middle class families, neatly maintained churches, chain stores and golf course-like lawns, sat on the ring.

Into this environment stepped a thirteen-year-old boy, slowly walking down the bleached-white concrete steps of his parent's home in the Maple Grove suburb of Minneapolis, which, along with St. Paul, constituted the "twins" of the greater Twin Cities Metropolitan area. A green Dodge Caravan idled on the wide, clean street, and a spindly, newly planted tree stood in front of each 2500-square-foot vinyl-sided home. The distinct clicking sounds of water sprinklers filled the air while homeowners hopped into vehicles and sped away to careers, sometimes casting glances toward their neighbor's property.

Carol and Robert Norris sat together in the Caravan as they called out simultaneously to their son, James. The June sun startled young James as he closed the locked house door behind him and sauntered onto the lawn. His head drifted down and his steps slowed, as if a great chain was dragging him against his will. The last hour had been spent playing Nintendo, and he had been absorbed in his new game of Tomb Raider, one of the more popular video games as of late due to its sexual marketing. His eyes were bloodshot and glazed over from staring at the TV screen, and he squinted in the morning sun.

Every year James' father dragged the family along on his yearly ritual to visit his brother, Kevin. Kevin lived just south of the mixed hardwood and pine expanse in northern Wisconsin known as the Chequamegon National Forest. The closest town was a little village called Loretta, fifteen miles to the south.

"Hurry up now, James," shouted Robert, who impatiently stood in the mini van with one foot on the floorboard and another on the street. "We gotta move, pal."

As the last rays of light disappeared in the west beyond the mat of evergreen tops, the world was ushered into a void of darkness. The dark has always been that mysterious enemy of man, keeper and protector of the unseen and the unexplained. Even in these most modern of times, its very presence conjures up the fear of what may lay beyond the flickering flames of man's fires. James stared out the window as the van neared Kevin's home. The isolation of his uncle's existence jolted him. He had been here before but had never really noted the change in the land during the four-hour ride. The loneliness seemed more tangible this time.

The van passed a small farm on the west side of the road ten minutes out of Loretta. It was a dairy, and this evening, in the creeping darkness, a few Holsteins made a slow march toward the barn across an isolated field cut into the surrounding forest. Robert took a right on a narrow, gravel road one-half mile past the farm. The road was lined with dense oak and maple. They seemed to press in on the van and pull it further into the darkness. In this place the van seemed to be a foreign abstraction, an intruder in the solitude. The drive wound on through the gloom for almost two miles over hills and across a small stream before it banked sharply to the left and terminated in the front yard of Kevin's home, a log cabin.

What kind of a screwball would want to live here? thought James. He slumped out of the van just as a tall figure stepped away from the front door and stood on a well-worn deck.

"You're late as usual, Robert," was Kevin's greeting as he walked back inside.

"I am glad to see you too," replied Bob, rubbing his eyes.

A short dirt path led them to the cabin. The entire first floor was one big room, except for a small bedroom and a simple, unkempt bathroom to the left of the front door. To the right of the front door was the sparse living room with stone fireplace and kitchen at the far end. The floor was hard maple. A rugged spiral staircase led from the first floor up to a loft. Under the loft a traditional staircase cut through the floor to an unfinished basement. The ceiling rose high and peaked, and large windows faced north toward a lake. Below the windows two sliding glass doors opened out to the gray, weathered deck, which wrapped around three sides of the house.

"So I assume your drive went fine?" asked Kevin.

Robert shot a glance back at him. "Whatever," he sighed. "Do you honestly think the roads were fine on a Friday afternoon? Everybody and his brother were leaving the Cities and heading north."

"Well, if they just stayed out here like me they wouldn't have that problem, now would they?" remarked Kevin.

Robert smiled back and commented, "Ahh ... maybe a job would help in that regard, Kev."

Carol enjoyed a reserved laugh as she and Kevin exchanged a curt greeting.

"So, Kevin, did you have a good year with the maple syrup?" asked Robert. "I hope you have some left for us to bring home."

"Well, would you really expect anything less from me! It was the best year I have seen in a while with the early spring and all, got ten gallons. I guess these short winters we've been having have not been all bad. Heck, the sap started running in February. Pretty strange."

James sat down in a rocking chair that creaked, the way a rocking chair should and studied the atmosphere of the cabin. The walls were real yellowed pine logs, not imitation half-log siding like some homes. Deer racks adorned the walls along with the one musky Kevin felt worthy to keep and display. Above the fireplace hung a crucifix. James glanced at it. *Funny, didn't think Kevin was superstitious.*

"I suppose you're all tired," said Kevin, "I know I am. Bob, why don't you and Carol take the bed in the basement. James, you can have the loft."

Great, James thought, *the loft.* It was a place he knew well. The loft contained a skylight that faced east and magnified the morning sun so the place heated up like a sauna. It was not conducive to sleeping late. *Whatever Kevin sees in this dump is beyond me. I got better things to do on my summer vacation. The world is more than this.*

* * *

It was day three of the visit. The batteries were dead in James' pocket Nintendo, and he was sick of listening to the same old Nirvana and Pearl Jam CDs. It was a sunny day, and the clock above Kevin's gas stove flashed 1:30. Carol was out for a walk, and Kevin and Robert were fishing on a nearby lake. James couldn't take being cooped up in the cabin any longer. He had to go outside.

The thirty-acre lake in front of Kevin's, shown on maps as Mud Lake, was calm this day. Despite the unseemly name, its waters were spring fed and crystal clear. In fact, one could see whatever lurked under the waves down to ten feet. Kevin's house was the only cabin and private land on it. The rest of the bordering land encompassed the public domain of the Chequamegon National Forest. James moped around under the swaying jack pines and red oaks that made up Kevin's naturally kept yard, but the question of how to spend the rest of his day lingered in his mind. Usually his friends, the Twin Cities and even the larger culture handed him something to do. Here he was forced to think up something to do on his own, and this problem perplexed him. In the end he followed his mom's example and went for a walk.

To the west of Kevin's cabin was a neat row of red pine trees. James followed a worn footpath through the plantation out to a fenced clearing of clover and grass. From here James knew he could walk basically any direction and not venture onto any private land besides Kevin's. Kevin had four-wheeler trails running through his 200 acres of woods that would make navigation easy and fire lanes cut through the public land of the adjacent national forest.

On the far end of the clearing a rutted trail cut through a dense forest of birch and poplar trees. James followed the trail and felt the air grow cooler as he entered the woods. The sunlight became more reserved as well. Soon dark, gnarled oaks and maples mingled together with their lighter barked cousins.

He came to a deep ravine where a pleasant brook, emanating from Mud Lake, gently carved a snaking path through the tranquil forest. Being careful to watch his footing, James slid down the steep walls of the ravine to the brook's bank. Here Kevin had constructed a makeshift bridge out of old railroad ties, and James quickly made his way across. He arrived at the other side and looked back into the water. For a few seconds he lost himself. The place seemed special, as if it held a destiny all its own. He shrugged it off and continued on his way.

James followed the trail westward and then northward through Kevin's woods, never allowing the waters of Mud to disappear completely from view. He soon arrived at a spot in the woods where the trail seemed to end and the mat of leaves that made up the forest floor was disturbed. Looking down at the ground, he noticed the area was a regular crossroads of deer trails. They ran off in all directions like the spokes of a hub. *Wonder where these lead?*

James picked the path that seemed to be used the most and would be the easiest to follow. It headed straight north. Keeping his eyes fixed on the ground, he followed the path with interest, taking note of the scrapes on the ground where the animals had scrounged for acorns. Overhead, crows made their normal ruckus, alerting the forest to the presence of an intruder. James knew little about forest animals, but he was amazed at the abundance of animal sign, activity and life in the woods. Meanwhile the lake had disappeared behind the trees.

After some time, James hit a fire lane, which cut straight through the heart of the forest. He followed it in the direction he thought was east until he hit yet another well-worn deer path running towards where Mud

Lake should be. James veered off on that trail, hoping to catch up with a deer and see a glimpse of a tail or antler. Lost in James' journey was his sense of time. He saw no deer that afternoon, only an endless expanse of pine, maple and oak. Soon the sun began to burn orange in the west and still no lake appeared.

Where am I? worried James as the air grew cold and the twilight advanced. He stopped walking and tried to collect his bearings, but the oaks, maples and poplars appeared as foreign as another world. He ran a few paces back in the direction he came and once again scanned the surroundings. All was unrecognizable. Then his pulse and breathing began to quicken. He started to run as fast as he could into the enclosing gloom, madly searching for a familiar tree, log or rock. However, in the gathering shadows he failed to notice the deep gully lurking ahead. He reached the steep embankment and tumbled sideways down to the bottom.

For a second he lay at the bottom of the ravine and gazed skyward, momentarily unaware of the pain in his ankle, which he had just sprained badly. He reflexively kicked his legs wildly, making sure he was not paralyzed. *God,* he thought, *Where did that come from?* Lying on the dampened earth, he saw the first stars and planets of nightfall twinkling in the blue-black sky. Back in the Twin Cities they looked so benign, so quaint, like the woods he had been walking in this afternoon. But now in the darkness their glitter seemed ominous. Once again Nature had done her incredible switch. In an instant she had torn off her playful, innocent mask and threatened very life and limb. She was no longer controlled.

He clenched his teeth and pulled himself out of the gully with the aid of maple and oak saplings. Once out on flat land again he took a few deep breaths and limped forward into the night. A horde of mosquitoes followed. Soon, however, James saw a distinct break in the forest ahead. For a brief second he thought it was Kevin's. Yet his hopes were short lived. This place looked nothing like his uncle's.

Cautiously, James entered the tiny clearing of wet, knee high grass. His only companion was the ghostly whisper of the night wind.

It had such a distinctive, signature sound when it rustled the tops of the surrounding trees. On the opposite side of the field the blue moonlight spotlighted a stand of incredibly tall old-growth white pines not too far from the threshold of the clearing. The tops of the pines appeared as gloomy shadows cast against the dying light in the early summer sky. In front of the white pines was a dense grove of black spruce trees. The spruce were limbless up to about five feet. However, the boughs from that point up grew so thick and so long they reached from one tree to the next, giving the impression of a tunnel leading into a hidden, darkened world. A thin wispy veil of fog hung where the spruce met the clearing.

An unknown sensation crept over James. Whether it was fear or longing or curiosity, he could not tell. It seemed to be all these. And he found himself standing stone-like in the middle of the clearing staring at this most unusual of groves. The place seemed to be inviting him as if he knew it well and had been there before. *It could be a nice place to rest and wait for the inevitable rescue team. Maybe I should walk in?*

Slowly, James approached the threshold of the dense wood. He placed his hand on one of the spruce boughs and attempted to peer into the world beyond. Whatever lurked in the shadows was indiscernible beyond a few feet; all was clothed in darkness. He walked further, one small step at a time, stooping down to sneak under the fanning limbs. Some of the spruce needles had fallen to the forest floor and created a soft green conifer blanket that muffled his footsteps.

Silence enveloped the unknown domain, broken occasionally by the gusts of wind that ruffled the branches of the ancient behemoths before him. The full moon, which James had scarcely noticed up to now, provided some light, but further into the grove the spruce were so dense its meager glow could not hope to penetrate their shield. All sounds of the outside world faded away. *What is this place?* James thought, forgetting the pain in his ankle. *Have I been here before?*

After ten yards the spruce began to thin out, and the tunnel opened into a forest with little undergrowth where the ancient white pines towered toward the heavens. Fine, powdery dirt and scattered pine needles covered the ground. James sat down and nestled his back against a fire-scarred trunk and looked up at the night sky and swaying treetops. The white pines were knotted, giant beasts, and James couldn't even hope to lock his arms around them. Greenish blister rust covered many of them, strangely growing on the same side of each infected tree. The pines were ambassadors from an age lost to modern man. Now they supported James with his twisted ankle and tired feet.

Little by little a sense of belonging crept over James. He closed his eyes and searched his memory. *When have I been here?* Overhead, clouds now obscured the moon, shepherding the ancient grove into the most oppressive darkness James had ever experienced. All sensory input disappeared temporarily, except for the sound of James' heart and rhythmic breathing. The world slowed down; directions lost their significance. James, the boy, had seemingly been swallowed by the forest herself.

The call started faintly and far off at first, as if coming out of the inner recesses of the darkened woods. But soon the sound grew louder, building on itself with a crescendo more powerful with each passing second. It pierced the soul of a lost boy and all living things in between. A moment later, others joined the solo call and the night was alive. Even an urbanized youth like James knew the sound. It was an unmistakable low guttural wail that drifted effortlessly across the blackened landscape. It was the sound that could only come from wolves, embodiments of Nature herself, persecuted by some, worshiped by others, but always holding a profound effect over the mind of man.

James knew the wolves were no danger to him. His biology teacher this past school year had pounded that fact into him a million times. Mr. Higgins looked like an aging hippie with a ponytail and unshaven face. He would walk into class and spout off clichéd sayings like, "Only a mountain has listened long enough to know the song of the wolf." His desk was covered with stickers of the planet earth emblazoned with the words "Love your Mother," and he drove a Chevy Metro that got sixty miles to the gallon. *He had the whole tree hugger thing down pat, even down to his warnings about the coming disaster of supposed global warming and melting glaciers.*

As the howls continued, they seemed to draw nearer and become more intense. James shifted his weight against the tree and then tried to sit perfectly still. Suddenly, thinking he heard a noise, he jumped up and turned around to face the dark. He tried to sit down again but instead found himself looking in all directions. *This is ridiculous. Wolves don't kill people.*

However, something about the wolf cries and their haunting sounds resonated in the core of James' heart, stripping away all pretenses of rationality and destroying all preconceptions placed on him by modernity. Despite his reason, education and all he had been told to believe, he was now talking to himself, turning his head frantically, while straining to catch the approach of the fanged killers. Instinctively, he grabbed a fallen branch and hefted it in his hands like a club. But he was losing the battle of control. His breath came in fits and starts. *Go ... go ...*

James used the branch as a makeshift crutch and hobbled frantically out of the grove. The howling continued, and as James ran faster and faster, he began to pant and sweat. He entered the clearing and charged off to the right, not knowing exactly where he was going.

This time, however, he got it right. He stumbled out upon a paved road in an awkward, disabled sprint, and ran down its center without stopping to view his surroundings. Now he was gasping for air as if he had just finished one of the dreaded mile runs in gym class. His body could take it no more. Slowing down to a trot and then a walk, James placed his hands on his hips and struggled to catch his breath. Sweat poured down his face and his clothes were soaked as well. Then he suddenly stopped walking altogether and stood still in the middle of the road.

The howls were gone, replaced by the mundane racket of crickets and dull hum of mosquitoes. The pain in James' ankle had worsened, but he sucked it up and started walking again while trying to collect his thoughts. He was still shaking a little but no longer looking over his shoulder as he began to heap humiliation on himself for being so afraid. *I can't tell anybody about this. God, this trip sucks. I should be out with my friends right now enjoying my summer.*

James continued to hobble on, hoping a car would soon pass. Suddenly, however, he came upon a driveway on the left hand side of the road. For a second he thought it was Kevin's road. His hopes were soon dashed when he noticed there was no farm nearby. *What to do now? Perhaps there was an occupied home at the end, or maybe I should just continue to walk down the road? No. That is not an option. My ankle is killing me. Besides, maybe I'll end up walking in the wrong direction. God, Mom and Dad are probably worried sick. Hopefully there is someone down here.*

His favorite baggy jeans and Nirvana tee shirt were caked in mud with a few drops of blood, and with his limp he certainly didn't look like the kind of person a stranger would welcome on a dark night. The driveway wasn't that long, and as James walked the slender, gravel path, he could discern a faint light emanating from some point in the distance. It shone through a window and appeared to be an oil lamp, but it was a light nonetheless, and lifted James' spirit. Here was the welcoming abstraction of light, a beacon for the fearful, steadfastly leading him out of the naturally darkened dominion of the woods. He felt like he was being welcomed home.

The light came from a window in a tiny A-frame house, more like a shack, made of rough cedar siding. A floor jack positioned where the driver's tire should be held up a rusty Ford truck in front of a one-car garage adjacent to the house, and thin trails of smoke drifted skyward from a small rock chimney sticking through the shingled roof. A short stringer of crooked steps led up to the porch and front door of the house. The front door was conspicuously missing a screen partner.

Warily, James approached, always eyeing the window where the lamp continued to glow. However, he neither saw nor heard any other signs of life. He reached the steps and gingerly placed his right foot on the lowest one, causing it to creak loudly. *Perhaps nobody is—*

All of a sudden, without warning, the front door swung open and a large, human figure stepped out into the shadows. Even in the dim light James could see the shotgun in his hand.

"Who the hell is there," bellowed the figure.

Aghast, James tripped on the step, nearly falling. "Please, please, I am lost," he stammered.

The figure turned to look down at him and raised the gun halfway to its shoulder.

"My uncle is Kevin Norris," James continued. "I was out walking and my directions got messed up. I turned my ankle pretty bad." He pointed down at the ground for effect.

The figure stepped back and turned on one of the cabin's interior lights. "So, you're Kevin's nephew, huh?" the figure said in a reserved yet friendly voice.

"Yes, my name is James, James Norris," James said as he stepped closer.

"Well, in that case, go on in," said the figure as he took a step outside and invited James in with a broad sweep of his right hand.

The man eyed James as he hobbled inside. "Looks like a nasty sprain you got there, guy."

"Walking on it made it worse," said James as the man carefully placed the shotgun against a chair and flicked on another light, illuminating the entire interior of the cabin.

James blinked his eyes to adjust them to the light, and after a few seconds he was able to view his surroundings. The place was even more rustic than Kevin's. Dusty pieces of non-matching furniture lay scattered about and a small fire burned pathetically in the meager fireplace. Like Kevin's, deer antlers adorned the walls, except this person owned several more. A pot bellied stove stood idle in the corner. *This place is straight out of the 1800s. Who is this person?*

At last James' gaze rested on the tall man who had greeted him at the door. The man's large, brown eyes were somewhat sunken into his head, highlighted by high cheekbones. His face was weathered from the ravages of time and beaten hard. He looked to be sixty or seventy years old, but his body was very robust. A red flannel shirt covered his barrel chest, and his long, gray hair fell unkempt over wrinkled ears.

"My name is Shawn," the man said extending his hand. "I know Kevin quite well. He is going to razz you something fierce for this, but right now he is probably worried to death."

"Yes, my parents probably are too," replied James. "We're up visiting him."

"Where are you from?" asked Shawn.

"Maple Grove, the Cities."

"There is one place I wouldn't want to go. Those drivers are just nuts."

James smiled knowingly. "Maybe I should call Kevin's. My parents could come and get me."

Shawn took a deep breath and walked a few paces toward a sink. Then he turned to look at James. "I am sorry, James," he replied. "I don't have a phone, and, unfortunately, as you may have seen, my truck is out of commission. I am in the process of repacking the hubs and rotating the tires. I should be able to get it fixed by tomorrow morning. Then I will run you home. But, for right now, you are welcome to spend the night."

"How far is Kevin's?" asked James.

"Almost three miles," answered Shawn.

Great. Three miles from my worried parents and Grizzly Adams here has a broken truck and no phone.

Shawn grabbed a dirty plate and tossed a few pieces of meat and potato on it before offering it to James. James studied the meat intently.

"That is venison there, James," Shawn replied.

James looked confused.

"Venison would be deer meat, James," he said.

James wasn't really fond of wild game or the process that created it. The thought of someone killing and skinning out a deer in less-than-clean surroundings turned him off. But under the circumstances he couldn't argue. He accepted the food and offered a semi-sincere "thank you."

Shawn then filled a large bowl with cold water. He handed it to James along with a towel. "You better soak your ankle in here a while," he said. "That well water should be pretty cold. It'll help with the swelling. I am going to scrounge up some blankets and a cot."

James took off his Nike shoes and sat down in a rickety wooden chair. He gingerly placed his right foot in the cold water. Shawn was wrestling around in one of the overflowing closets when he called over to James. "How did you get so turned around? Did you enter the National Forest?"

James was embarrassed a little for getting lost but more so from being afraid of the wolves. "You know, to tell you the truth," James answered, "I am not really sure what happened. I was going to walk around Kevin's lake but got to following some deer paths until it got dark out. I turned my ankle and rested in a grove of pine trees until I heard the wolves howl."

"Wolves?" answered Shawn snapping to attention and cracking a smile, "they were rather active tonight were they not? You weren't afraid of them now, were you?"

James shot out a quick, "No!"

Shawn grinned, revealing shabby, neglected teeth. With an aborted yawn, he tossed James a few green blankets from the closet and made his way over to a couch next to the unused potbellied stove. A comfortable silence fell over the room, and the water soaking James' ankle began to warm. He was beginning to feel relaxed and somewhat content. Looking around the cabin again, he noticed Shawn did not care much for appearances. Assorted outdoor equipment such as snowshoes and leg-hold traps lay scattered haphazardly throughout the house, and Shawn's dirty dishes from his evening meals were piled high next to the sink. A small bed lay unmade in a corner.

Shawn reached up behind him and shut off the electric lights. Now only the eerie glow from the fire and the oil lamp fell over the one room shack. It wasn't completely dark, but it caused James to relax even more. Shawn then took out a pipe and packed it with apple tobacco very deliberately. Looking satisfied, he lit a match and the sweet, distinct smell wafted through the room. He squinted his eyes as if in deep thought.

"Well, that's good that you weren't afraid of the wolves because it's nice to have them back in this area after so many years," said Shawn finally.

He seemed to be recalling memories and speaking very thoughtfully, smoke being the catalyst. "The wolf is a wonderful creature," he continued. "I believe that the wolf coming back to this area foreshadows a day when man and nature can live together. Perhaps a new world, a new synthesis, between nature and man is taking place."

The old man's low, solemn words reverberated off the house's walls, and his wise eyes bore right through his young guest. James just sat there confused, staring at his soaking ankle, the words barely registering in his head. *That is all so cliché. He's probably going to light up a bowl and start talking about how everything is one and we need to get on to a higher plain.*

James' gaze shifted to a painting Shawn had on the wall depicting a lone timber wolf against a backdrop of mountains with its nose to the wind in a snowstorm. Shawn caught his stare.

"I like that picture too," he said, setting his pipe down. "The wolf is my favorite animal. It is so enigmatic, so powerful and predatory, yet it is socially similar to us humans. There are some that are solitary, mainly young outcasts finding their way, but most form groups and work together to survive."

Shawn puffed a cloud of smoke from his pipe and ran his hands through his unkempt gray hair. "I am no biologist myself, James," he said, "but the mythology and folklore of the wolf really fascinate me. Do you know that in Paleolithic times wolves used to follow the hunting bands of humans and wait in the shadows around campfires for scraps of leftover meat? But when agriculture was introduced, the wolf became a dangerous predator of domestic livestock instead of a revered companion. The danger was equated with evil when Christianity arrived, for the wolf would prey upon man's sheep, the symbols of God's children. Soon the wolf was thought to be the Devil incarnate."

Shawn closed his eyes, exhaling more smoke, drawing his words out slowly. "Thus, the wolves were persecuted and the wilderness that is their home subdued and conquered. However, not all cultures or traditions view the wolf in the same way. Native American traditions often view the wolf as a friend or teacher. Some Indian myths even say man and wolf have the same eyes."

Why is he telling me this? Guy must be lonely. From the looks of this place he doesn't get a lot of visitors.

"You know, James," Shawn continued, "there is an Ojibway creation myth where the wolf is said to be man's brother." Shawn paused for a second to pack another bowl of apple tobacco. He struck a kitchen match, lit the pipe and fixed his eyes upon the smoldering embers in the fireplace as the smoke curled about him. He inhaled deeply before speaking.

"It is said that Original Man and Wolf walked the earth at the beginning of time and came to know all of her. In this journey they became very close to each other. They became like brothers, and in their closeness they realized that they were all part of the same creation."

Shawn broke his gaze and leaned toward his young companion, his face alive with conviction. "Then one day the Creator said to Man and Wolf, 'You are to separate your paths, for you must go different ways and what happens to one will also happen to the other. Each of you will be feared, respected and misunderstood by the people that will later join you on this earth.'"

"Is that not the truth?" asked Shawn.

James failed to answer, trying to comprehend the meaning.

"Man went the way of the civilizations and its man-made abstractions. He tried recreating the world in his own image, thus separating himself from nature while the wolf stayed true to her purity. But we are still brothers with the wolf. Like I said, maybe the wolves' return to this area signifies the coming of a day when we can walk with our lost brother again. Maybe the circle will be made complete."

Shawn turned to face the fire once again as the flames reflected in his eyes. A small open-faced clock chimed, signaling midnight, and James yawned. However, he knew Shawn had much more to say. Shawn's eyes, his whole being in fact, radiated a quiet intensity and revealed the soul of a master storyteller. He was a keeper of a lost art and able to weave magic secrets with only his tongue. His ability to arouse even a little interest in a boy accustomed to more staccato stimulation was extraordinary.

"James," Shawn said, "the wolf takes on all sorts of personalities and characteristics among the many myths and stories of the world's peoples."

"You mean like Little Red Riding Hood, Three Little—"

"Yes," Shaun interrupted, almost jumping off the couch. "Those are the childhood stories everyone hears about the evil wolf at the door. But the wolf can be a joker, a trickster, a teacher, a fool, a killer or a destroyer depending on the myth or folklore in question."

The old man's eyes grew bright and animated, and he shook his head from side to side. "Such a wondrous animal," he said almost to himself as he set his pipe down. "James, to contrast the story of wolf as man's brother at the beginning of the world, I will tell you the story of Fenris, a wolf in Norse mythology, and his role at the end.

Fenris was the illegitimate offspring of the trickster god, Loki. He was monstrous in size and incredibly fierce. The only god he trusted was the god of War, Tier, who fed him daily. However, the other gods and goddesses saw Fenris was becoming unruly, and they decided he must be restrained. An ordinary rope or chain could never hope to contain him. So they made a magic rope as thin as a strand of a spider's web, fabricated from all the unseen mysteries of the earth like the roots of mountains the sounds of fish breathing and the noise cats make when they walk However, Fenris would not be bound unless one god placed his hand in his mouth. His friend Tier was the only one to sacrifice himself, and in Norse mythology he is often depicted with only one hand."

James found Shawn's intensity frightening, yet strangely compelling. For the first time he was witnessing the ferocity of feeling that comes when one believes a story to be not merely entertainment but truth. Shawn leaned close to James, the dancing light from a mysteriously revitalized fire illuminating his face with a hellish glow. Only after several seconds did he continue. He spoke softly now, almost in hushed tones.

"So Fenris was bound ... or so they thought. But all things must end, James, and it is told that at the final battle between the gods and the forces of evil, Ragnorak, Fenris will rise again. First will come a terrible winter called Fimbulvetr. Snow will drive from all quarters. The sun will be of no use. Great wars, floods and famines will ravage the land, and brothers will kill each other for gain."

"The end of the world?" asked James.

"The end of this world," answered Shawn before continuing, now with more passion.

"The whole surface of the earth will tremble and mountains will crash down. All fetters and bonds will be snapped and severed. Fenris will break free. He will advance on the home of the gods with wide-open mouth, his upper jaw against the sky, his lower jaw on the earth. His mouth would gape even wider if there were more room, and his eyes and nostrils will blaze with fire. The gods will be destroyed in this final battle while two other terrible wolves, Skoll and Hati, will swallow the sun and moon. Then the sky will turn black, and the earth will sink into the sea. The bright stars will vanish from the heavens, steam will rise up from the conflagration and a high flame will play against heaven itself."

Shawn's arms were now high above his head. His voice boomed

into the night and seemed to shake the entire shack. Then, as if suddenly self-conscious, he quickly dropped them to his side and turned his gaze back toward the hissing and popping of the fire.

"But a new world will arise, James, arise from the ashes of the old. The new world will be fair, eternally green. The sun will have borne a daughter to take her place. Two humans will have survived to continue on the race of man. From out of the destruction, out of the disorder and chaos, new life will emerge."

James leaned back in his chair and looked at Shawn with wide alert eyes. Shawn could tell that he had made an impression on his young visitor's mind, but he also knew that James, like most young people, had a limited attention span.

"I hope I am not losing you too much, guy," said Shaun. "As you can probably tell, I really enjoy telling these stories. I don't get visitors too often, seeing I am out here by myself."

"The stories are, um, interesting," James said.

Shawn smiled. "Well, I'm glad you find them interesting, James," he said. "I think you are different than most kids these days. Most of them would say that these stories are old or boring or unbelievable."

"No, of course not," laughed James.

The fire began dying away, like the intensity in Shawn's eyes. Yet, he was not quite finished. "You can learn a lot from these stories, James, for they sleep in you, in me, in everyone," he said. "They just need to be reawakened. People today are adrift, told to create their own reality. We are told society makes us who we are. And what do we have to show for it?"

Shawn answered his own question. "We have the mess of modern society. Just pick up a daily paper if you need any proof. If only we could reconnect with the lessons found in the great stories and myths, like the stories I told you tonight, the stories of Original Man and Wolf, of Fenris."

"Why is that important?" asked James.

"It is important because these timeless stories take you to a place beyond yourself," answered Shawn. "They center the individual in his proper context and give meaning to his life, showing him how to live and what we all must go through on this journey called life. They are not literal predictions or historical facts, but a way of explaining the world around us through symbols that contain a truth all their own. When life is seen mythologically, or religiously for that matter, the ordinary, the mundane, becomes a spectacle. But in today's world we no longer have such myths or rituals. Disorder is the result. We need a new story that holds true to the myths of old but still resonates meaning for all the peoples on our rapidly shrinking globe."

James now looked confused. Shawn was speaking over his young visitor's head; however, Shawn was a good conversationalist, which meant he knew how to listen with more than his ears.

Shawn stood up and placed his hand on James' shoulder. He tilted his chin down toward him as if seeking some unspoken acknowledgement of trust. "A new world will come about, James," he said. "Man has grown separate from his Creator and the timeless laws of nature that are His will at work, just as he was separated from his brother, the wolf. Man has fallen from God's garden and sought to recreate the world in his own image. In the process, the truth so often found in the great myths has been forgotten, replaced by strip malls and the garbage pit of television. This is the cause of the troubles we see today, the troubles that haunt the diseased mind of modern man. But one day man will return to the truth. From what man falls from, man is destined to return in the end."

"But what will bring about this change?" asked James, his natural curiosity heightened.

"A new world will be brought about by a hero, the one man who sees the modern world as it is. Fate will force him to go on a journey where he will retreat from the sick society and die to his self only to be reborn in spirit. Then he will receive a revelation that will bring man back into accordance with Nature's God. He will return to society with his message to recreate the world anew, and the old, corrupt world will be destroyed. And this experience of the hero will be but a metaphor for the struggle and potential of all," answered Shawn.

"Sounds kinda like the story of Fenris."

"What I have told you, James, is a symbolic separation and return to the ultimate truth embodied in the natural law, one wolf at the beginning and one wolf at the end," said Shawn locking his eyes on James. "And those stories, James, those stories rest in you … live them."

A soft night breeze drifted in through one of the cabin's open windows and breathed a few moments' life back into the smoldering flames of the fire. Shawn withdrew his hand from James' shoulder and nodded, satisfied with what he had done.

"So you believe in mythology?" asked James.

"I don't really believe in mythology in the literal sense," Shawn answered. "We are talking here about a different level of knowledge and truth. Besides, what is belief? I can believe anything I want, just like I can sleepwalk through the motions of life. I can say I believe in God. I can say I believe in Jesus Christ. But what is belief without action? What matters is how you live your life in accordance with the natural laws created by God. I don't believe, James, I live."

Shawn breathed deeply and settled back on the couch. He closed his eyes for several minutes.

"Well, James," Shawn said finally, "the cot is in that closet by the barrel stove. I'll wake you in the morning."

And with that Shawn abruptly stood up and walked over to his unmade bed. He sat down, took off his flannel shirt and very deliberately lay down to sleep. Snoring commenced within seconds. James found the cot and set it up but lay awake as he thought of Shawn's words. *What does he mean to live those stories? They are just old myths. What do they mean for me? And what of all this talk of the end of the world?*

James Norris quickly forgot most of what Shawn said. However, this night a seed had been planted deep in the hidden, inner regions of his mind. For the first time in his life he had been exposed to the idea there was a world beyond himself. Nonetheless, soon James was occupied with other worries. *That new version of Tomb Raider should be coming out soon. I'll have to check it out. Does Missy Carter really like me? Will the Vikings finally win a Super Bowl this year …*

And as James drifted off to sleep, it was those thoughts that washed over his brain like so many waves upon that gold nugget of sand imparted by Shawn. The power of the stories, the importance of the experience, was pushed away and hushed by life. In two days he would be back in the Twin Cities. Once again he could partake in his video games, his relationships, his malls, his movies and the Internet, all amidst those vinyl-sided dwellings adjoining the soccer fields. All the stimuli that was needed to prevent boredom and loneliness awaited him. These were the things that mattered. It was time to return.

Chapter 2
Life Denied

It was the dreamtime, a time owned by random firing of electrical impulses in the chemically controlled brain, nothing more than the ultimate triumph of chemistry. Dreamtime, it is said, contained no mystical significance. It was just pure and simple science at its finest. However, no matter how many white-shirt scientists had prodded and poked at it, the dreamtime still brought relief from the daily toils of work, relationships and bills. Sleep still served its purpose as worries melted away in the adventures to far off places, or they were rendered unimportant by the more pressing dangers of demons or monsters. If only he could stay here forever in this state, but he knew it wasn't real as he flew over the sea and glided effortlessly and free through the wisps of clouds. Soon he was falling, falling toward the light that grew more intense by the second.

* * *

The screams of the dreaded alarm clock awoke the man from his coma-like slumber. He hated mornings but, at least, held out the hope that he would gradually grow accustomed to them as he grew older. It had something to do with changing circadian rhythms he was told. But at the age of twenty-five, James Norris knew no such comfort. He threw off the covers and stared at the ceiling for a few seconds. *Only a dream*, he thought. Instinctively, he reached his arm across the bed as if seeking a hug. But lying next to him was only a pile of blankets and a pillow. She was nowhere to be found.

James arose and walked into the living room of his one-bedroom apartment in Richfield, Minnesota. He quickly found the TV remote and began to go through the morning routine of channel surfing some seventy-five possibilities of enlightening and entertaining stimulation. The clock above the TV console flashed 6:32 AM, Monday, September twenty-seventh. James quickly found CNN Headline News. The anchorwoman with her stern but falsely compassionate voice spoke to James and the rest of her captive audience.

"The situation is not getting any easier for the people living in the midst of East Africa's worse famine in almost twenty years. African leaders are pleading for more relief aid at today's summit in Nairobi."

The TV broke to a clip of the UN Secretary General shaking hands with an unknown East African leader. The voice of the anchorwoman rang like a bell, "The UN Secretary pledged his support."

James had been following the story for some weeks, even though strife in East Africa was nothing new. Famine was but one topic in the steady stream of bad news CNN was covering, but this was the norm ever since James started watching TV. Events such as famine, war and crime were aberrations. That is what made them newsworthy and sellable.

The anchorwoman continued looking important and sounding even more so. The next story was about the presidential campaign trail heating up. *Oh, great. Now I get to listen to the candidates manufacture issues to grab the public's attention.* President Donaldson was involved in budget negotiations while the front running Democratic challenger, William Beecham, was at a campaign rally in Illinois stressing the need for more federal dollars to put additional police officers on the street. James looked over to the bathroom door, purposely ignoring the campaign news.

This was the time she usually turned the shower on after reminding James to hang up the previous day's used towels.

James sighed and returned his attention once again toward the eye-candy newscaster. *A remorseful man knows no relief but distraction.* She launched into the next story as if acting on James' command.

"The severe midwestern drought is entering its fifth month. However, this week's forecast calls for dry conditions and record high temperatures once again for the entire mid-section of the country."

Same old news, same old news. James walked to the refrigerator and poured a glass of milk for breakfast. She would always drink two glasses a day. Yet, he continued to look at the TV, now flashing the local Twin Cities weather report. *Another hot one. Almost ninety degrees the last week of September, unbelievable. Probably will not even have winter this year.*

"No need to hunt for those winter clothes, Kristin," he sighed while looking toward the bathroom door.

But nobody answered. The ghosts of shattered expectations maintained their awful silence. James grabbed the now empty plastic glass and tossed it nonchalantly into the sink next to a host of other dirty plates and utensils. *How did I screw this up?* However, now there was no more time for regrets. He had to shower and dress the part of a young, corporate accountant.

Kristin Crandon and James Norris had broken up for good over a week ago. The initial spark was a dispute over whose turn it was to make the bed, but the two-hour squabble morphed into a full accounting of the couple's problems and forever ended the three-year relationship. That same night she had left for her mother's in Chicago. The first two days James got by well enough. His work saw to that, for it was the busiest time of year. However, with each proceeding day, the apartment got quieter and quieter, and the Miller Lite tasted better and better.

Moving in together sounded like a good idea at first. All of their friends were doing the same thing and heading down the fast track of cohabitation, marital bliss and happily-ever-after. However, reality fell pitifully short of once fairytale-like expectations. The experiment lasted six months and each fight got worse until the final conflagration. It was such a contrast from their first two and one half years together, a time that witnessed only one major disagreement. They had met their senior year at the University of Minnesota during a homecoming party. She was a sociology major and James was an accounting major, but after graduation she decided to follow her dreams and become an interior decorator. James entered the business world.

However, Kristin was not the only one gone. James knew he would probably never see her parents again. The Crandon's were fun people, and when the relationship was going good, James thought he'd make a great son-in-law. He especially enjoyed the feeling of family when they were around. It was a feeling that had been taken from him when his own parents died tragically in a car accident five years earlier, leaving him with no brothers or sisters and only a widely scattered extended family.

James showered, dressed and jogged to the parking lot in front of his apartment complex. It was filled with Hondas, Saturns, the occasional Lexus and a slew of sport utility vehicles. Most everybody in the complex was in their twenties and thirties, but the occasional forty-something divorcee was mixed in among the youth. Many lessees were single and looking for partners in what really amounted to a glorified dormitory filled with young professionals eager to go out and show how their college education enabled them to tell others what to do. Sometimes James referred to the complex as a yuppie training ground. But it was a term he kept to himself. Kristin never thought it was funny.

James had a forty minute commute through rush hour traffic to his job at Litchfield, Taylor and Faust Accounting in downtown Minneapolis. He had worked with Litchfield ever since he graduated from college over two years ago. It was the first company that had offered him a job, and the pay was decent. However, recently, he'd been thinking about a few of the elective courses he took in college. He especially liked the ancient philosophy class, and the European history class had been interesting as well. Sometimes at work he'd look away from the computer and remember Dr. Stevenson's discussion of Plato. He'd smile on the outside and second-guess on the inside, constantly asking himself if he'd made the correct career choice and life decisions. *Plato can't pay my rent,* he'd often think. And it made him feel better, if only for a few hours.

Rolling down the windows a bit, he sped out of the parking lot in his Honda Prelude. The low morning sun hit his eyes, and he put on a pair of dark driving sunglasses. It was going to be a beautiful, hot day. *A great day to be at the office.*

Before battling the cell phone-toting masses on 35W North, the freeway that would take him into downtown Minneapolis, James stopped at a Phillips 66 for ten gallons of unleaded at a cost of almost fifty dollars. Despite the promise of more Alaskan oil flowing into the world supply, gas prices were leaping to record levels. Nobody expected such a pinch so quickly, and various conspiracy theories abounded as to why the price was so high. The price increases were hitting the SUV-driving parents especially hard, although all Americans were feeling the squeeze. But this sort of storm had been weathered before.

Amazingly, James pulled into Litchfield's parking garage right on time in bustling downtown Minneapolis. Many a young recruit, fresh from college, would consider himself to have "arrived" if he worked here amongst the sharp office buildings. It was 7:30 AM. He had a quality group meeting at 8:00 regarding some new LIFO procedures in the food industry.

James walked smartly up to the front of the office building rented by Litchfield and a host of other companies. It looked rather intimidating with its darkened glass facade. He made his way to the elevator and quickly punched the button for the third floor. Soon the elevator doors opened, and he could smell the freshly vacuumed carpet of his working world.

The third floor was essentially one big room divided into manila-colored work cubes. A few coffee machines and water coolers lay scattered about, but the only true office belonged to James' boss, Mary Statler. It was positioned right across from James' cube. However, he had no worries this morning. She was not in yet, and he was on time. With catlike quickness he walked to his four-foot by four-foot kingdom and flopped down in the blue office chair.

The E-mail messages were piled up from the weekend, and he quickly scanned some of them. Today would be yet another stressful day. It was the time of year when some clients' annual reports were due. Also, semi-annual performance reviews, prepared by Mary, would end up on desks soon. To make matters worse, there were rumors floating around of possible company layoffs.

After working for a few minutes, James' attention soon wandered from his cubicle, and he gazed through the open door of Mary's office out to the great city beyond her windows. The temperature across the street at a Wells Fargo Bank flashed ninety-three degrees Fahrenheit, not unusual for a September day the last few years. James' daydreaming almost caused him to overlook the small flock of pigeons that clung precariously to the ledge just beyond the window barrier. Over the past few weeks James had grown to like them; in fact, he could identify by name the four outside right now. *Fascinating creatures, wild animals adapting to the city. They could live anywhere.*

James sighed deeply and turned back to his burden—the computer. The pre-workday slacking was over. Suddenly, a knock came from the outside of his cubicle. Litchfield employees were supposed to refer to them as offices, but James didn't buy into that reasoning. *They were cubicles. An office has a real wall and a real door.*

"Come on in," said James. It was Mary.

"Good morning, James, how are you today?" she said wearing her whitened corporate smile.

"Working hard, as usual," replied James as he arched his back over his chair and stretched out his arms. He then let out a deep, drawn-out breath.

Mary continued, "James, the quality control group has been canceled for today. Instead, would you please be in my office at 11:15, okay?"

"Sure thing," replied James pretending to not care.

Mary left quickly, and James stopped working immediately. Individuals were only called to her office if there was a big problem. She preferred to stay away from the power trip that a closed-door meeting could fuel. *Mary was actually a pretty good manager in that regard,* thought James. *But what did I do wrong? Maybe I'm not setting the world on fire, but I'm getting things done.*

11:10 AM. The time on the computer leaped out and distracted James' gaze from the pigeons. For the past three hours he had tried futilely to get some sort of work done, but the thoughts kept roaring through his head at breakneck speed. Four trips to the Pepsi machine and five trips to the washroom did little to help focus his attention on the accounting tasks. A few co-workers had stopped by to chat and ask how his weekend went. They were all smiles.

Mary was out at the moment, thus providing James the opportunity to look through her open door out to his winged friends. He stood up smartly and walked three cubes down to his co-worker, Tim Foldfarb. Two other co-workers were already gathered there on an impromptu break, Fred Baldwin and Alice Humphrey, both in their mid-twenties like James. Despite the fact that Tim's cubicle was one of the smallest in the entire office, people enjoyed hanging out there because it was so colorful. He had expressed his interest in his heritage by decorating the cube with African tribal masks and woodcarvings.

"Hey James," Tim cried, "you're late today. You already missed our Vikings bitch sessions. Now it's time to pick on the Twins."

Tim loved sports, and his mind seemed to revolve around all things that dealt with football, baseball or basketball when he wasn't talking about his two kids or wife. James gave him a token listen, but he couldn't pretend to like sports talk for too long.

"I'll tell you this," said Alice, a twenty-seven-year-old brunette who was living the single, independent life. "If you guys don't stop talking about sports, I am going to leave this little group and join my sisters in the real break room to discuss sex and shower curtains."

"Well, we can discuss shower curtains too," laughed Tim, his six-foot-three, 275-pound frame jostling about in his chair.

Tim's intent to bring laughter to the cubicle, however, did little to relieve James' anxiety. Nor did it appear to influence Fred Baldwin, who just drank his coffee with a blank stare. His eyes shifted back and forth in obvious agitation. Alice was about to ask him what was the matter when he suddenly blurted out, "Any of you guys see those moronic animal rights protestors at the capitol yesterday? Seems they were talking about banning bear hunting. I can't believe it. I mean, it's goddamn ridiculous."

Alice, Tim and James looked down. Fred had the reputation in the office of being the resident hick, the antithesis of the urban, cultured Litchfield employee. He was obsessed with ducks, deer and anything outdoors. James, however, really couldn't understand what people like Fred saw in hunting. *Fred would have to wake up to the twenty-first century. People are evolving beyond that state of mind.* Mary then appeared at her office door and caught James' eye. The time had arrived.

Mary closed the heavy oak barrier behind her with a solid thud. James found himself staring at the pictures of cats Mary kept on her office walls next to the obligatory framed inspirational quotes like "There Is No I in Team" with a picture of a rowing team. Mary was a heavy-set, well-rounded woman in her mid-thirties with dancing eyes and a beaming smile. It was the perfect cover for unbridled ambition.

"Have a seat, James," she chirped. James sunk into the black leather chair across from her polished maple desk. "Pretty nice weather today, huh."

James started to sweat. "James," she continued, "I'm sure you are aware of the upheavals here at Litchfield because of the current economic conditions."

James could only muster a feeble, "Yes."

Mary looked him straight in the eye. "James, there is no easy way for me to say this so I'm just going to come out and say it. I'm afraid we are being forced to cut some jobs for restructuring. It seems the guys at the top think we are overstaffed and can do more with less. It is the same old story. This is something I think you should hear from me before the rumor mill gets going."

James slumped in his chair, and his professional straight back wilted. There no longer was a reason to play the part. In the darkest parts of his mind, in places he didn't want to acknowledge, he knew this day was coming. But he knew he had only himself to blame. By not climbing the ladder faster, he had placed his head on the chopping block. Now it was time for corporate America to go about its cyclical job elimination. It was called downsizing or "rightsizing" in the politically correct euphemisms of corporate culture. Nonetheless, the fact of the matter was that Litchfield, Taylor and Faust just didn't need him anymore.

Mary continued on, even though James was no longer listening. "James, you deserve the truth. Your job will no longer be needed here at Litchfield, Taylor and Faust. I would love to reassign you and keep you on, perhaps in another division, but with the restructuring plan it is not feasible. I am sorry, James, you are not the only one. Please clean out your desk. It has been nice working with you."

James stared blankly at the floor as the horrible grip of failure began to seize his being. *It is not supposed to be like this. My life is falling apart. First it was Kristin. Now it is Litchfield.*

"I understand," James finally said, now directing his speech at Mary. "I appreciate your candor."

Mary stood up and extended her hand. James took it weakly and tried to look into her eyes, but they were focused beyond James, as if she was trying to pierce the oak veil of the door with her gaze. Beyond that barrier the accountants worked and built careers while in here those same careers met their fate.

"Today?" James asked.

Mary simply shook her head in the affirmative and opened the door for James. "I'm sorry," she said.

All James' energies were now focused on getting out of the building as quickly as possible. He walked toward the elevators, feeling utterly alone in a building full of people. The whole process felt like it was running in slow motion. His head was pounding, his hands were numb and the room of cubicles looked to be stretching onward to the horizon while closing in on him all the same. His co-workers receded and talked in slurred, foreign tongues. James just stared at their questioning faces with blank eyes as he continued his grim march. Strangely, however, James felt a sense of liberation that accompanied his failure. It was almost a masochistic glee, like a quarrelsome student would feel after being sent to the principal's office. But liberation, like Plato, does not pay the bills.

Once in the parking garage he made his way to his Honda and sped away from his aborted corporate accounting career at Litchfield, Taylor and Faust. Everything was a dull fog. However, he knew where to find relief.

Chapter 3
Refusal Of The Flesh

James knew where he was going, and it wasn't home. No, he had another plan. He peeled out of the parking garage and came precariously close to running a red light on Hennepin Avenue. Today he could hear Gary's calling. Gary's was a bar/restaurant in downtown Minneapolis that he used to frequent with his former co-workers during Friday night happy hours. And today, faithful as always, he hoped she would be there serving up the poison. Her name was Kim.

James liked Kim, perhaps not as a long-term partner, but she was fun to be around. At twenty-two she was an aspiring artist at the University of Minnesota. She was always quick with a comeback to any gentle razzing and loved all sports or, at least, pretended to. In fact, she played field hockey for the university. Her divorced father was an engineer for the Cargill Company, and the familiar taste for status undeserved could be detected in his progeny. James didn't dare guess how much she spent a week on make-up, eye shadow and bleach for her long blond hair, which seemed to change to a different shade daily. But he also thought it strange that someone who supposedly loved to play rough, manly sports would be so obsessed with her girly looks.

James, after parking his car in a nearby ramp, strolled casually into the bar. Kim caught his eye almost immediately.

"A little early today, James, don't you think?" she said. Her brilliant white teeth reflected the indoor light. "You're not starting to be a three martini lunch man now, are you?"

Kim's magic worked once again. No matter how rotten a day James had, no matter how horrible he felt, Kim always made him feel a little better, albeit temporarily.

"Nothing unusual, just a little thirsty," James replied.

He didn't feel like telling Kim about his predicament. Kim was supposed to take him away from reality, not force him to confront it. But she did have a strange way of always relating other people's problems to her own, as if she craved the attention that comes with sympathy.

"No class today?" asked James, as Kim handed him a glass of Miller Lite, his usual drink as of late.

"Nope, got my schedule arranged so I can work Monday and Fridays," she said in a sing-songy voice. She then placed her elbows on the bar and let her feet slide apart on the floor under her weight like she was doing the splits. "I'm thinking of changing my major to marine biology. What do you think I should do?"

"Do what makes you happy," said James as he took a rather large swig of Lite.

Kim righted herself, smiled and bounced up and down a few times while shaking her head from right to left.

"Then that's it," she said. "I want to be a social worker and help poor kids."

James joined in the laughter and made eye contact with her as she quickly turned away. He was pretty sure she knew Kristin was no longer in his life, and he made sure the drinks kept coming as he eyed the collage of pop culture iconography that covered every square inch of the bar's walls: pictures of movie stars, car parts, old advertisements and athletic jerseys. Once in a while he checked out the TVs, all seven of them. ESPN's Sportscenter was the current showcase. The talking head and his good-looking female companion were jabbering incessantly about the minutia of some holdout NFL star's contract negotiations. Between the actual news bits, obnoxious Gatorade and Nike commercials drove James' gaze away from the screen.

Time rolled away quickly as the alcohol took effect, and James' tongue became looser and looser as more Miller Lites met their end. Soon his pledge of stoicism was forgotten, and his guts were spilling unchecked as Kim lent her ear between making drinks. No subject was untouched— his firing, Kristin and the state of the world. Kim feigned sympathy and tried to match him with her miseries, mostly boyfriend and relationship difficulties.

Soon the after-work crowd began to roll in, all smiles and camaraderie, most in their mid-to-late-twenties, ambassadors from the world James just departed. They sat down within earshot and talked of promotions, water-cooler rumors, office politics and the housing market. James tried not to listen but to no avail. He was getting restless and an urge he had not sensed since college surfaced. Inhibitions had disappeared, soaked up in the ten Miller Lites. Kim stood in front of him now cleaning out a glass. *I must look like hell,* he thought. But he did it anyway.

"What time do you get done tonight, Kim?" he asked, taking care to pronounce each syllable as best he could.

"Six," came Kim's cheery reply as she punched up an order on the computer register and quickly shot back a smile. "Why do you ask?"

The moment of truth had arrived. "I was wondering if … um … maybe … "

A smile formed on Kim's crimson lips. She obviously relished the attention. James tried to regain his composure. "Do you want to go to dinner, coffee or something after work?"

His heart was now racing, magnified by Lite. But the reply came without hesitation.

"Sure, why not," said Kim as she rushed to fill another glass of beer and almost ran into her fellow bartender, Rich.

She had done a good job of concealing her excitement. In reality she had been waiting for this day ever since James first became a regular at the bar. He was a man with a college degree, a real job and a future. He was even her age. It all fit. However, James was like no man Kim had ever dated in her long history of relations with the opposite sex. Her old boyfriend, Greg, had no education and couldn't hold a job longer than three months, and her boyfriend before that was a part-time flagman for a road maintenance crew and full-time drug addict. She always seemed to attract guys who were rough around the edges and not very good for her mental or physical health. In fact, Greg had done jail time for attempting to steal a car. Many a night she lay awake pondering her disastrous relationships. It consumed her. She called it "the game." Then after work two nights ago, in a moment of clarity, she realized she did not have a current boyfriend. For the first time in two years she thought of suicide, despite her Paxil prescription. But what she didn't want to admit was that dating losers made her feel powerful. These were guys she could boss around, and they dumped on her the attention she craved. Now James had arrived. Life had meaning again.

For the next hour James tried not to act nervous or uncomfortable. Kim's quick acceptance of his offer somewhat unnerved him. *If she did this with me, what was preventing her from doing it with some of the other guys she met on a daily basis?* However, the wonders of alcohol soon erased such nagging doubts.

At 6:15 she pranced up to the empty stool next to him with a plate of shrimp and French fries. "I've got to eat something now," were her first words.

"Must be one of the benefits of working here, huh," said James. "Get a free dinner after every shift."

"You bet," laughed Kim. "You hungry? I can have Rich sneak you something from the kitchen.

James looked at his latest empty beer glass. "No thanks," he said.

"Do you hunt at all?" Kim asked.

"What?" answered James not sure where this conversation was heading, "you mean hunt animals?"

Kim dunked a French fry in ketchup. "Yes!" she exclaimed as she swallowed it in one gulp. "I love these French fries."

James shook his head no, not yet catching Kim's energy level.

"I love hunting," Kim said. "Last year Greg took me out deer hunting with his friends. I used my grandfather's old 30-30. It shoots awesome."

"Did you get anything?" James asked.

"No," Kim replied, "but someday I'll have a big rack on the wall. It was so funny though. Cabela's doesn't have women's hunting clothes in my size so I had to wear men's. I looked so dumb because they were too big. I was like walking up to people going, 'Hey, how ya doing?'"

James smiled as she continued to ramble. "Next year I am going to buy a Browning PBS shotgun."

"At what distance do you zero your 30-30?" asked James.

"What?" Kim asked seemly annoyed James had dared to speak.

"Oh," James continued, "I'm not a big outdoorsman, but I've got a buddy at work who always talks about sighting his hunting rifle. I was just curious what distance you sighted yours in at?

"Are you testing me?" asked a cautious Kim.

James let it go.

"Are you going deer hunting this year?" he then asked.

"Well, since I'm not seeing Greg anymore, I don't know who is going to take me. We used to hunt on his Dad's land."

"Can't you hunt on public land by yourself?"

Kim scoffed. "I don't like being alone. Last week I made my

mom come over and stay with me all day when I was sick."

"But I thought you were tough?"

This time it was Kim who kept quiet, and the silence revealed the true reason for her interest in the outdoors and everything else.

"Hey, that guy is kind of cute in a bad sort of way," said Kim pointing to a young man in a goatee wearing some sort of heavy metal shirt. "Have you seen some of the new stores at the Mall of America?"

"No, I—"

"I went shopping there yesterday. I think I am going to go back tomorrow. My friend works as a security guard there. Maybe we can kick someone's ass together."

"You know, I've not been there for a while."

"Do you like to dance?" Kim asked suddenly. "I love to dance."

She began shaking her shoulders and waving her head from side to side, which created a blonde storm of hair. Then she put her arms out in front of her and moved them in a circle with the gyrating motion of her body. James hadn't danced since college, and he didn't even enjoy it then. Mingling with all the people on the dance floor who flared their arms around in some strange upright sex ritual set to mind-numbing trendy music repelled him.

"Sure, that would be great," he said.

"Right on," Kim replied.

The longing for companionship overrode his personal dislikes, and the exaggerated sex drive once again trumped all.

"Where do you want to go?" asked James pulling out his car keys.

Kim butted in abruptly. "You are not driving anywhere. How many beers did you have? Besides, I love to drive."

She neglected to mention her three speeding tickets and two accidents the past two years.

"Hey, it's ladies night at Coconut Charlie's. I'll bet the party there will be awesome by later tonight," she said

"That's not exactly the most romantic place in the world," James replied.

Kim threw him a stern glance straight from one of her favorite cop shows. "And when did romance enter this particular picture?"

She then giggled a fake laugh and set off towards the door, proudly displaying her tight white Playboy tee shirt and midriff for the wandering eyes in the dinner and happy hour crowd. James followed.

Coconut Charlie's nightclub was on the other side of downtown Minneapolis. It was known as a happening place every night of the week, and Monday would be no exception as the lonely and rhythmically impaired grinded together, looking for love and companionship. Kim drove James' car and left her white Grand Am at Gary's. She parked in the closest available ramp and led James away by his arm toward the neon outline of Mr. Coconut Charlie himself, plastered on the front of the brick complex. The night was still young, and James half expected Coconut Charlie's to not even be open yet. However, as he and Kim approached the front doors of the establishment, a deep, chest-penetrating bass thump began to grow louder and more assertive. The pair were ushered through the door by two bouncers in white undershirts that stretched over their chests as well as their protruding paunches. Once inside, James saw that the shindig was in full swing despite the fact that the sun had disappeared only an hour earlier. A wave of humanity flowed to and fro in an uncontrolled spasm on the dance floor. Each individual moved his or her body in rhythm with the melody-devoid, beat-obsessed tunes. Girls in tight shirts stood over tubs of iced beer, taking care to squeeze their shoulders together as they bent over to retrieve glistening, cold beer bottles. The bizarre smell of alcohol, smoke and cleaning solution drifted through the stifling, humid air.

Young singles and college students who were coordinated enough didn't hesitate at all to jump into the fray and move to the music, while the divorced and the thirty-somethings desperately tried to cling to some vestiges of youth as they gulped their drinks and avoided eye contact in the dungeon of hormone infested dreams. It was retro-nineties music night at Coconut Charlie's, and the tune of the moment was from the Spice Girls. Cheers and screams erupted in the club as the speakers radiated one of the group's timeless tunes. The whining voices almost sent James to the door. He remembered the days when this sort of music was popular. Now it was a laughingstock, gathering dust on the trash heap of pop culture only to be revived at laughable retro nights and lame dance clubs. *Pop culture is always changing. And this is the culture, the belief system, which has consumed the world.*

James stared out at all the souls on the dance floor. *What will last? Nothing. So here I am.*

He almost forgot about Kim while he was preoccupied in his musings. Turning to look at her, he noticed a disgusted look on her face.

"What is the matter?" asked James.

"All the guys are staring at me," Kim exclaimed. "Why should I have to take that?"

James shrugged off the comment.

"Hey guy, let's go," Kim said after her latest attention-grabbing statement. She grabbed his arms and pulled him towards the floor. James resisted.

"Let's get a drink first," he said.

Kim put her hands on her hips and pouted.

"No, you said you would dance. Princess Kim says dance!" she demanded.

"Just one drink, please, Kim," replied James as the two wandered up to the bar and grabbed a pair of stools vacated by a departing couple.

A pretty girl with glitter on her face bounced forward to take the order, her tight cropped-off tee shirt revealing she was not hired for her drink making knowledge. Kim offered her an obnoxiously girly "Hi" as she looked down on the floor. After James ordered two Lites she revealed the reason for her actions.

"That bitch is too fat to work here," she said.

James was puzzled, but he didn't want clarification. The Spice Girls quit their whining, and the DJ mixed in some new music by the rock group Thorn.

"Never heard this before," said James reaching for his Lite.

"Loser," she scoffed.

James returned to his beer.

As the minutes wore on, James began to feel the club revolve around his being. The entire place seemed blurred and distorted, and he withdrew into self-contemplation, which suffocated his urge for companionship. An unexpected commotion built up behind him, and he slowly spun the stool around to see a line of young women standing up on top of another bar opposite the dance floor. They joined hands and danced together as men below cheered them on. Smiling ear-to-ear, reveling in the power of their sexuality, they became the focus of the obscene world. For one or two songs in a dark, noisy bar their existence mattered.

Isn't there more than this? Is this all that I'm going to amount to—a single accountant doomed to hang out in pathetic clubs?

The beat continued to pound James' brain, and, combined with the laughter and the revelry of the crowd, it produced a sickening ugly roar, which reached to his very soul and forced the question. *Why can't I be like them and enjoy myself?* Anger, rooted in unseen, unacknowledged places within, welled up to the surface. He began to hate their worship of the flesh and their lack of larger questions. And sitting here, neglected in his contemplation, sat the living representation of all this nonsense.

James abruptly turned and looked at Kim who was methodically swinging her legs off the stool with a goofy grin on her face. James stared straight through her. A moment of clarity in a day of disorder had arrived. The laughter and screaming emanating from the feel good dancing mob began to drift into the background.

"Do you believe in God?" James asked.

"Yes, of course, I do?" she answered with a sneer on her face.

James retorted probingly, "And what do you think God is?"

"God is anything you want it to be. What does it matter as long as you are living the life prescribed by your personal God?"

James was not satisfied, but it was the answer he expected. "What do you think of religion?" he asked.

"I don't know," replied Kim. "You know they all think they are right and everybody else is wrong. I think, you know, everybody has, like their own personal God. Everybody sets, you know, their own morals. All the religions do is fight among one another. But, James, I know all about the Bible. My Mom used to make me read it-yeppers—!"

She raised her hand up to James' face and moved her neck in some sort of hip-hop gesture. However, it seemed James had sparked her interest and turned her mind momentarily away from dancing. Now it was her turn to ask a question.

"Since we're on such deep subjects here, James, what do you want out of your life?" she asked as she put her hands on his knees and tilted her head to one side.

"If I knew the answer to that question, I probably wouldn't be here," James replied.

"And what is that supposed to mean?" Kim sneered. "You know, you take this philosophical stuff way too far sometimes. You think too much. That's your problem. You just got to let stuff happen."

She took her hands off his knees. "I'll give you my answer though," she said. "You want the meaning of life? The meaning of life is having fun and being happy. That is why I want kids. I think they'd be a blast. And, you know, the only thing better than having kids is making them."

She suddenly leaned forward and kissed James softly on the lips. Her verbal attack had disguised her true feelings. However, James was taken back.

"Come on," she said teasingly, rubbing her hand slowly up his thigh, not caring at all that people might notice. "Let's leave and go to my place. I'll let you get out of dancing tonight." Again she kissed him.

James hesitated at first, but he began to kiss back, albeit haltingly, as the thoughts swirled and tormented his mind amidst the dull thump. He was frozen on a fence between two worlds. It was time to decide. He pulled his lips back from Kim and moved his body away slightly to view her face in the pulsating, multicolored lights, now dimming as the sound of a computer generated dance song engulfed the club.

James sensed time's perpetual rhythm waver. From his barstool the flaying of the bodies on the dance floor became like slow motion, as did the female bartenders doing their attention dance. Whether it was the effect of alcohol or something else, James could not tell. And in this surreal environment, this world he perceived, his attention again focused on Kim and the seductive smile on her lips. Her face had changed. No longer did it belong to a smiling blonde. It was wrinkled and aged. To his utter horror her affliction continued to worsen. James began drawing away from her as the wrinkles transformed into hideously rotten skin. Her once silken white flesh became reddish-black and seemed to writhe and move across her face before falling off in bloodied sheets. Eyes caved in, revealing hollow sockets as her hair grayed and quickly fell out en masse. White teeth fell out one by one, making a distinct clinking sound as they bounced off the tiled floor. Viscous, thick blood poured out of her gaping mouth as her entire body began to shrivel. The bones of her skull and cheeks ripped through the remaining shards of rotted skin that tore away before turning to dust. Kim the beautiful was revealing her true identity. Flesh was all she was.

The hideous, disintegrating figure leaned forward to kiss James again. In that second, that flicker of time, a decision was made. *No, this is not all there is.* An indescribable, vague feeling engulfed his being and shocked him out of his vision. He would seek a different, neglected path. Where it lay he did not know, but it was certainly not here. Nor was it with Kristin or in the world of Litchfield, Taylor and Faust. Instead it lay somewhere in the fog of his consciousness. But no longer would he play the part. Sex was of the body and the body was of death. He would not be another casualty.

He turned away with revulsion and pushed off Kim with his left arm. However, his instinctive shove was stronger than intended. "What the hell is the matter with you?" yelled Kim as she fell from the barstool.

James didn't bother answering her question because he barely knew himself. Angry, liberated, yet broken all the same, he stood up and stumbled toward the door. The flesh had been rejected, the suitor refused.

The night air felt refreshing on his slick, perspiring skin brought on by the combination of the crush of people and the effects of alcohol. He shook violently and tried to regain his composure, not exactly sure of what had transpired in the club but knowing full well he had to leave as soon as possible. Kim never followed, and James was alone as the chaos of Coconut Charlie's deteriorated in the background. But it was too early to return home. It was now time to drive.

Kim still had the keys, but, luckily, James kept a spare under the car in a lock box. The parking garage was filled with Sunfires and Grand Ams owned by the young beer drinking, dancing regulars. They sat ready to be taken home by their impaired drivers. Tonight James would join them.

James slumped into the driver's seat and sat silently while trying to collect his thoughts, still sweating profusely. He turned on the radio, and immediately the hip-hop thump of 101.3 KDWB hit his ears. It was more than he could take. Shutting off the radio, he started the engine and eased the vehicle down the spiraling ramp toward the street. He flipped the attendant a twenty-dollar bill and peeled out to the street without waiting for change. Anger was his diagnosis; speed was his prescription, a release through the gas pedal. James punched the accelerator and headed west.

The IDS skyscraper, alight in its nocturnal glory, shone like a modern lighthouse aflame in the sea of commerce. The adjacent buildings, smaller in stature but no less brilliant in their radiance, took their rightful secondary places on the skyline. The spires of St. Mary's Basilica were barely visible among her more modern friends. James ran a red light one block after leaving the garage and sped toward Interstate 394 W, which would take him toward the great 494/694 beltline that encircled the entire Twin Cities. He hit the onramp going eighty miles per hour. The authorities were no longer a going concern.

Once on the freeway, the content individuals in their SUVs and minivans flew by James like a blurred streak in his rearview mirror. He was a target for a DWI or worse, but he no longer cared. The all-encompassing rage still gripped him as he turned south off of 394 W onto 494.

The carbon copy chain stores and franchised restaurants flashed by unrecognized as James pressed south on the 494 beltline. The speedometer now read ninety-four miles per hour, yet he kept the wheel steady in his drunken state. After some time, 494 curved gently to the east, and James continued to press on past all the glass-encased hotels and sprawling car dealers. Soon he neared Twin Cities International Airport, and a huge complex alight in megawatt splendor lay in all its grotesque vastness to the south. It was the Mall of America, the "Mega Mall," complete with its artificial "Underwater World."

Underwater World lay in the bowels of the complex. It was a world packaged for progressive, human consumption. Here glass tanks contained a myriad variety of fish including sharks and other predators that swam side by side with their prey. People could walk through the tanks in enclosed, air-conditioned walkways. The employees of the aquarium fed the sharp-toothed carnivores; otherwise, they would be tearing apart the pretty little tropical fish that delighted parents and kids alike. Allowing the natural predator-prey relationship to take place would be real yet politically unacceptable. It would destroy the sanitized version of the natural world that modern, twenty-first century Americans accepted as truth. And the "Mall" could ill afford to expose crying children and their doting parents to reality, for its very livelihood depended upon separating them from that reality and promising it back through the products its stores offered.

James liked the mall in his younger days. He looked out the passenger window and remembered the constant screams and cries from the indoor amusement park echoing thru the canyons lined with stores peddling every conceivable product. In his mind's eye he saw the TVs flashing in all the shops, making it impossible to escape the controlling, powerful images of name-brand attraction beaming directly into his brain, and the throngs of teenagers spending money they didn't have while walking slowly down the halls checking out attractive members of the opposite sex. The girls wore tight tube tops that cost much and covered little while the boys showed off their baggy jeans and backwards ball caps.

He watched the glow of the mall of malls pass thru the corner of his eye and tried to purge his mind of its memories. And, yet, not so long ago, before the realities of the world had hardened his outlook, he probably would have been in there tonight.

After passing Twin Cities International Airport on his left and crossing a bridge over the Minnesota River, James faced a choice. He could either continue on 494 and the giant loop around the Twin Cities or head north on Interstate 35 E into the heart of St. Paul. He decided on the second option, and as he crossed the grand Mississippi River, the bright lights of Minnesota's capital came into view. Here the regular fifty-five miles per hour speed limit slowed down to forty-five miles per hour and charming residential neighborhoods lined either side of the freeway. Weakness now took over. The anger was working its course, and James began to realize just how reckless and stupid he had been. He slowed down to the posted speed limit.

Then it came into view, rising above the busy center of the capital city. James always liked its position, holding supreme command of the skyline. It had yet to be dwarfed by governmental or economic concerns. Shining spotlights reflected off its refurbished dome on this warm evening. St Paul's Cathedral had steadfastly held its ground on a proud hill overlooking St. Paul for almost a hundred years. Unlike the newer sister city of Minneapolis, here in St. Paul, the religious pillar of civilization held its premier position.

James exited 35 E. Ever since he was a small boy he had wanted to visit the heights of the cathedral at night. Tonight he would finally realize his wish. He parked his Honda, not bothering to lock it, on a quiet residential street a few blocks away. Slowly and deliberately, shaking off the effects of the alcohol, he walked around the outside of the massive structure to its front doors, where a short series of steps cascaded down to the street below. Beyond the street was an open grassy yard on a hill. A worn dirt footpath led across it.

At the bottom of the hill across 35E was downtown St. Paul and the symbols of the economic pillar of civilization. The huge Xcel Entertainment Center was buzzing with activity this evening. Its lots were full and an audible hum could be discerned from inside its confines. Next to the Xcel arena stood the skyscrapers of business and commerce.

To the east of James' position the Minnesota state capitol building, that grand monument to the governmental pillar of civilization, shone like a piece of the celestial moon placed on earth. James let his eyes wander, breathing slowly, before he sat down on the highest of the cold, granite steps with his back to God's house and his gaze upon the city. Alone.

So here I am, he thought, looking out upon the city, which sang its muffled song of the night. *Where is the ambition, the will?* All he could think of was his failures at work and home. And at twenty-five he felt old and adrift, unable to locate his center in his own personal world. *Detached.*

He turned to find a young couple had taken up residence on a sidewalk bench not far from where he sat. They laughed, and he tried to ignore them. He thought of Kristin and marriage or, as the educated called it, domestic partnership, which sounded more like a business relationship. It was now nothing more than a legal definition to be easily created and dissolved by the whims of the courtrooms, not a higher order or truth. *Something has gone amiss on the road to happiness. Yet is it not my responsibility to figure out what I am to do with my life and where I am to go? I want to be happy. But how?*

He turned to face the enormous cathedral, cast in an odd glow by the surrounding floodlights, as if expecting an answer from God. He didn't oblige. Looking once again upon downtown St. Paul, he found it gave no answer as well.

Suddenly, the shuffling of footsteps broke James' train of thought. He turned to see a disheveled, older man approach him. The man seemed nervous and would look over his shoulder every few seconds. James noticed the man slip a needle into his pocket. As the man drew near, James saw that he was not old at all. The effects of his drug use had taken a terrible toll.

"Got a buck," the man pleaded hopping back and forth on his feet.

"Sorry," James replied.

Surprisingly, the man left with no argument. He took one quick glance over his shoulder before jogging down the steps toward downtown St. Paul.

James forced a brief smile as he thought of the anti-drug zealots who actually believed they could snuff out the use of such substances. *Didn't they know what the drug represented? It wasn't pain and misery but the hope of an experience that transcended the daily and ordinary. Through the needle or the pipe a spiritual experience could be quickly and easily achieved by anyone with a few dollars and a disregard for the law. There was no need to labor away on some desolate island denying oneself the pleasure any human is indeed entitled to.*

Spirituality could be found in one's personal God. Isn't that what I believe? How can there possibly be some sort of universal truth? Everything is relative and capable of being deconstructed. Reality, like that damn English professor used to say, was a social-political construct designed by one group to oppress everyone else. Even truth itself is suspect.

So there he sat. No answers came, only regrets and questions and gloom. And the steps of St. Paul's became the scene of James Norris's greatest failure of all. The voices of the young couple disappeared, reverberating off the granite walls of the cathedral. James started to feel cold, and soon the shivering began. Tonight there would be no easy solutions or grand revelations or life changing commitments. So with his head down, he shuffled back to his unlocked Honda. It was time to go home.

James wisely stayed off the main freeways on his return trip to his apartment. Instead he crept ever so cautiously through the stilled, darkened St. Paul and South Minneapolis streets. He never once let the speedometer rise over the posted limit and dutifully obeyed all stop signs.

Once back at the apartment complex, James found an open stall and parked the Honda. He shut off the engine and sat for a few seconds in silence, looking across the still-green apartment complex lawn to the hushed suburban homes on the opposite side of the street. The largest one, now highlighted by an array of soft porch lights, belonged to the Johnson's. Mom and dad and kids were now all tucked away securely in their warm, clean beds. The grass in their yard, a temple to suburban landscaping that would make the greens keepers of Augusta National envious, was a brilliant shade of green with no hint of deviation in color. Even in the pale light of the surrounding streetlights it was a sight to behold. It was all a quarter inch high. Tim, the father, was even known to measure it with his ruler, and not a hint of invading crab grass could be found. Such an encroachment attracted the scrutiny of his wife, Tiffany, and the wrath of Tim's weed killing chemicals. Every weekend the majority of their time would be spent on similar endeavors: cleaning, fixing and perfecting, making sure the universe of their three acre lot was orderly, neat and compartmentalized.

Perhaps the Johnson's are doing the work of God, producing order in a world of chaos. No. The reality is that if the Johnson's died tomorrow, not a soul on this planet would give a damn about their lovingly cared-for home and yard. They are doomed to the same fate as everything else. All is time-bound and meaningless, even the Johnson's own lives. It is all the daily details that prevent Tim and others like him from realizing the ultimate senselessness of their actions. And not so long ago I probably would have tried to keep up with them.

Only the hum of the refrigerator interrupted the silence in James' apartment. He untied his tie and tossed it onto the living room floor before shuffling into the kitchen to fetch a bottle of Heineken. A vivid green light on the microwave flashed 1:00 AM. He slowly thought through his possibilities. None were good.

Unable to focus, James returned to the living room and fell onto the sofa opposite the TV. The remote, for a change, was just where he thought he'd left it that morning, wedged between the cushions of the sofa. He turned on the box.

The colored light flickered thru the somber, darkened room, casting his face in a weird, rainbow-hued glow. Methodically, he clicked through the channels as the images bombarded his senses and raced toward him at dizzying speeds. Again and again he hit the button, and the guts of society were beamed into his brain. The images and sick sounds seemed to come ever faster: the Gatorade commercials, the explosions, the cop shows with stern female lawyers marching out of vehicles, the talking heads, the so-called news, the empty sportscasters, the obnoxious sitcoms, the scantily-clad buxom blondes with guns. On and on the channels went. Nothing.

James was not quite sure what happened. It was not like he consciously thought through the motion. Perhaps he did it because he had set the empty Heineken bottle on the coffee table and it was in his way. But in one swift, almost athletic, motion he hoisted the bottle over his head and sent it on its final journey into the screen. The monster was slain.

James walked across the room and opened up a window. The inviting, cool night air rolled into his home with the low roar of the slumbering city. He shut the lights off, and the fresh breeze combined with the darkness to bring peace from the toil and misery of that day. Tomorrow he would begin to pick himself up, but for what purpose he could not yet begin to surmise. However, sleep did not come easily. As the alcohol ran its course, James found himself waking several times throughout the night, shaken from his slumber by what he thought was a distant, sad cry.

Chapter 4
The Community Left

The early morning routine was no more. No longer did the clock screech its awful chorus, and James lay in bed the next day until almost 9:30 AM. It had been months since he enjoyed such a simple treat. Such are the unexpected joys of unemployment.

His head throbbed from the Miller Lite and each breath was like a dry wind blowing across the parched landscape of his mouth. Yet, despite the lingering effects of his intoxication, he remembered everything that had transpired the night before. All the images, all the thoughts were burned into his brain. *Need a drink of water,* he thought as he righted himself in bed.

It was then that the phone rang, and James reached across the motley mound of blankets and covers to answer.

"Hello—"

"James, I'm so glad you are there," said the man on the other end of the line. "My name is Bob Wilkerson up here in Spooner, Wisconsin. I'm sorry I'm the one who must deliver you this news."

James froze up. His brain began reaching desperately for more horrible events that could befall him.

"Please continue," he said.

"James, I am the lawyer handling the will and estate of your uncle, Kevin, who I regret to say passed away yesterday."

Kevin is dead. Old Kevin. God, what next? And to think I never bothered to call him at all since his birthday last June.

"How did he die?" James asked.

Bob answered, "As far as the coroner knows it must have been natural causes. His neighbor, a ... Martin Steiger, found him dead on his kitchen floor. I bet it was his heart."

James said nothing in reply, but his mind flashed images of the hated youthful excursions to his uncle's. He could see the loft again and hear the whine of mosquitoes.

Bob continued, "Kevin left strict instructions in his will to be cremated and buried on his land without a funeral. Martin, I believe, is arranging that as we speak. But, James, that is not the real reason I need to talk to you."

"Go on," answered James, the words falling ever so apprehensively from his parched lips.

"Well, James," Bob said, "you are the family member I needed to get a hold of. Your uncle's house and land were paid off years ago, and in his will your parents were named first beneficiaries and you were listed as second beneficiary of his assets. But I know your parents died a few years back, and I don't think I told you then that you were now the primary beneficiary of Kevin's estate."

James now saw where the conversation was headed.

"James, that means you have inherited Kevin's property. It is now in your hands," Bob said.

James didn't know what to say. He certainly appreciated his uncle's unexpected gift but was confused all the same. It was another headache, and his mind was already saturated with trivia. This only added more water to the sponge. *Do I want to keep it, sell it, let it appreciate?*

"So where do we go from here?" he asked Bob finally.

"There is a lot of paper work and legal dealings we have to go over,

James, but as soon as we take care of all that, the property is yours. Then you can do with it as you choose. When can we meet?"

"You ever get down to the Twin Cities?" James asked.

"Well, I'm going to be in Woodbury on Thursday."

"Great, why don't you give me a call when you get into town," replied James. "Then we can arrange to meet somewhere."

"Sounds like a plan to me. Will you be working?"

"Alright, thanks a lot," said James as he quickly hung up the phone.

James fell back onto the bed and covered his eyes with his hands. *Kevin died. Yesterday, Kevin died. Alone. Well, I guess that is fitting. He relied on himself his entire life and nobody else. But still it's sad. Just like Mom and Dad. I never had a chance to say good-bye.*

James pictured Bob as a typical small town lawyer doing child custody cases, divorces, wills and property law. *He was probably short and fat with a mustache and got along with everybody in town. He's probably a happy guy too.*

Two hours later James finally arose from his bed to shower and grab a bite of leftover, cold Papa John's pizza. He meandered into the living room and tuned his stereo to hard rock radio 93.7. Pearl Jam's *Black* was the tune of the moment. While munching on the limp slice of pepperoni, James' eyes fell across the room to an open closet door and an old moving box, stacked high with assorted papers and worn notebooks. The album sat on top of the pile.

It was ordinary enough, just a skinny binder of hard green plastic emblazoned with gold star stickers. He used to get the stickers for academic accomplishments in elementary school, and back then they seemed like the most important things in the world to him. Now he had all but forgotten about them.

James reached down to pick up the album before flopping onto the couch. The pictures inside were from his teenage years. They included some of his senior pictures and snapshots of his aborted football career. Intermingled were pictures of his mother and father on various trips, special occasions and get-togethers, along with other family members he met once or twice. His eyes scanned the pages quickly. Suddenly they stopped. They were locked and drawn toward the picture stuck under the protective sheath of clear plastic in the lower left hand page. It was a picture of him, his mother, father and Kevin outside Kevin's cabin. James was wearing his usual Kevin visit scowl while his mom, dad, and Kevin flashed smiles. *Looks like it was taken the year I got lost, the year I heard those wolves and met that old guy. What was his name?*

While staring at the picture all the poignant sounds, smells and sights of the cabin came back to him again. *Kevin lived such a different life from mom and dad ... and me.* He gently placed the album on the floor and lay down on the musty couch. Above him the ceiling fan circled lazily and triggered thoughts. *It is tempting. And it is mine. Could I do it now? Do I want to do it now?* A galactic tug-of-war was taking place.

Minutes ticked away. Then, all of a sudden, James jumped to his feet in one very ungraceful motion and in a half-hearted triumphant voice declared the victor to the ghosts of his former life. "Why not?"

It will only be for a little while, he reasoned. *Maybe I can get things sorted out there. It can't be any worse than this, childhood memories be damned. If I were to cash out my 401K, I could probably live frugally for some time. I guess I'll be getting some unemployment too.*

James grabbed the album and once again stared at the picture, his eyes falling onto Kevin's smiling face as if the odd man himself was pulling him away to his retreat in the east. *I'll head out there as soon as possible. And maybe I'll return a better person.*

* * *

Friday, October eighth. During the past fortnight, supposedly the start of fall, the mercury had reached an average of eighty degrees

Fahrenheit each day in the Twin Cities. Hot sun scorched the earth and anything that dared to enter its path. Temperatures across the entire United States were above average, and across the Atlantic in Europe summer-like weather reached from Dublin to Moscow. Along Alaska's Arctic coast massive thunderstorms formed, not unheard of at these latitudes the past decade, but positively unbelievable so late in the year. Endless summer seemed a possibility.

James had spent the past two weeks preparing for his move from the comfortable confines of Richfield. Some of his belongings were placed in storage while everything else was loaded into an eight-foot U-Haul trailer that could be pulled behind his Honda, once he had Sears install a trailer hitch. He decided against casing out the cabin before his move. In times of distress, leaving the scene of pain takes precedent over foresight.

The money factor was somewhat of a worry, but he believed he could hold out for up to six months before he had to find another job. Along with unemployment he did have some savings including $15,000 amassed in a Vanguard growth fund given to him at high school graduation. However, after much mental wrangling, James decided to leave his 401K untouched. The tax penalty for early withdrawal was too painful. Nevertheless, his responsible planning for retirement had been thrown out the window. He rationalized that at twenty-five he could worry about such concerns at a later date. Short-term exigencies had won out.

James awoke on the floor and rubbed his eyes before looking out the east facing living room windows for the last time. Outside the sun's rays were hopelessly trying to penetrate heavy, sullen clouds, and from James' sheltered vantage point the weather seemed cooler, harsher than what he had grown accustomed to the past few weeks. His back ached, the just punishment for packing his bed early, and the condo was barren except for a few random chairs and kitchen utensils. James had decided to leave them for the next lessees—a newlywed couple. As he struggled to his feet he smiled wickedly and wondered if this apartment would witness their meeting a fate similar to his and Kristin's.

Nobody was there this morning to see him off, no goodbye calls, no farewell waves, as if he was some sort of reject from this vibrant metro area of over two million people. His unpacked radio alarm clock flashed 11:00 AM. He had slept in embarrassingly late. Noon rush hour would soon be in full effect. He had time to kill.

James sat down again passively on the floor and tuned the clock radio to 92.5. *Gimme Shelter* by the Stones was playing for the millionth time, and today James just didn't want to hear it. He flipped the radio over to AM and tuned in 830 WCCO news talk. The topic of the day was the presidential campaign trail leading up to the November election, which James, being a typical self-absorbed patriot, knew very little about. Commentators remarked how the latest polls put Democratic presidential challenger William Beecham almost five points ahead of Republican incumbent Henry Donaldson. James had little trouble seeing why that would be so from listening to the brief, twenty-second sound bites. Beecham's voice exuded a confidence rarely heard in a modern politician. Crowds cheered in the background amidst his fist-pumping pledges and catchy slogans filled with words such as "change" and "renewal" and 'rebirth." For the first time since the campaign started James had the opportunity to really listen to Governor Beecham. There seemed to be a consistent theme running throughout all his policy suggestions—order and security now, even at the expense of individual liberties and freedoms. He was a man who supposedly had the answers for the problems and fears of the average person, namely, put more faith in people like himself to solve those very problems. And in these times it was a sales pitch many people were buying.

Two hours later the time arrived. James gathered up the clock radio and a few sloppily packed duffle bags and walked smartly out of the apartment complex to the Honda. He checked his pockets for the cabin keys that Bob had given him last week at their meeting and never looked back. It was a four-hour drive northeast to Loretta.

The mid-afternoon traffic was light as he skirted the Minneapolis downtown and headed north on Interstate 35. He soon noticed that the leaves, the warm weather notwithstanding, had begun to feel the urge, that age-old message, to turn radiant colors of orange, red and yellow. Some had already completed the process and were falling dead onto the road before him. A few trees already bared their skeleton branches and boldly waved their stark, naked bodies in the brisk northern breeze. They placed this ride in such a contrast with his summer trips to this place when he was young. Back then the leaves were usually on the trees, and the countryside teemed with life and growth. He would have been with his mom and dad, never alone. There was so much promise in those days. His whole future lay ahead of him. Now he drove onward in silence—alone, fired, banished.

He traveled out of the Twin Cities past all the new developments, multiplexes, Targets and Menard's growing at breakneck speed upon the vanishing open space around the metro area. At the suburb of Forest Lake, twenty minutes north of Minneapolis, he turned east on US Highway 8 and drove through a patchwork of towns that all ran together as if they were connected by one long main street. The towns were built near a chain of lakes that once had been the refuge for those hoping to escape the urban life but still live close enough to its charms. But now it was but an extension of that ever-expanding metropolis to the south. Houses, docks and boatlifts plastered all the available shoreline.

Further north at the town of Taylor's Falls, US 8 crossed the St. Croix River into Wisconsin. Here rapids had cut a deep gorge and highlighted devilish outcroppings of weathered rock. James looked down from the bridge to the raging foam and sheer cliffs. A few hardy climbers were inching their way up one of the rock faces with ropes.

Once across the river, James continued into Wisconsin past the farmers in their fields harvesting what meager drought-ridden corn they could. The Twin Cities classic rock radio station he was listening to began to fade as static intermingled with the Beatles and the Eagles. James shut the radio off and let the sound of the engine facilitate his contemplation. In a trance-like state, his eyes zeroed in on the highway, and the Honda continued its great rhythmic pulse of the empty road. The thoughts came like a flood, complementing the solemn weather. They washed his soul in shades of gray and colors of even darker persuasions.

Maybe I'm kidding myself. I'm not going out here to rest a short while so I can come back to the Cities and further my career. Maybe that is only a rationalization. I just don't know what I want. I want something else, something beyond what everyone I know seems to strive for. But what?

At the village of Turtle Lake, he turned off Highway 8 and headed north on US Highway 63. He passed an Indianhead Sport Shop and Community Motors Auto Repair on the outskirts of the town of Cumberland and gazed down at his fuel gauge. It was on E.

Ahead he spied a Kwik Trip convenience store at the intersection of US Highways 63 and 48, the epicenter of the Cumberland metropolis. *What a pitiful excuse for a stoplight,* James thought as he eyed the flashing red beacon placed at the four corners where the highways met each other. He chuckled to himself as people pulled up to the four-way stop and couldn't figure out who had the right-of-way. However, he soon lost his flash of cheerfulness when he saw the price of gasoline. It was five dollars and fifty cents a gallon.

Two old farmers—their overalls gave them away—stood outside of the Kwik Trip building near the parking stalls. One leaned up against the side of a battered red early-nineties Ford pickup truck. They both wore straight-billed red Cenex hats that blended in nicely with the red suspenders that stretched over their expanded bellies before hooking snuggly on their grease-spotted jeans.

As James approached them on his way inside to pay, he could smell the potent scent of dairy barn, a blend of hay and animal, rolling off them A Green Bay Packers logo was proudly displayed on the back windshield of the Ford truck. James ranged within earshot of their conversation.

"I suppose a guy could believe him. He sure seems to have the right medicine," said the taller and fatter of the two as he played with his key chain.

"Doesn't matter," said the other man, "nothing ever changes so I'm not going to vote. They're all the same, just a bunch of crooks. As long as I get paid, I'll be happy."

"Ain't that the goddam truth," said the fat one. "Say, we gonna get any rain?

"Don't count on it," said the skinny one. "Sounds like we got heat coming again next week. Say it may get back near ninety."

"Something sure is amiss," replied the fat one. "The atmosphere is changing or something."

James watched them talk and laugh as he paid cash for the gas and returned to the Honda.

The skies were still a pale smoky gray as James traveled out of Cumberland. Fellow travelers on the highway became fewer and fewer, and the rural driveways and houses were placed further and further apart. Lakes were tranquil, fields and woods dry and vacant. This time of year the weekend cabin owners didn't venture north to their summer playgrounds with their boats, jet skis and related toys. The land was left to the locals. Even retirees began to pick up and head to their snowbird winter nesting grounds in Florida and Arizona so they could escape the inevitable chilling wrath of winter. *I wonder if they will keep going south if these wimpy, warm winters continue? I can't remember the last time we had a real winter. At least that's the way it seems.* He shifted his weight in the car seat, cracking his back in the process, before settling back into his driving position. *I wonder if all this global warming stuff is real? The weather guys can't even tell what will happen the next day much less the next hundred years. I have my doubts, but only time will tell.*

With great disregard to his highway safety skills, James looked skyward through the front windshield at a v-flock of Canadian geese as the road began a series of roller coaster rises and descents. Here the recurrent fields began to fade away, and in the distance all James could see was the canopy of the forest as it stretched northward and merged into the oblivion of the horizon. He was on the divide that marked where the farmland ended and the forest began. The red oak and maple snuggled up to either side of the road, giving the impression of standing sentries guarding a pathway on an ancient imperial road. In some spots, their branches touched the branches of their brothers on the other side of the road, creating the perception of a tunnel under which James advanced as if he was being propelled along his route, in majestic grace, with an unseen force pushing and building behind him. Dry, reddish-gold leaves were falling in front of his vehicle as he rolled up the crest of the hills and down the opposite sides. He imagined the leaves as petals being thrown at him by the tree guardians on the sides of the road, urging him onward to the purpose that was but a faint light in his unconscious.

After some time his eyes ventured to the right side of the road as he passed a tidy white church abuzz with activity tucked into a grove of hardwoods. There was a funeral taking place, and in the cemetery adjacent the church a small gathering watched the blessing of a casket. The grass in the cemetery was a gray brown, and giant, leafless white oak trees protected the final resting place of life's victims. "Continue," he whispered to himself. "Kevin's cabin is not too far."

James passed through the town of Spooner and turned east on US Hwy 70. He passed a few stores but decided not to stop, for his trunk was laden with food he bought at Cub the past week. The scenery here became more familiar, and the latent memories from bygone trips drifted back into James' head. Looking out at the landscape a half hour out of Spooner, James noticed Big Sand Lake on the right side of the road and the sign a little further east welcoming all to the Lac Courte Oreilles Indian Reservation, one of five major Ojibway reservations in northern Wisconsin. The tribe operated a casino on the north side of the reservation near Hayward. Here on the south side of the reservation, however, there were few noticeable houses or businesses, which was typical of this stretch of highway. Small towns further along the route, like Radisson, Ojibwa and Winter, boasted a gas station or two and little else. By now the farms had all but disappeared, and the forest was becoming oppressively dense and grave. Also, more red and white pine intermingled here with their hardwood brethren.

James pulled into Loretta at 5:00 PM and turned north on County Road M at the town's flashing red stoplight. He was now on Loretta's main street. To his right stood a tiny brick building housing Anita's café, and Freddy's IGA General Store sat to the left adjacent a building that once housed a realtor but now lay vacant. In fact, quite a few businesses in town were defunct. Several "for sale" signs hung idly in dirty windows. Looking out of the sheltered realm of the Honda, James began to understand that these rural areas were economically worse off than the Twin Cities. Yet, even here the interconnectedness of the cyber age extended its inviting hand. The personal computer business, PC Doc, owned by a Ret Baine, still was a going concern. A battered truck was parked out in front of the drab shop. Two bars finished the parade of businesses toward the north end of Main Street—Lyle's Pub and the Watering Hole. The neon Miller and Old Milwaukee signs invited in the regulars for their Friday night shift. *Why did every village in this state over three people need at least two bars?* thought James. *God, it even looks like some of those closed businesses used to be taverns.*

At the end of the pot-holed strip, set against a backdrop of quaking aspen and facing down the main street, stood the Loretta Town Hall. It was a decrepit building of peeling red paint, the victim of an age in which people's civic duty is accomplished through CNN and Fox News instead of antiquated town meetings requiring face-to-face contact. Going to a town meeting and actually seeing your neighbors required travel out of one's chair, and who had the time for that? To the right of the hall was a Willy's Sport Shop. Willy's windows contained proud displays of hunting rifles and fishing tackle complete with gargantuan musky lures. Next to Willy's were a few unkempt two-story houses and a small Marathon gas station. One house was for sale. Immediately past the houses was a weathered "Welcome to Loretta" sign facing north. It was barely readable, but James could make out the faded words "Don't Forget Loretta Fun Days July 26, 27 and 28" below the greeting.

There could be no more startling contrast between Loretta and the cosmopolitan, urban Richfield. But this was to be James' closest town, his home of sorts, where he could open a PO box and purchase food and other necessities. James snuck a quick peek in the rearview back at the village. He had no memory of this place from his youthful trips. Robert and Carol always drove straight through without stopping, and by this time in the drive, James was usually asleep or absorbed in a video game. In those days, James viewed Loretta just like any other small town in the United States—boring.

At the town hall and Willy's, M veered slightly to the east before continuing straight north beyond the Loretta welcome sign. A ramshackle town park littered with rusted playground equipment lay just north of the town limits on the left-hand side of the road. Two grimy boys seemed to be enjoying themselves on the swing sets as they pumped their legs, trying desperately to swing higher. A run-down but defiant collection of trailer houses were on the opposite side of the road. Adjoining the makeshift trailer court, ten-foot piles of poplar and maple logs were stacked next to the highway. James rolled down the driver's side window and drank in the sweet, distinctive smell of freshly cut timber. The logs were destined for a small chip mill just barely visible over the piles and through a dense patch of fir trees. A sign on M signified the operation as Jackson Timber, and stated that the company manufactured pulp, wood fuel and other timber related products. James noted a large conveyer carrying the logs to their final destination in a massive pole shed. Some of the logs came out of the mill as finished wood chips and were blown by a giant snow blower-looking device into waiting semi-trailers. Adjacent to the processing shed was a trailer house that doubled as a maintenance shop. Two front-end loaders raced hurriedly, almost recklessly, about the mill.

Kevin's cabin was still fifteen miles and a thousand potholes away north on M. Here the forest hemmed in the road as it gradually followed the terrain over lazy hills and through cool, shadowy tamarack swamps. Ten miles out of town he passed a restaurant on the left side of M tucked into a cozy red pine grove overlooking a placid lake, and, not surprisingly, the little sign out front read Cozy Pines Restaurant and Bar. A tiny green marker fifty yards past the bar signified the waters as Grassy Lake. The establishment didn't look to be busy this day. Only a Ford truck and Chevy Impala were parked outside.

Two miles further, James spotted the small dairy farm and pasture. It was a meager operation but heavily invested with sweat equity. The listing red barn was decorated with the words "Steiger's Work Till You Drop Family Farm." Across the road lay another fenced-in field used for grazing the Steiger's dairy cows. Past the farm, M made a sharp turn to the left. A gravel road turned off to the right at the corner, and there an ominous Dead End sign was placed in a most conspicuous position. It was badly bent, however, and looked to have lost a fight with a snowplow. James recognized it immediately.

He turned onto his road and listened to the dull crunching sound that the gravel made under the wheels of his Honda as the huge oaks and maples looked solemnly down and judged him with silent testimonials. The road climbed a hill then dropped down a long steep grade, which curved sharply to the right at the bottom, only to traverse another diminutive hill. James negotiated the ruts and washboards of the drive with care. At the bottom of the second hill, James could see the lake where his cabin rested. Here a winding creek normally ran under the road through a rusted culvert, but it was essentially non-existent due to the drought. Finally, a half-mile later the road made a sharp left into Kevin's driveway.

It was still standing just as he remembered it, complete with the weathered logs that made up the frame construction of the dwelling. Jack pines and oak trees covered the yard and made sure grass mowing would never be a concern. For a second he sat in the driveway running the engine as nightfall fell silently upon the landscape. He was home.

James exited the Honda and slammed the driver's side door. The noise echoed rudely through the stilled forest, and he almost felt bad for shattering the evening quiet. He took a few moments to savor the fall air and watch the sky continue to turn an imposing grayish black palette before studying the cabin and yard with amazement. The place had not changed at all, and it all contributed to the poignancy, a palpable presence that surrounded the dwelling.

James walked over and lifted the unlocked door to the garage. Inside, rusting away, sat Kevin's 1990 black Dodge pickup. It was no worse for wear, complete with Kevin's collection of tools scattered in the bed. He picked up a tire iron and hefted it in his hands before traversing the dirt path that led across the unkempt lawn to the cabin's front steps. They were in poor shape and sang a bizarre welcoming chorus as James ascended them. Before entering, James walked around the decaying porch to face the lake, and, just like twelve years ago, there were no other man-made structures on it. *Pretty unusual in these times when people were willing to pay six grand a foot for lakeshore property in their mad rush to carve out their little piece of heaven among the woods and water.*

The honk of geese overhead momentarily broke the silence, and James looked up at the roof to spy the octagon window. Some ancient, rusting lawn chairs were relaxing on the porch. Peeling paint fell onto the deck as James ran his hands over their wire frames. Empty bird feeders lined the twenty-yard path that led to the lake. The same instruments also hung on the porch next to plastic, stern-looking owls designed to scare woodpeckers. A battered rowboat and wooden dock lay in the cool waters of Mud Lake. *Lake level seems down. Because of the drought, I suppose. God, why would you call a clear, spring-fed body of water Mud Lake? There seemed to be nearly a thousand of them in Wisconsin and Minnesota. People just didn't have an imagination.*

James was somewhat anxious to start unpacking, but first he walked around to the west side of the house, which faced the woodshed where Kevin kept his winter supply of warmth. Beyond the shed, the plantation of red pines still partially blocked the view to the field beyond The neatly planted red pines, despite being a slow growing tree, were starting to grow into each other and crowd out some of their smaller, sun-starved neighbors. Soon James began to shiver in the sharp air, and he walked back around the porch to the front door. He put the key in the lock and opened it.

To his surprise the cabin was pleasantly in order. The bedroom and the bathroom on the first floor were arranged and clean, furniture in its place and boxes stacked neatly. It was as if the cabin anticipated his arrival and organized itself as welcoming as possible. However, as James ventured down to the chilled, gray slab basement he saw quite a different picture. Fishing tackle and an assorted ensemble of ill-ordered flotsam and jetsam were strewn everywhere. Halfway down the flight of polished maple stairs, he shook his head and turned around. He didn't want to deal with it right now.

Craning his neck upward, he spied the loft or, as he used to refer to it, the sauna. The fireplace still stood seriously on the east side of the cabin. Its smoke-darkened chimney ascended thru the ceiling. This fireplace, however, was not the main heating source. A massive fire-breathing wood stove in the basement fulfilled this task. Electric backup heat was also available. Kevin had installed a recessed drop box on the west side of the cabin so wood could be pulled directly out of the woodshed and placed below ground at basement level. A trap door in the basement gave access to the box, which saved time, labor and back problems. James had yet to make his mind up about the use of wood heat. The entire process from cutting the tree down to cleaning the chimney to starting the fire seemed like a major-league headache. He didn't think too much of Kevin's tiresome saying "The man who heats with wood is twice warmed."

The stainless sink and the kitchen area crowded the northwest corner of the cabin, and the old maple floor creaked as James walked over and opened up the fruitwood-colored cabinets. Immediately, the sweet smell of cedar escaped from their interiors. The dining room adjoined the kitchen and boasted only a small round table for meals. *When you're a family of one, what did it matter? But all in all, it appears I have everything I need. Perhaps Kevin wasn't so impoverished after all. Looks like he even bought a new Whirlpool refrigerator.*

James returned to the living room and slumped into a heavy, light-brown recliner next to the empty fireplace. He threw his feet up on a rickety stool and surveyed his surroundings. The old rocking chair and a green-brown couch faced him. Kevin's deer racks and the big musky still stood watch. A gun rack holding a 30-06 bolt-action deer rifle and twelve-gauge pump shotgun hung on the wall.

Sitting in the chair caused James to grow tired almost immediately, and for the first time that day he felt truly relaxed. He decided he would move nothing in tonight but instead relish the reality that this cabin was his to enjoy. He had never owned land before. Now he was the sole master of some 200 acres of woods and field. Yet, behind the novelty of it all lay the cold truth.

I'm alone and the future is murky. Is this escapism, some sort of perverted Buddhism? The bottom line is I have to get back to work. I'm not meant to stay here.

Hunger suddenly clawed its way into James' stomach. He walked over to the refrigerator and opened its freezer portion, digging through some assorted packages that were marked "steaks" with a black marker. Despite his limited knowledge of wild game, he knew it was venison left over from one of Kevin's successful hunts. He grabbed a six-pack of Heineken and a bag of potatoes from the Honda and prepared to make his first dinner at the cabin. Within a matter of minutes James had the steaks defrosting under the broiler with neatly sliced potatoes frying on the stove and two empty Heineken bottles on the counter.

And he was feeling rather proud of himself when the knock came to the door.

"Who is it?" he called above the sizzling meat.

There was no answer, but he could see the figure standing on the porch. He turned down the electric stove and walked over to the door. Neglecting to sneak a look out the window, he opened it.

"James Norris?" asked the forty-something man who stood outside.

"Yes," answered James. "What is the matter?"

"Hello, I'm Martin Steiger, and I own the dairy farm out on M. I was a good friend of your uncle, and Bob Wilkerson said you were going to be up here sometime. The wife and my son and daughter have been looking after the place."

James extended his hand. Martin's grip almost crushed his fingers.

"Come on inside," James said.

Despite Martin's vice-like handshake, he was not a physically imposing man. He stood five-foot-ten with a medium build and close cut black hair. Tonight he wore a flat-billed Green Bay Packer ball cap and a red flannel, which was ripped and smeared with grease. His dark brown eyes held an intense energy, and he stared at James with a penetrating, squinting gaze that made James feel a bit uncomfortable on the receiving end.

Martin continued talking as the pair walked inside. He didn't bother to stop to take off his shoes.

"Your uncle was a great guy. Him and me were pretty good friends."

"Beer?" James asked.

Martin grimaced. "Twist my arm," he answered.

James tossed him a bottle and an opener out of the fridge. Martin caught them, and took a seat in the recliner opposite James in the rocking chair. He opened the bottle nonchalantly and studied the label. For a few seconds nobody said anything.

"What is this stuff?" Martin asked finally.

James replied, "It is Heineken, a European beer."

Martin scoffed, "Looks like yuppie beer to me. Sure ain't Old Mil."

"Old Mil?" asked James.

Martin looked at James like he was a naive two-year-old. "Yeah, Old Milwaukee, the best beer there is."

This guy is serious. However, James held his tongue. The first visit with his new neighbor was not a time for an argument. Besides, he saw that Martin seemed to be enjoying the beer anyway. The bottle was half empty.

"Kind of tastes skunky," said Martin.

"Well, you sure seem to like it," James answered. "You got half that bottle gone."

"What can I say," Martin laughed. "Guilty as charged. I like beer. It is not a crime."

"I suppose that is your stuff out there in the trailer?" asked Martin changing the subject.

"Yeah," replied James. "I'm going to wait till tomorrow and start moving some in."

"You need any help?"

"Well, most of the stuff is pretty light, but I suppose I could use some help with a few of the heavier things so I don't end up killing myself."

"That's right. You don't want to break your back when you don't have to. I'll tell you what. I'll come down tomorrow evening after I get my work done and give you a hand. Then maybe you could meet my wife and family and go out to dinner with us at Cozy Pines."

"That sounds great," answered James somewhat glad he was not entirely alone out here.

"Yeah, I don't know if my wife's going to like me having a new playmate down here," Martin laughed. "You know what she's going to say if I end up doing stuff with you. But you gotta get away sometimes, right?"

James sat silent for a moment. "I don't have that problem right now," he said.

"You divorced?"

"No, not divorced, just got out of a serious relationship."

"Tough break."

Martin's friendliness surprised James. Yet, he also sensed some secret anger inside him, like he was only friendly up to a point and then there was a line of separation one should not cross.

"Bob told me you were an accountant at Litchfield, Taylor and Faust. Where did you go to school?" asked Martin.

"I went to the U of M."

"That's funny, because I wanted to be an accountant too at one point in time," said Martin. "I went to UW Madison for two years but dropped out and went in the Army for three years till I blew my knee out. The old man needed help back here on the farm, and the rest is history."

"So what exactly are you going to do out here now?" Martin continued. "You just doing the R and R thing, or are you going to stay here permanently?"

"You know, I am really not sure," answered James. "I just needed to get away from the Twin Cities. My girlfriend and I weren't getting along. My job fell through, just too many memories there, you know. I was lucky enough to get this place because Kevin named me the second beneficiary in his will. My parents were the first beneficiaries, but they died a couple years ago in a car accident."

"I think you're going to enjoy it out here," said Martin, cracking a sly smile.

He then stood up from the chair and walked over to the sliding doors facing Mud Lake, barely visible in the gathering gloom. "Geez, this sure is a nice place," he said, "Great view of old Mud."

"I'll tell you what," said James. "After coming out here from the Cities, it's going to take a little getting used to."

"Think you can handle the silence?" Martin said turning to face James. "You know, there is no mall around the corner, no Metrodome, no zoo, no sporting events, no movies. I hope you hunt and fish."

"I've been thinking about fishing, maybe hunting. But I don't really know a whole lot about it."

"Why?" Martin snapped. "You are not one of those animal rights activists are you?"

James laughed. "No, no I've just never really been exposed to it."

"Well, we may need to change that," replied Martin. "Up here we don't care about dead deer hanging from trees out in our front yard. We are not like you guys down there in the Cities."

James was a little unsure about how to interpret that statement, and he decided not to continue the discussion on that avenue. He found Martin's stereotypical rant against city dwellers somewhat annoying.

"I'll have to introduce you to some of our neighbors," continued Martin. "They may have a thing or two to teach you on your little adventure here. You know, I am not sure if you remember, but one time we actually met before. You were probably twelve or so. Anyway, you were hiding out in the cabin, and I was helping Kevin cut some wood out by the shed."

James rolled his eyes back in his head in a desperate search of lost recollections. "Oh yeah, I remember that vaguely now," he lied.

"Well, James, it was nice meeting you. I'm going to head home," said Martin as he extended his hand and made his way towards the door. 'We will see you tomorrow, okay. If you need any help, just give me a call. My number is seven-five-two, fourteen hundred. It is also in the phone book if Kevin left you one here somewhere."

"Thanks," James answered.

Martin opened the door. "Have a good one," he called out as he jogged down the steps and climbed into his black Ford F-250 diesel pickup. As the distinctive rumble of the diesel faded into the night, James was left wondering who this man was. *He could simply be a friendly neighbor. But he seemed to have an intense side to him that became evident when we talked about hunting. There was something more to this man.*

However, James' thoughts quickly turned to the neglected venison defrosting in the oven, which was now smoking away and setting off the annoying high-pitched whine of the smoke alarm.

Chapter 5
The Realm

James finished dinner quickly as the night won its temporary battle over the remaining holdouts of light and completely covered James' surroundings. He didn't bother to wash the dishes but instead sat in front of the non-existent fire contemplating his situation. Sleep, however, soon cast its irresistible spell, forcing his eyelids closed as they became heavier and heavier. The urge to rest prevailed. Slowly he ascended the spiral staircase and fell into the king-sized bed, which, by luck, was still covered with sheets and a blanket. Despite the relentless thoughts in his head, sleep quickly overtook him.

* * *

Wandering, in search, the man traversed the forlorn and starkly gray landscape. A melancholy chill hung in the air as a moisture-laden carpet of clouds conspired with the onset of evening to host the impending shroud of night. He did not know what he was searching for. But he felt as if he had lost something important, something essential.

The man continued on his strange journey, now walking in a deep, cool wood. *What am I looking for?* he asked himself again and again as the frustration grew within him. It was something he could not view with his eyes, yet it was known all too well, its shapeless form lurking somewhere in the surrounding murkiness. Fleeting signs and flashes of forest animals seemed to disappear like ghosts. Images raced through his mind, but not one showed its face clearly, all foreign and vague.

Breaks in the canopy alerted him to a thinning in the forest ahead. And soon there was a place set before him, a place markedly different from the landscape. Recognition failed him, yet he could not resist its inviting charms; escape was impossible. So he stepped closer to its realm.

It was so recognizable. Guardians stood on the threshold and giants lay within. An icy wind emanated from its dim entrance, chilling the man and stopping his advance. He paused for a few seconds, his thoughts disjointed. And slowly it made strange sense. In fact, he did know the place. It had changed only slightly, adapted or evolved into a bizarre shape, and he knew the dangers of its inner womb.

The man stood at the entrance as the conflict tore him apart. Above, a rhythmic drone like one would associate with the meditations of monks in foreign lands began to rise and fall with the sporadic gusts of wind as it built upon itself. "Enter, enter, enter," the voices seemed to be saying. The man took a few clumsy steps toward the realm and closed his eyes. *I must cross the threshold...*

But then a fear began to swell within him, and he stopped outside of that sacred, magical place. *I'm not ready*, he thought, *something has to change*. So there he stood—paralyzed.

Suddenly, unmistakably, his surroundings brightened. A faint star from within the womb of the realm seemed to grow ever brighter as its presence moved toward him. He walked forward, no longer afraid, as the blinding white light began to envelop and flood him with its brilliance. The great light now totally concealed the realm and grew ever fiercer, causing the man to squint and cover his face with his hands. Looking through his fingers, the man could barely make out the source of the light. It was radiating from what seemed to be a window, an octagon window cut into the soft blue sky.

* * *

James bolted out of bed with cold sweat streaming down his forehead. He was shaking uncontrollably and his heart threatened to pound out of his chest as he gazed out the octagon window to the risen sun. He tossed himself back on the bed and tried to catch his breath. *Never, never,* he thought, *have I had such a realistic dream.* Every sight, smell, sound and sensation was imprinted in his memory. He even pinched himself to verify his actual flesh and blood existence.

After the initial relief of realizing it was but a dream, James began to criticize himself for being afraid. Yet, he could not deny it was the most eerie experience he had ever known. However, the scientific training of his college years told him dreams were nothing more than random electric impulses in his resting mind. They signified nothing and meant even less. And one couldn't argue with science.

James threw off the blankets and stood up to face day one at his new home. There was work to be done. As soon as James made his way down the spiral staircase and touched his bare feet on the chilled maple floor, the night's tribulations had all but been forgotten. He poured a glass of fresh two-percent milk he had brought from Richfield and silently sat down at the circular oak kitchen table. The table, which had come from the grandparents James never knew, was worn badly. Shallow, darkened scrapes and grooves cut into the pale grain gave testimony to a tough but loved existence. They were half-moon shaped, and James guessed they were imprints from drunken games of quarters that Kevin and his underage friends played when his parents were away, thus leaving the brand of adolescence forever etched on the table's face.

In quiet contemplation, he gazed out at the festival of color and pine trees that was his property. The day was in stark contrast to yesterday's day of arrival. Brilliant sunshine and clear blue skies greeted James. *Nice to have some variety,* he thought. It was a perfect beginning to a new day.

Unpacking and organizing the cabin was to be a tortuous task, but James hoped the warm sunshine would make the job a little more pleasant He was determined to redesign the cabin in his own image, which meant relegating some of Kevin's belongings to the basement. Yet, James was no interior decorator. In fact, if he was to be totally honest with himself he despised the entire activity of decorating and the people who spent the vast majority of their short lives agonizing whether or not their bedspread was color coordinated with the latest fall fashion and their toilet matched the shower curtains. However, even decorating-adverse James felt that the cabin needed a little sprucing up.

After putting on some torn Levis jeans and a tattered ugly green flannel shirt, James begrudgingly started the task. However, he soon realized he would not need many of the things he had brought out in the U-haul. Either there was simply no room or Kevin had already provided them. Items he brought out that he didn't need would have to be tossed in the garage or in a small storage shed which lay next to the woodshed. In no time, James was immersed in the job, running back and forth between the cabin, U-Haul and garage.

In fact, James was so busy that he almost didn't hear Kevin's antiquated rotary phone ringing inside the cabin. Like a startled bird, he jumped off the garage floor where he had been sitting and sprinted towards the cabin. He got to the phone just in time.

"Hello," he answered in a breathless voice.

"Yeah, James, this is Martin. You still up for dinner tonight?" came the gruff voice from the other end of the line.

"Sure, sounds great," replied James still not sure what to think of this newfound friend.

Martin continued, "I'll be down tonight at five-thirty or so after chores." He then hung up.

James' first day flew by in a mad dash of unpacking, assorting and arranging. The few assorted leftovers James had brought from Richfield sufficed as lunch. He was beginning to feel a little comfortable out here, but by no means did he feel settled. Really, he was still struggling with the realization that this place was his home for the time being. *But for how long? I gotta look through those Star Tribune employment classifieds soon.*

Martin arrived at James' cabin exactly at 5:30 PM. This time he drove a red Grand Prix sedan. His wife and two kids were in tow. Martin hopped out of the car in the driveway and didn't bother to shut the door, so the pinging of the open door alarm could be heard wafting over the still waters of Mud. With long strides, he walked over to James who, at this time, was standing outside of the garage surrounded by a mess of moving boxes. The scene resembled a trailer park after a requisite tornado had done its work.

"James, I would like you to meet my wife, Katie," Martin said as a shorter dark haired woman approached James and extended her hand.

She had dark eyes and skin that gave her a Mediterranean appeal, and behind her eyes lay the same fierce determination discerned in Martin. She shook James' hand firmly.

"And this is my boy, Steve," Martin continued. "He is sixteen."

Steve was a shorter version of his old man, right down to the straight back and squinted eyes.

"This is my daughter, Marie. She is fourteen," Martin said, pointing toward her.

Marie and Steve shook James' hand firmly as well. Marie looked like the black sheep of the family and showed almost no resemblance to her mother. James would almost have guessed she had been adopted, for she had blonde hair and was extremely tall and skinny with high cheekbones. *Interesting mix of children.*

Martin jumped into action and quickly helped James move some heavy boxes to the far end of the garage. Then James and Martin moved a table, couch and desk out of the U-Haul and placed them haphazardly in the garage as well. Martin didn't even break a sweat while James was panting in the seventy-degree temperatures and worrying about the dull ache in his lower back. Nonetheless, in short order the group was all packed into the car. No sooner had James taken the front passenger seat Martin threw the car in gear and tore off down the road leaving a pile of dust in his wake.

"Saturday night is the prime rib special at Cozy Pines," announced Martin as he approached the bar. "Its one heck of a deal, I'll tell you, boy, nine ninety-nine all you can eat with salad bar, usually brings in a big local crowd."

The lot was full as James and his dinner companions pulled in. It was a gravel lot with an aged pine log fence ringing three sides of it, and some of the logs were falling down in places.

"You ever eaten here before?" asked Martin as threw the car in park.

James shook his head. "I just got here. You know that," he laughed.

With his distinct giant strides, Martin approached the entrance and forcefully opened the front doors as if to announce his presence to the entire establishment. There was no entryway into the restaurant. Immediately one stood amidst tables and booths with the bar off to the right and a spacious dining room to the front and left. The dining room had large windows that gave diners a view of Grassy Lake. A beautiful stone fireplace was cut into the far left wall. After the entire group entered the restaurant, an older woman walked over to greet them.

"Out on the town tonight there, Martin?" she asked.

"Just with the family and our new neighbor here, James Norris," he said. He motioned for James to come forward. "He is Kevin's nephew and moving into Kevin's cabin. So we are out here showing him the sights."

Martin turned to look at James. "James, this is Ann Bakke," he said. "Her and her husband, Ray, run this place."

James shook her hand. She had warm yet weary eyes that seemed to radiate the thousands of stories told within these walls. "It's nice to meet you," she said with a slight smile while grasping her burning cigarette in her left hand.

The group decided on a table overlooking Grassy Lake at the far end of the dining room. It was an idyllic view with the fall sunset bringing out different hues and colors in the lake water that one could never see any other time. Only the undulating wakes of a few scattered boats broke the calm. While walking ahead of James to the table, Martin was grabbed by a husky man in a black Fraser Papers jacket. The man and his large wife set down their beers in unison.

"You too good to call anymore or something?" the man said.

Martin smiled as his family continued on to the table.

"What, you three sheets to the wind?" Martin said. "I see you every goddamn day on that grader like you are king of the world."

"You ornery old bastard," the man laughed. "Say, I seen that big twelve over by Johnson's."

"Really?" Martin questioned. "He'll probably die of old age. That bastard will disappear here in a few weeks. Only way a guy will get him will be luck."

"You got that right, boy," the man replied. Martin swung around to face James.

"James, this is a man you don't want to piss off. He is Isaac Stelsky, and he takes care of the roads here in Williams Township."

The big woman stared at Martin as she took a drag off a Marlboro Lite. Martin gave her an amused look. "And this is Isaac's lovely wife Meg," he said.

"Asshole," Meg replied, laughing as her portly frame shook in the chair.

"James is Kev's nephew," Martin continued. "He's living in the place now."

James shook hands with his new neighbors as Isaac pointed at Martin. "You remember how Kevin always used to stop here every Friday for a six pack of Old Mil," he said. "Hell, a man could set his watch by him. Five o'clock and he'd be here. But, I'll tell you, he was one hell of a guy."

"Well, I'm gonna go get some dinner," Martin said. "See ya round, Ike."

James dutifully followed his host back toward the table. But it was a long journey. Martin exchanged hellos with no less than half a dozen people in the restaurant. It made James feel a little uncomfortable, as if he was an outsider sneaking into some private club.

"Hey, Martin, you hear Mike Hodgekin's boy hit a bear with his truck?" said an older bespeckled man sitting at a booth drinking a beer with a red and white label.

"Yeah," Martin replied, "stupid bastard gonna mount it."

And on it went table to table.

The chosen table was somewhat apart from the rest of the dinning room, an annex in the corner, with a circular booth. Martin and James took their seats on the ripped but comfortable plastic coated brown cushions.

"You need menus, guys?" Martin asked Marie and Steve.

They both shook heads in the negative as James studied his surroundings. The restaurant had a look all its own, unique but common at the same time, with shiny, yellowing pine walls, mounted walleyes and northern pike, deer racks, collector bar mirrors advertising every brand from Hamm's to Old Milwaukee to Miller, replica guns, knives, pictures of family members and cute quotes saying things like, "If you sprinkle when you tinkle, be a sweety and wipe the seaty."

Yet the scene didn't overwhelm. It wasn't the colossal pop culture trash heap that hung on the walls of a place like Daimon's or Applebee's, places that served as a shrine to transient fads and consumer goods that evoked some sort of romantic nostalgia. *At least here you could still make out spaces between the items hanging on the walls. And here people actually talked to each other, seeing there is not a TV hung up in every corner, just one in the entire place and that is in the bar.*

Martin pulled out a pack of Marlboros from his worn red flannel shirt pocket. "All you can eat prime rib," he said as he lit up. "I'll tell you what, though. The prices aren't what they used to be. Used to be a hell of a lot cheaper, but that's the way it goes, I guess. Too many swampys and mudducks driving the prices up."

James looked at Martin. "What is a swampy … mudduck?" he asked.

Martin, Kate, Marie and Steve burst into laughter. James turned sheepish.

Martin gathered his composure, looked at James and started laughing again. "Look in the mirror," he said finally, sending more laughter chorusing around the table. Now James was getting annoyed, and Kate was compelled to step in.

"Swampys and mudducks are Minnesotans who have lake cabins in Wisconsin. It is not a term of endearment," she said.

"Why swampy or mudduck?" asked James.

Martin, now straight faced, chimed in. "Because yuppie Minnesotans say they come from the land of ten thousand lakes. Hell, they even print it on the license plate, but the fact is Wisconsin has more lakes than Minnesota. Minnesotans say they got ten thousand lakes because they count every swamp and mud hole as a lake, hence the term mudduck or swampy." Martin then exhaled the Marlboro Man's vice. "Screw 'em," he growled.

James laughed off the comments and grabbed a stray menu that lay on the table near the wall. He opened it and saw that not one meal was over ten dollars.

"What else is good here besides the prime rib?" he asked.

"Walleye is all right," said Kate before Martin could speak. "Since Martin can't catch any, we come here. In fact, I think that's what I am going to have."

Martin shot a sorrowful glance in her direction. "That wasn't very nice," he said with a grossly inadequate pout.

"You guys getting ribs?" asked Kate looking at Steve and Marie.

"I'm old enough to make my mind up," snapped Steve in a fit of teenage self-assertiveness.

Martin took a long drag from his cigarette and looked at James "He wanted to go out drinking tonight with his friends, but I said he should meet you."

"I don't drink with them," yelled Steve, attracting the attention of a few other patrons.

Martin rolled his eyes back. "Yeah, right," he said.

"I just want to have a life," a more subdued Steve said with his eyes fixated on the table.

"Just leave him alone, Dad," cautioned Marie.

These people were certainly up front, James thought to himself as he pretended to read his menu.

Ann sauntered over to the table taking out her order slip in the process. She tapped her pen on the table as if she was ordering everybody to attention.

"Well, what's it gonna be?" she said.

Dinner arrived exceptionally quickly, distracting the diners from their lively conversation that touched on all sorts of topics from sports to the prospects of actually having snow this coming winter.

"Fish all around," said Ann as she set up the folding tray holder and began passing out the dishes with the baked potatoes and French fries on the side. Old Milwaukees were passed out as well to everyone, including underage Steve and Marie. Kate handed a plate to Marie who took it carefully and placed it in front of her while poking it with a fork.

"Damn it, Marie," snapped Martin, "eat it or I will."

Marie yelled back, "I'm just seeing if it's done."

James tried to divert the conversation back to other matters as Ann smiled knowingly and walked away. "You know, I think I'm going to try deer hunting," he said.

Martin cut him off. "Great, you can come over and help us on drives. We got some great swamps for you to walk through." He then glanced at Steve who chuckled in return.

James had heard about deer drives from Fred back at Litchfield. He imagined them to be nothing more than a bunch of drunks stumbling through the woods in a paramilitary line as they chased a terrified creature to certain death.

"It's a possibility," he replied.

Throughout the evening James' thoughts began to drift back to his dream the previous night. *So vivid and real. And the feeling ... that presence ...*

He wasn't sure where the question came from. It just popped into his head without warning, and he spoke the words without really consciously thinking.

"Do you guys have any wolves around here?" James asked the Steiger family collectively.

Steve opened up his mouth like he was about to speak, but he made eye contact with Martin and clamed up.

"Yeah they are 'round, unfortunately," said Martin with his mouth full of walleye. An intense fire in his eyes welled up, and James knew immediately he had hit a nerve. "I've lost a few calves because of those things. I just don't understand."

Martin stopped chewing and sat his fork down. He placed his elbows on the table, swallowed hard and pointed at James. "Our forefathers killed the wolves because they were competitors," he said. "They attacked cattle and the like. But that was when people actually had brains. When I was a youngster those damn things began making their way back into the state, must have been like the eighties or early nineties. Now the wolves at least have stabilized population-wise. But … ahh … shit, I don't even know if that is true. There is probably more and more of them every year I just don't understand why we need 'em. It is all because some fuckin environmentalist, liberal wackos from the Twin Cities or New York are telling me how to live. The fact is the wolves kill deer and kill livestock. That is what they were designed to do and don't give me no bullshit about how they only kill the sick. Hell, I've seen the carcass of a twelve-pointer that had been picked clean by those things. Now, I'll tell you, James, I am not some ignorant old timer who is worried about being attacked by wolves while I am going out to get the mail. My problem is that it just seems like this land is being given back to them. And for what? During this process, I am struggling to get by, even with the higher milk prices. I'm the loser in the end. Ahh … fuck, I just don't know. I don't know if I can coexist with wolves. Hell, I just don't know."

As if by instinct, Martin reached into his flannel pocket for another Marlboro. He had scarcely taken a breath the past minute during his verbal rampage.

James sunk back into the booth somewhat shaken by the tirade. Martin had talked non-stop, his voice getting louder and louder like he was doing some sort of Adolf Hitler impression. The rest of his family just continued to eat.

"I heard wolves howling once as a kid," said James, not yet wanting to change the topic completely.

Martin picked his fork up again and speared the last bit of walleye on his plate. "Even though I don't like the creatures," he replied as he spit out small white pieces of chewed up fish and bone, "the cry certainly is an unforgettable sound. I've probably heard them five or six times."

Soon dinner was finished, and Ann strolled over to request they clear the table. It was an unusually busy night and space was needed. The group moved to the bar and all ordered more Old Milwaukees. James watched as numerous friendly faces came over to chat with the family. He was coming to appreciate the fact he had a close neighbor he could talk to, despite Martin's intensity and flashes of anger. And he saw it as a plus that both Martin and Kate were college educated and could easily converse with him on a number of subjects. Kate was a nursing graduate from the University of Wisconsin-Eau Claire and currently worked in nearby Hayward at the hospital. But, for now, as the group stood at the bar, the conversation was limited to the more pressing topics: fishing, local gossip and weather. The recent drought was a favorite complaint.

Steve and Marie were bored stiff, and they made their way over to the video games by the front door. The machines, a Ms. Pac Man relic and a worn Galactica, were well over twenty years old. Behind the bar stood Ray, a giant of a man, six-feet-five inches tall with frying-pan hands, deep-set eyes and long, frazzled gray hair. He talked up a storm while Kate introduced an endless stream of neighbors and strangers to James. In the right corner of the bar was the TV. It was tuned to CNN, no sports tonight. The images from the presidential campaign trail were flashing on the screen, and nobody was paying attention, nobody except Martin.

James looked down the bar at him. His eyes were glued to the screen. Amid the flag-waving, presidential hopeful William Beecham trumped up his credentials and his vague, yet nonetheless persistent, call for "national rebirth" amid uncertain times. The details, the specifics, apparently were to be revealed at a later date. During the entire CNN clip, Martin never shifted his gaze, and James thought he seemed to be squeezing the Old Milwaukee can like he was about to crush it any moment.

He abruptly hit the can a few times on the bar, causing the sound to echo throughout the establishment. Then, in a flash, as the TV story changed to some meaningless entertainment topic, Martin eased up noticeably. James' natural curiosity was aroused. *Who was this Martin Steiger?* he thought. It was time to find out.

"Beecham seems like he has the power of destiny on his side, huh, Martin?" said James as he approached his new friend.

Martin tensed up like his entire body was preparing for a fight. He turned in his barstool to look at James.

"That man is the most dangerous person on the face of the planet," he said in an acid-laced voice. "I know what he stands for, but I bet you think guys like him mean safety?"

Martin never let James answer.

"Bullshit, he stands for the surrender of freedom for safety's sake, and the complacent idiots of this country are going to let him do just that. I'll tell you this, James," he yelled pointing his finger at the TV, "Those who would surrender their liberty for the sake of security deserve neither liberty nor security."

He looked up at James with a wry, quizzical look as he set his beer down. "You know who said that?" he asked.

James shook his head.

"Ben Franklin, that is who. I tell ya, Beecham simply is a creature of the times. He plays on people's emotions and tells them what they want to hear, like he can solve all their problems for them. I don't understand how people could be so stupid to give up their God-given rights inherent in the very order of nature for mere safety."

Martin then turned away from James and picked up his beer as if he was sure his sweeping verbiage had thoroughly trumped his new neighbor's ability to retort. However, he soon found out he had underestimated his young friend.

"But don't times of crisis and uncertainty like we are living in today require some governmental steps that may, perhaps, reduce a little liberty?" asked James. "Besides, what do you find so abhorrent in Beecham's proposals? I know he wants to raise some taxes and increase some police powers, but that all sounds reasonable to me."

Kate spoke up this time. "I don't think this is necessarily a time of crisis. I mean, I agree that the economy is not so hot, but the question is if short-term, feel-good legislation is worth sacrificing our liberty for. I say it is not, because liberties lost are never regained. It is the start of a dangerous slippery slope. Where does it end? The fact is, we must never give up what our ancestors worked so hard to achieve. Eternal vigilance is the price of liberty."

More than the union symbolized in their wedding rings, Katie and Martin were a union of ideology, James thought. *They stood shoulder to shoulder when it came to politics. I am sure they have a lot more to say.*

But there would be no more such talk tonight. Marie and Steve were about at the end of their boredom rope. Right now, they were doing three-sixties on a couple of barstools and staring out into space. Kate stepped in to save them.

"It's getting pretty late for us old folks," she laughed. "Tomorrow is just another work day for us."

She spoke loudly while looking straight at Martin, who ignored her by striking up a conversation with Ray and another older man two stools away. Kate rolled her eyes. "Could take hours to get him out of here," she sighed.

Nonetheless, within a few minutes Martin motioned to the kids with a strange pointing gesture and started to walk toward the door. On the way out he then shook hands with several other assembled neighbors. James had already forgotten half of their names, but he did his best to remember and act friendly. And as he strolled to the parking lot, the names Bakke, Larson, Stelsky, Stevens, Wesley, Rosenbach and Kaufman all stuck in his mind.

The five left Cozy Pines and drove quietly through the desolate, darkened countryside. All kept an eye out for the glint of light in the ditch that forewarned of the deer soon to cross the road and total out the vehicle. Marie and Steve were dropped off at the Steiger farm along with Kate as Martin drove James home. Martin watched the taillights of Steve's pickup disappear in the rear view mirror of the Grand Prix as he raced back to Loretta and his friends. Martin shook his head.

"That idiot kid doesn't understand the price of gas, but, hell, it is his money. He'll learn," he said.

Soon Martin pulled into James' driveway, and the headlights of the car cut through the surrounding darkness and spotlighted the cabin. However, they did little to make the cabin more inviting. James was soon to be alone again, and it naturally spurred conversation.

"Do you really think, Martin, we are becoming a police state?" he asked.

"God, I hope not, I really hope not … " answered Martin.

Martin shut the car off. Immediately the headlights winked out as well. Outside a stiff breeze whisked up from the north, clearly audible through the closed car windows.

"You know, James, I think I know what you're thinking," Martin said.

"What do you mean?" James asked.

Martin smiled knowingly. "I am not no militia guy, ok," he said. "I'm not calling for a revolution or anything. One must be realistic about these things. I mean, look at me. The fact is that I rely on government help for the dairy farm sometimes. Damn feds have their hands in all aspects of the industry. But one thing you must never forget is that behind the cloak of law, power ultimately rests with who controls the weapons, and this power must always be checked or tyranny is the result."

"Well, maybe," James said as he opened the door of the car. "Thanks for showing me the neighborhood."

"Have a good one, James," replied Martin. "I'll be in touch, introduce you to some of the other neighbors around here."

And with that, Martin started the car and disappeared down the road, leaving James alone, once again, to absorb what he had learned.

James slowly approached the cabin, taking care not to trip in the dark. Once inside, he turned on the electric lights and took a second to survey the mess of boxes and memories scattered throughout the living room.

In all his time spent in the Twin Cities with all the constant noise of the presidential campaign on TV and radio, James never had such an illuminating conversation with any of the supposedly educated people he knew and worked with. Here, out in a place that was ridiculed for being the home of hicks and the uneducated, he had been exposed to issues and viewpoints surrounding the campaign that he had never even bothered to think about. It wasn't that he agreed with Martin completely. In reality, he thought Martin was overreacting a bit, and he did think Martin's political leanings were right wing to the extreme. However, Martin had introduced James to valid concerns concerning Mr. Beecham and what his repeated calls for security meant for the abstract notions of liberty and freedom that were constantly tossed about in the American political theater. These thoughts occupied him as he made his way up the spiral staircase. Luckily, out here, in his new home, he did have time to think about such matters. But, for now, sleep beckoned.

Chapter 6
Teachers

The man made a few steps towards the realm and that threshold between this world and eternity. The air was growing cooler by the second, driven by winds from inside the inner womb. Yet he was still frozen in hesitation, teetering on the edge of decision. *Enter or run,* his mind screamed. *But why? What lay beyond in that most sacred of places?*

But it was not to be. The light was drawing closer, beating down on him with all its intensity. His body warmed quickly and sweat began to pour down his face and neck. Turning his head, he stared into the blinding glow streaming in through the window.

* * *

James hit the floor running and actually took a few steps before he even knew what was happening. It was a Sunday morning. It had happened again.

Things were beginning to settle down, so to speak, in the mixed hardwood and conifer forest of northern Wisconsin as the season rolled into late October. The trees were now bare, and the dead leaves left a crisp brown carpet around James' cabin. Many times the past few weeks, James had awakened from a broken sleep caused by the strangely fascinating nocturnal adventure. It didn't happen every night, but it did possess a strange sort of consistency. He would always remember standing in front of some mysterious place full of a sense of dread and indecision.

He had long since pitched out the terrible alarm clock. The horrendous mechanical device had been replaced by the sharp honks of southbound geese. Days rolled by in an unbroken stretch of quiet. Most of James' time was consumed by rearranging the cabin, which did actually take some work. Nevertheless, these days would soon be coming to an end. There was only so much he could do out here. Then the work of how to rebuild his future and career would begin. His computer still sat unpacked in the garage, and, surprisingly, he didn't miss it at all. The urge to be plugged in and deluged with useless information had dissipated like the long days of the summer season. However, he was acutely aware the computer was an invaluable, and neglected, tool in his job hunt. But, for now, he was content to be informed by the radio or the small talk that drifted through the smoke-filled confines of Cozy Pines. He had been down there a few times since his night out with Martin and enjoyed talking with Ray and Ann. However, he as of yet had no other people to talk to besides them and the Steiger family.

It was the third Sunday of October. Brilliant clear, crisp blue skies lay overhead as the warm southwest breeze signaled to all dwellers of the northern latitudes that Indian summer was here after the first frosts of the year, which had been almost three weeks late and just barely caused the mercury to dip into the low thirties. James guessed the time to be 7:00 AM. He didn't think he was going to be able to do this—get up early—once he got out of his work routine. However, on some days he forced himself to do it.

Slipping on a worn pair of slippers, James sauntered down to the basement to stoke up the coals in his main heat source—the immense wood stove. He had gotten pretty good at making fires and keeping them well fed at night, which, due to the warm weather, was the only time the cabin needed a little heat. It was a chore, however. There was always work to be done, either moving the wood into the cabin, starting the fire or cleaning up the mess of wood scraps always covering the basement floor. James hoped burning the oak, maple, birch and poplar that Kevin had worked so hard to split up would save money on the monthly electric heat bills.

James decided that this Sunday would be different. For too long his universe had been confined to the cabin, which did little to alleviate the general feeling of melancholy and doubt concerning his future that was always with him. He had neglected so far to go out and explore the surrounding countryside, as he would have done when he was younger. Today he was going to change that; he was going to make a point of wandering.

After a light breakfast of milk and bagels, James put on a red and black Hudson hat left behind by Kevin and his cracked Rocky hiking boots. His jacket was a light red flannel over a pure white t-shirt. He didn't bother to lock the door as he strolled out to meet autumn in all its glory.

Today he would walk the boundaries of his land. *My land, I just can't get used to that.* Only a solitary puff of cumulonimbus cloud to the north broke the blue. It was a lone survivor, separated from its brethren, of a distant unsettled t-storm. The familiar sound of dry leaves dancing in the wind on their final journey across his driveway into the woods beyond greeted him as he walked down the front steps.

"Maybe I should rake," he said aloud sarcastically. "Yeah, right."

He looked skyward as if expecting a response from Kevin himself and smiled as the memories of the man who made this day possible returned. *I wonder if Kevin really expected that me, of all people, would end up with his cabin?*

The blast of a shotgun echoed across the countryside as James laced up his boots in the front yard. He made a mental note to get a hunting license, but no deadline was set in stone for the task to be completed. It would get done in his own time, unlike the demands of Litchfield, Taylor and Faust that required work to be done yesterday. Here time flowed smoothly and fluid instead of in fits and starts.

He began his journey by walking to the east. The adjoining forest in this direction was a mix of oak, maple and large poplar. Several massive poplars were lying on the forest floor, torn up by their roots in recent winds. Upon closer examination, he saw that many of the trees had blackened, hollow trunks. *They look so robust and strong from the outside, but inside they have rotted away.*

The hardwood forest soon gave way to a low-lying tamarack swamp. It should have been a boggy mess, but due to the relative absence of rain over the summer it was now dry enough to walk across in most parts. The ground was soft under James' feet as he traversed the spongy and potentially dangerous bog. He took great care not to fall into the blood-black pools of water still collecting around the decaying rotten trees and stumps.

In the summer this place would be inhospitable and totally alive with mosquitoes, but thanks to the wimpy, late frost they were long dead, and humans could actually enjoy the silent land, as could the red squirrels. James took a few seconds to watch their antics of whirlwind chases and incessant chatter. Deer tracks pressed deep into the mud crisscrossed the swamp.

Upon reaching the far eastern edge of the swamp, James turned north. Once again, oak, poplar and maples dominated the forest. He was now to the east of Mud Lake and still on his land. However, the land directly east was private, and through the woods James could make out a barbed wire fence. Suddenly, the blast of a shotgun broke the forest calm again. *Sounds close. Probably people in the National Forest.*

James stumbled ahead through small briar patches and blackberry bushes, which seemed to cluster together in spots where younger, smaller trees grew. He took care not to let the thorny branches swat him in the face or attempt to catch a free ride by sticking into his flannel. When he was younger he used to like to pull back the blackberry branches and let them fly like a catapult into a trailing companion. He recalled how he would laugh to himself as he heard the "whack" across his dad or mom in days gone by. But now he was alone. Those games were impossible to play.

Just as James thought he was nearing the National Forest, the blast of a shotgun split the air yet again with its distinctive baritone crack. The shot was very close and actually caused James to hit the ground. He jumped up immediately and instinctively felt his body for buckshot. With a hawk-like gaze he scanned the shadows of the surrounding forest and for a brief instant he thought he heard the crunching of leaves. Then he took a few halting steps forward and stopped. Slowly moving his head to the right, he caught the glimpse of a baseball cap up on top of a slight ridge of aspen slashings directly to the east. And soon he could make out the figure of a man. James mustered his courage.

"Who is there," he yelled in his most commanding voice.

There was no answer. James rapidly, yet cautiously, strolled over to where he saw the capped being. The solitary hunter was now fifty yards away with his back to James, and a shotgun was tucked under his armpit. James shredded his inhibitions, and he ran to catch up to the intruder.

"Hey, hold it, guy," he yelled.

The man wheeled around but said nothing. He removed his sunglasses and walked deliberately towards James, taking care to point the muzzle of the shotgun down toward the forest floor. James started to wonder if maybe it wasn't such a great idea to distract a man while hunting, but the fact of the matter was, this was his land.

One dead rough grouse hung limp from the man's belt, which was also holding up the man's straight 501 blue jeans. He wore a tattered blue and white flannel that appeared to have survived many hunting seasons. The man's dark hair stuck out around the brim of his hat. Surprisingly, the hunter spoke first. "Hello, how is it going?" he said.

James ventured a few steps closer and folded his hands across his chest.

"Not too bad," he replied. "What are you up to?"

"Just a little grouse hunting in the aspen here," said the man. "This is where they are, you know. It is tough though, stuff is thick, and I've got no dog."

"You seen many?" asked James?

"Few," the man answered. "I got this one while trying to fly back through that stand of young oak trees back to the west of here toward that shallow ravine. You know if a guy were to come back here with a dog he would really mop up. They are in here."

The man talked and acted as if he belonged here on James' land. And for a brief second James wondered if, perhaps, he'd stepped into the national forest. But he decided he had to assert himself anyway.

"Excuse me, but my name is James Norris," he said. "My uncle was Kevin Norris, and I now own this land."

In a second the man's face changed to a look of sympathy.

"Hey ... I ... I'm sorry, man," he said. "You know Kevin always gave me permission to hunt here, and I hadn't heard of anybody buying the place yet so I just assumed it was all right. Sorry, I'll get out of here."

"Don't worry about it," said James. "I don't care if you want to keep hunting here. I may hunt a little too, but if Kevin said you could be here than it is okay by me. By the way what's your name?"

"My name's David, David Marquette," he said in a quiet, unassuming voice as he extended his hand out to James. "I live about two miles up M past your road at the place to the right. It is the blue and gray rambler. My little chunk of land adjoins the national forest so I like to wander through to Mud Lake and around into these slashings of Kevin's—or yours."

"What do you do for a living?" asked James.

"I'm a water quality specialist."

Dave, who had been holding the shotgun in his left hand, moved it to his right hand and flipped it over his shoulder. "So do you live here full time now?" he asked.

"Yeah, I am sort of on a sabbatical I guess you could say," said

James. "I'm not real sure when I'll be leaving. I used to work at Litchfield Taylor and Faust as a corporate accountant in the Cities but recently got laid off."

Dave put his sunglasses back on and shifted the shotgun again to his opposite shoulder, and it was during this brief pause in the conversation that James finally noted his features. Dave was not tall, but he did sport a thick, chubby face and broad shoulders. His hair was jet black, and his cheekbones were set high on his face, accenting large eyes.

"Awesome day isn't it?" James said restarting the conversation.

"Really couldn't ask for better, but, God, is it dry. We need rain The forest is like a tinderbox," Dave answered.

"Like that everywhere," James replied.

"You seen that Dateline special last night on the farms in Nebraska and Kansas. It is like the Dustbowl. I don't know what is going to happen, man."

James, suddenly, felt out of touch. He had watched little news since his, more like Kristin's, TV met its rather unfortunate end. "No," he replied quickly. "So what does a water quality specialist do?"

"I check for mercury concentrations, things like that," said Dave.

"Mercury?"

"Yeah, it is a problem with some lakes. Mercury falls in the rain from pollution and contaminates the fish. Bigger fish have more of it than small ones, but, still, some concentrations in lakes are so high children and pregnant women shouldn't eat anything out of them."

"Shame."

In the brief conversation James sensed Dave would be a good neighbor. He found him so quiet and laid-back compared to the argumentative, intense Martin. In fact, James thought his personality to be the polar opposite of the dairy farmer's. He was a different teacher with a different message.

"Well, Dave," James said. "I'm getting pretty hungry, think I'll header home for lunch. You want to join me?"

Dave replied, "You know that's an idea, but I think I'll be going home myself. The wife gets pissed if I stay out too long. Maybe we should get together sometime and have a beer."

"What's your wife's name?" James asked.

"Jessica," said Dave. "Maybe I should invite you over so she'll actually cook a meal for me."

The pair let out a good laugh that echoed through the silent forest, and the two neighbors quietly parted ways.

* * *

He was so close, only a step or two away from breaking the threshold into the realm. The icy, bone-chilling wind emanating from that most special of places gathered speed, as overhead the voices continued their rhythmic, hypnotic chant. *Do it. Enter. Just step into the place.* He closed his eyes and took a step forward before stopping. He tried to step back, but now something was acting on him, pulling him in. Horror. Then light.

* * *

James opened his eyes, and desperately tried to catch his hyperventilating breath as tiny beads of sweat slid down his face. Yet again the dream had come, the first in three days, and it was the most intense one so far. He sat up in bed and tried to ponder the meaning of it all. It was truly a frightening nightly experience, made even worse because he didn't know when it would happen. Each dream had been a little different, and each time it progressed a little further, as if a story were slowly unfolding.

It was 8:00 a.m., Wednesday, October twenty-sixth and time for James to face another day of "taking it easy." However, he seemed to have more and more work to do every day, such as getting the cabin ready for winter, tinkering with Kevin's truck, making calls back to the Cities, arranging different details with his investments and calling the bank. One conspicuous thing he didn't do was look for work. The last two days had been spent mostly in the garage trying to figure out the workings of a Dodge 318 engine.

Am I happy? Not really. I need to face up to my situation, maybe go back to the Cities. I can't stay here forever.

With one slow, rather reluctant motion, James pulled the woolen comforter and sheets off his still shaking body and stood up to face the morning. Once downstairs the daily dose of morning milk was poured, and James wedged his back into one of the shaky wooden chairs at the table. He arched his back and listened to his spine crack like an old man's. It was a bad habit he could not quit. The sharp sound of acorns falling off the splendid oak trees onto the cabin roof reverberated throughout the kitchen. Some were so loud they sounded like gunshots to the uninitiated. Beyond the north-facing windows, a gathering of black and white chickadees congregated around one of many bird feeders James had stocked up with feed. In a frenzy of life and activity, the tiny birds prepared for the inevitable winter, a winter James didn't want to think about, by attacking the mixed shells and thistle seeds in the elongated red plastic tubes.

James thought he might be slipping into a depressive state. In fact, there were probably quite a few people who upon meeting him would say he needed some sort of help. However, the instant gratification promised by the modern happy pills was a cure he literally and figuratively could not swallow. *There had to be something to be learned in all of this. But I have to find work soon. Doesn't that define who I am?*

James precipitously snapped out of his malaise and began to gather his things for a trip to the general store in Loretta. Due to the price of gas these days, James decided to always shop there when possible, despite the limited selection of goods compared to the larger towns of Spooner, Hayward and Park Falls. While in town he was going to purchase a hunting license and maybe learn a thing or two about how to actually engage in that activity. He laced up his Rocky boots and stepped out to meet the day.

His Honda sat unused and neglected in the driveway. He'd only driven it a few times since he moved out here. Instead he had fallen in love with Kevin's beaten Dodge, despite its gas-guzzling ways. It sat next to the Honda in the driveway in all its rusted glory. James opened the door to the truck, and it let out a welcome all its own, a dull, protracted squeak. As James jumped inside, the leaf springs flexed generously, causing the truck to groan even more. He turned the key and punched the gas all the way to the floor. After a few coughs and false starts, the engine roared to life and shook the body of the truck. The noise was intense due to a plethora of holes in the muffler and catalytic converter. Soon a cloud of blue smoke caused by burning engine oil enveloped the truck, and James jammed the transmission into drive. It was to be a twenty-minute ride to town.

James took in the scenery as he approached Loretta on M. Overhead a smattering of high clouds warned of possible, and much needed, rain. The temperatures were in the 70s, and a few mosquitoes were flying again like spring had arrived. James slowed down as he neared the chip mill. A front-end loader raced around the yard as usual, and James watched it intently, so intently he almost crossed the centerline and caused a Ford Bronco going northbound to hug the opposite shoulder.

Freddy's IGA General Store was the largest establishment on Main Street as evidenced by the new, lighted sign on its facade. It welcomed all to come in and browse through a surprisingly diverse stock of necessities from Rice-a-Roni to spark plugs. James parked out front on the street next to a rusty Ford Ranger that was guarded by a large and slobbery Newfoundland in the bed. The dog looked at James with his big, sad eyes that seemed to be saying, "feed me." James patted the dog's massive head, and the dog immediately rolled on his back, expecting the full tummy rub.

James laughed, "What a watchdog."

The new sign outside the store was a deception, for inside the store was unkempt. *No reason to stay all spic-and-span when you are the only game in town.* He was dying for a good steak, but a quick scan of the meat department's prices quickly changed his mind. The drought in the Mid-West was beginning to pinch the pockets of the hamburger-loving public.

Fresh vegetables were in their customary short supply, and the ones that were available were bruised or dry. Such was to be expected. This wasn't Cub Foods; this wasn't Byerly's. There were no intermittent sprinklers showering row upon row of watercress or lobster tanks for kids and mothers to gawk at while shopping.

The store was quiet inside. Only three patrons wandered the five aisles. James wandered as well, tossing what he thought he might eat into the cart until it was full. In aisle four, the assorted condiment and cereal aisle, James stopped to grab a box of Honeycomb, a cereal he had enjoyed since he was child. He barely noticed the man standing next to him looking at a box of corn flakes. James threw his cereal in the cart and proceeded toward the checkout, but the man abruptly grabbed James shoulder.

"Hey, aren't you that guy that lives in the Norris place?"

"Yeah," replied a somewhat startled James as he took a step back from the man.

"Name is Ken, Ken Dresser," said the stocky, thirty-something man with glasses. He extended his grease-covered hand.

Ken wore a black down vest over a flannel and a black Jackson Timber hat. He stood five-eight on a good day and weighed 200 pounds. His cheeks were ruby red like a drinker, and he talked with a deep, raspy voice. Blonde, unshaven whiskers protruded from his face.

Ken continued, "I used to party with Kevin once in a while. We got just a fuckin' pie-eyed shit-faced a few times. I live over on W past Francis's place. It's the trailer to the left with the ugly Newfoundland out front when he is not catching a ride in my truck."

James looked out to the street. Sure enough, the Newfoundland was gazing into the store at his master as if to remind him not to forget his dog food.

"You buying the place?" asked Ken.

"Got it in the will."

"Nice, that place is awesome."

James continued, "I'm kind of staying there for a while. Taking it easy."

"So am I today," said Ken, "took vacation. I work up at the chip mill. I'm the maintenance foreman."

"Really. That place looks interesting. How long you worked there?"

"Too long," laughed Ken. "Been there since I graduated from high school sixteen years ago. Each day I go in at six and leave at three, for some goddamn reason." His eyes looked beyond the lone cashier toward the street and his faithful canine.

"It can't be that bad," said James.

"I don't know," answered Ken as he tossed his cereal into the cart. "Where else is a guy gonna work?"

James shrugged his shoulders and for a second was worried he had touched on the wrong subject. He tried changing the conversation.

"What is your dog's name?" he asked.

"Butch," was Ken's one word reply before continuing on the previous thread of discussion. "I guess I'm pretty lucky though. Ain't married. That mill needs me, and the Jackson's pay me pretty good, fifteen fifty an hour. We did a lot of belt splicing yesterday. That is a real bastard. The clips keep breakin' on our debarker line. There has got to be some product to smear on 'em to protect them."

James shook his head. *How the hell would I know?*

"But what I wouldn't do for some excitement," Ken continued. "I'll tell you what, man, one of these days I'm going to move to the South Pacific and live on an island. Or maybe I should join some guerilla army somewhere, die in a war and go out in glory instead of this slow way. You want to take my job?"

James feigned laughter, masking a sort of pity he felt for Ken.

"You'll love it on that lake," Ken said. "Got public on three sides no neighbors. You are lucky. My Dad and I used to clean up on the crappie down there in years past. I think it has been slow recently."

"I really have not been out yet, to tell you the truth."

"What?" questioned Ken, "too busy moving in?"

"Something like that."

Ken rubbed his chin and looked out past the cashier. "Supposed to be a nice day again tomorrow. I'll be at work ... "

James left Ken with his thoughts and began to make his exit toward the cashier. He almost made it to the front of the store before Ken spoke again.

"See ya later, James," he yelled. "We will have to get together sometime and chase women."

James laughed.

"Eighty-five eighteen," said Penny the cashier, with her name printed on her nametag for all to see. James paid in cash. He had spoken with Penny a couple of times over the past few weeks. He knew she was a widow but had a large extended family. Penny punched the register and gave James the change from his five twenties.

"Any rain coming?" asked James.

"God, we sure need it," she said closing the register drawer. "I swear half the damn country is burning up."

"Yeah, not good."

"How is the cabin coming along? You getting settled?"

"More or less. How are your new grand-daughters? Twins, right?"

"More than a handful for their mother," laughed Penny.

Ten minutes later, James left the store.

Having accomplished his grocery duties, it was but a short jaunt down Main Street to Willy's Sport Shop for the requisite purchase of a hunting license and equipment. Peeling brown stain on aged cedar siding enclosed the small shop where thousands of fish stories must have been told over the years. The front door was propped open, and a small bell jingled as the screen door slammed behind James. The place reeked of minnows, and the faint bubbling sounds of aerators in the live wells could be heard even from James' vantage point by the front door. The floor, which was made of some sort of old wooden planks, creaked under James' feet as he walked towards the lone, sixties-era register. Pine walls were plastered with the mounted bodies of walleye, musky and northern that kept a stoic watch over their domain and the tall tales contained within. The fish kept secrets well, never tattling on the fibbing fisherman who actually caught three instead of thirty-three, and they fit in nicely along with the assorted bar mirrors. Behind the register hung a few long guns, which appeared to be old cowboy-type lever actions. There didn't seem to be much of a planned layout in the store, for equipment was scattered indiscriminately throughout the establishment. James looked at some of the strange contraptions: huge plugs painted in bright colors with giant, deadly treble hooks, spinners, beads, reels and lead weights of all sizes.

Nobody came to help as James approached the counter and register. There didn't appear to be anybody else in the store. However, there was an entryway behind the counter into another room with a large "Private" sign hanging above it. A glass display was built into the counter, proudly displaying arrows and a few handguns. Next to the register were some small cards, and James picked one up to examine it. It was a business card for the sports shop with the names of the owners—Willy and Nancy Rosenbach. James lifted his eyes to the rows of dusty liquor and wine bottles on shelves behind the register. A cooler filled with beer stood in the far right corner of the shop.

James then heard a door slam in the room behind the register. In walked a man. He was average height but carried a huge potbelly, which alone weighed seventy-five pounds. It was the most distinguishing characteristic on the sixty-five-year-old frame of the man. His suspenders worked strenuously to contain it. He had a balding head and chewed a cigar. His face was chubby with large round eyes, and his hands were small and meaty. He wore a tight white tee shirt, which hung down to about his belly button, and he apparently saw no shame in exposing the bare skin between his waistline and his shirt. On the top of his head was a black cap that was just that, with no advertisements at all. The man's cigar was not lit, but it was badly mauled. He was chewing it now as he looked at James.

"What can I do for you?" Willy asked.

The cigar muffled the words as it failed to leave his clenched mouth.

"Need a license," James said.

Willy walked over to the register and clasped his hands together.

"Well, what kind of license do you need?" he asked with more than a hint of sarcasm as he rested his elbows on the display case, obviously annoyed at James' undetailed request.

"I'm going to hunt some grouse. Okay, well, I don't know, maybe deer too."

"So, what kind of a license do you need?" asked Willy again. This time he sounded even more annoyed. James stammered then stuttered. He felt embarrassed in this new territory. *Deer or grouse?*

Willy cut him off. "Listen, guy, let me make a guess here. You've never hunted before in your life, have you?"

James smiled. It was a good time to be self-effacing. "You are an observant man," he replied.

"I've been in this business awhile, let me give you a little piece of advice," said Willy. "You can learn a lot about someone just by observing him. No one today seems to just want to sit back, lay low and observe. I know when someone comes in here and talks a good line but really don't know bullshit. Here's what you want."

Willy reached behind the counter and pulled out a pamphlet of hunting regulations.

"You need a sportsman's license. Now on that license you can hunt small game, you know, squirrels and stuff like that. You can also deer hunt with a gun and fish. It's about fifty-five bucks resident."

Willy was already reaching for a pen.

"It sounds good," James said, swallowing his wounded pride and wallowing in more than a little humiliation.

"Well, all that I need there, guy," Willy said, "is a drivers license and a hunter education card."

Luckily, James had been reading a little out of an old regulation book Kevin had left behind. Reaching into his wallet he pulled out his Minnesota driver's license and decrepit Minnesota hunter education card he got as a reluctant teenage Boy Scout.

"I live here now, past Grassy Lake out on M in Kevin Norris' old place. Been there about a month now," said James.

"No kidding?" asked Willy. He looked interested and sat the pen down. "I knew Kevin. He was a good man. And I suppose you are a Wisconsin resident now, uh?"

"Guess you could say that," answered James, not wishing to dispute Willy's assumption as he handed him his license and hunter education card.

Willy studied them intently. "I'm sorry there, guy. Unless you have a Wisconsin license, I've got to charge you non-resident fees."

"That more expensive?" asked James.

Willy laughed. "You bet your ass it is. Now I need two hundred forty."

James felt deflated. "Visa okay?"

"This isn't the Middle Ages," replied Willy as he began punching in James' information on a tiny computer that printed licenses and was linked directly to the DNR.

"Why don't you give me three twelve-gauge boxes and a couple boxes of thirty-aught-six while you're at it," said James.

"What kind do you want, what length, what grain?"

"You seem to know more about this than I do," answered James as he looked Willy in the eye and tried to play his game. "What would you suggest?"

"Well, that's going to depend on what you want to shoot and how you want to shoot. But in my opinion, Winchester are the best shells a guy can use."

Willy reached for the license that was printing off of the computer and grabbed James' Minnesota edition VISA card at the same time.

"If you want to hunt deer," he continued, "I'd go with about a one eighty grain for the aught-six, and twelve-gauge for grouse with, I don't know, maybe number six lead shot should be alright. But I need to know what length you need too."

Willy paused for a second and removed his cigar. "Hell, you don't know what you're doing anyway so anything I sell you may or may not work. Either you are going to love it or you are going to hate it, and it is going to be my fault, so just take this box here and these damn aught-six shells and go do something."

He proceeded to set four boxes of shells down on the counter and smile as he figured the bill. "Three hundred forty bucks and forty-five cents, guy" he said.

James just shook his head, but he was getting rather annoyed. He didn't like being made fun of anymore than the next person.

"I got the prices all memorized," said Willy. "That is how I can ring you up so fast, even figured in what Uncle Sam wants too."

James signed the sportsman's license and then the VISA slip. "Nice to meet you," he said to Willy as he extended his hand.

Willy shook it, almost breaking James' wrist in the process. He looked at James with patronizing pride, much like a coach looks at a young athlete with potential. "Yep," was his reply as he let go of James' hand. And as James walked out of the shop, Willy's eyes never left him. The cigar was still in his teeth.

It was early afternoon, and James had nowhere to go. Now that he had a license, he was free to hunt, and a little crash course on the ins and outs of this activity would be made possible by the myriad of books Kevin left in the cabin. However, today he was not content to go straight home and start studying. James climbed into the Dodge and took a quick look back down the main street before departing. Lyle's and the Watering Hole had the most vehicles parked next to them. After all, this was Wisconsin.

James soon arrived at Cozy Pines, and despite the early hour, two Ford trucks were already parked outside. Bits of straw were stuck in the grills, giving vivid testimony to their role as farm vehicles. James walked in the front door amidst Garth Brooks'*Calling Baton Rouge* playing on the jukebox. The staccato knock of a pool ball on pool ball broke the baritone of Garth in the dim afternoon atmosphere. Three figures James did not recognize stood by the pool table in the bar area. Two of the figures looked similar, but one was slightly shorter and stockier. James guessed him to be twenty-years-old and the skinner, taller man to be twenty-five. Both wore padded flannel shirts; both held Old Milwaukees. The third figure stood between them ready to take a shot at the pool table. His shaved face was like worn leather, and chopped light brown hair stuck out from his Green Bay Packers hat. He had a scrawny build but was taut and muscular. A pair of glasses hung from his overall pocket. The two younger men teased him as he shot.

"Grandma shoots better pool than you," the skinnier boy said.

The man missed, and he let out a curse followed by laughter. He was more than friends with these two young men. He was their father.

These guys must be dairy farmers like Martin, James deduced. *I think dairies are the only farms in the area.*

James was right. However, the size of the farms here paled in comparison to the large operations further south in Wisconsin. Only the small operator worked here surrounded by forest, and, unfortunately, the small operator was not the rich operator.

Ann was behind the bar, and she poured James a Leinenkugel's before he could sit down. Recently, he had grown to like this beer. He had tasted it before in the Twin Cities once or twice, but here it was a staple along with Old Milwaukee and Miller. However, Leine's, as it was known tasted more like a European or German beer. It was a little stronger, a little darker, than your typical American lager.

"Where have you been the past few days, James," Ann asked.

He sat down and took a swig out of the glass. "Been busy."

"I bet," laughed Ann.

"Hey, I went shopping today," James said as he glanced over at the men playing pool.

Ann walked out from the bar to join them and engaged in a lively discussion with the elder man, who kept glancing over at James. James shifted nervously on his stool and surveyed the assorted antler racks on the walls. He knew he was being talked about, and he didn't like it.

But then someone set a beer bottle down on the bar to his right and disrupted his attempt to concentrate on being ignored.

"James, James Norris, nephew of Kevin?" a man said.

It was the elder pool player extending his hand.

"Yeah, glad to meet you," replied James accepting it.

"My name is Paul Larson. I was good friends with Kevin."

"It seems most people around here were."

Paul laughed. "I'll buy you a beer."

"Why not."

The two young men soon joined Paul. "James, I would like you to meet Mike and Aaron. Mike is twenty and Aaron is twenty-five. I might give them a hard time, but they're pretty good guys, not many of them left."

James shook both their hands and congratulated himself on his powers of observation.

"Kevin and us used to get together and drive deer," said Mike, plopping his 200-plus pounds down on the stool to James' left and proudly showing off the beer in his hand.

"I knew Kevin for almost thirty years," Paul went on. "He even worked with me sometimes, since he never seemed to have a steady job, but you probably know all about that. He sure got a nice place there. That's where you staying?"

James answered, "Yes, I got it in the will. Right now I'm sort of out here relaxing for a while."

"That's what we try to do sometimes," said Paul, "but only for a short while, it seems, with all the work we have to get done before winter. We are wasting time sitting here, but you can't work all the time, you know."

"Don't tell me about relaxing. I'm doing all of Mike's work," added Aaron, standing loyally next to his father.

Paul looked at James. "Don't mind Aaron here. He is just upset at seeing all his friends get married, and he's still single hanging around with me. I tell him there is no hurry; a fella can wait."

"I'm not sure if you're missing a whole lot, either," added James in a fatherly type tone. "I just got out of an engagement. Luckily though, you know, we didn't make it official."

"Sorry to hear that," said Paul. "I've been with my Angela twenty-seven years. She works as a dental hygienist in Park Falls."

"And what do you do?" inquired James before he realized just how stupid a question it was.

"Well, haven't you figured that out yet?" said Paul. "I'm a dairy farmer, unfortunately. I own the farm on the right down one-and-three-quarter street a mile before Martin Steiger's place. Same road as Larry Wesley, by the Thompson's old place."

James looked confused.

"You know Martin?" asked Paul.

James shook his head in the affirmative.

"Well, just take that gravel road to the right before his place, and we're right down there. It comes right into our driveway."

Ann passed out four more beers.

"At least he ain't going to be a mudduck now," said Mike while he nudged Aaron. "Now he can hang out here with real people instead of those yuppie weekend warriors who blaze in and out."

Mike grinned at his father and turned his attention back to his beer while Ann turned the volume up on the TV. The anchorman's voice rose above the conversation.

"Democratic presidential candidate Howard Beecham continues to promote his bold policy initiatives as he travels through the swing midwestern states of Minnesota, Wisconsin and Illinois."

"Great," huffed Aaron between sips of beer.

"I ain't ever going to vote," said Paul, cutting off the rest of the anchorman's soliloquy. "Shit, they are all a bunch of crooks, nothing ever changes."

"As long as I survive, that's all I worry about," Ann said.

Paul acknowledged her by nodding in her direction and continued. "Lawyers and politicians used to be shot back in the good old days. Now they're running the show. All they care about is money and power while I bust my ass year in and year out for less and less. Those sinful bitches tax the hell out of everything so they can send money to foreign countries. And they are never satisfied."

"It's damn near communism," said Ann. "We get taxed so much we sometimes want to give up, and all the damn regulations just ain't worth it."

James glanced over to Ray who had just appeared from the kitchen. He jokingly flexed his arms for Paul. "Got my yearly physical tomorrow," he said. "Think he is going to say I got forty years left in me."

"I don't even know why you go to those goddamn quacks," said Paul as he placed his queue stick on the bar. "Just to have your temperature taken costs a thousand bucks."

"Costs are so high because you are paying for the doctor's tuition," replied Ray with a blackened smile before winking at James. "What's going on, James?"

James smiled back.

"You know how to run this new spreadsheet you put in the computer last week?" Ray asked Ann.

"Don't ask me," snapped Ann. "You know I hate that thing."

"Well, tell me how the hell you figured out how to install the program," laughed Ray as he reached into his coveralls and pulled out a fresh pack of Basic cigarettes.

"Shut up," said Ann pointing at him in mock anger and balling up her fists in a mock boxing pose, "you're walking on thin ice."

Behind James, the door slammed abruptly, echoing through the establishment. James' head whipped around to see the twenty-something girl race into the bar. Her blond hair looked unkempt, blown in fall wind. She took care to shut the door behind her.

"Sorry, I'm late, Ann," she said with out-of-breath gasps as she raced behind the bar and into the kitchen. She stood five feet, six inches tall with a stocky yet athletic build. Her name was Nicole Kaufman. She was twenty-five-years old, and James had never seen her in his previous forays to the bar.

Nicole had grown up in the area and now lived with her mother, Betty, in a small house two miles south of Cozy Pines. She also had a four-year-old son, Matthew. Nicole never noticed James as she exited the kitchen and began setting the tables. James watched her for a second and wondered.

Ann lit up a cigarette in unison with Ray, and soon the owners and the patrons' attention was focused back on the TV filled with the usual newsworthy events: poor economy, drought, starvations, presidential campaigns, shootings and all the other symptoms of a distressed world. It was enough to make anyone depressed. But not here. Through it all, those assembled laughed, drank and talked. Those problems were worlds away and not influencing the lives of the seven people at Cozy Pines Bar and Restaurant. They were only images on a screen.

Yes, the world was getting smaller, thought James as he withdrew from those gathered around him. *But does it really affect everyone equally? In reality, the images on that damn TV were nothing more than static. God the world is a baffling place. Perhaps it is better not to even acknowledge it. Maybe some of these people were on to something? Had they already crossed through the territory of concern and realized just how insignificant their lives were, perhaps come to some sort of quiet revelation that they could only change small things? To worry about things that they could not change would slowly lead to frustration, and maybe change wasn't all it's cracked up to be, anyway?*

Nevertheless, the world sooner or later catches up to everyone This is inevitable, an absolute certainty. For miles away from the autumn woods of northern Wisconsin, events were unfolding that would shape the worlds and lives of those gathered at Cozy Pines.

The temperature reached 100 degrees in New York City that day warmth unheard of so late in the year. In Colorado a massive 35,000 acre blaze fueled by bone-dry conditions threatened posh new housing developments west of Denver. And across the globe, off the coast of India, NOAA computers were indicating the birth of a severe cyclonic storm.

Ray reached for the remote control that lay on the bar. He nonchalantly flipped off the TV and let loose a puff of smoke that leisurely wafted out of his mouth. "Seen many deer, Paul?" he asked.

Chapter 7
Indications Of Change

It was November fifth, and the security light outside James' cabin was illuminating the season's first cautious flakes of snow. An Alberta clipper, compliments of Canada, had swept down quickly from the northwest, wiping out the record seventy-degree warmth that had settled over Wisconsin and Minnesota the past week. In normal years it would have been a precursor of wintry things to come, but this year—in fact, the past ten—was far from normal. The nightly array of stars, which James had grown accustomed to viewing, were now obscured by the blanket of clouds brought in by the fast-moving clipper. A northwest wind howled furiously, almost convincing James to stay home this evening by the fire instead of traveling the four miles to Cozy Pines. However, loneliness is a powerful motivator. He quietly cleaned the dinner table of his potato and baked chicken meal and rubbed his tired, bloodshot eyes.

The dream had come again last night, and, as usual, it was just a little different than its predecessor. This time he had actually started to enter the mysterious place before waking up. The experience continued to frighten and intrigue him at the same time. He had heard of people having recurring dreams and always scoffed at them. Now, in a strange way, he sympathized with them. Worried, but still fascinated, James tried to shrug it off. He was in no mood to visit a shrink, and the dream was almost becoming manageable, like an integral part of his routine.

Time. James had plenty of it out here. Recently, he had tried fishing a little out on Mud in the old aluminum twelve-foot fishing boat—unsuccessfully. Additionally, he had experimented with Kevin's shotgun and 30-06 in anticipation of deer season a few weeks away. The thought of wounding a deer disturbed him and motivated him to go out and practice but he still had a lot more shooting to do to feel really comfortable. He often contemplated how his views concerning this activity had changed so rapidly in the past few weeks. His change was radical, almost as if this place compelled its visitors to view nature not as one would in a zoo, as a sideshow or a laughingstock, but experience it in its entirety, with its beautiful juxtaposition of innocence and cruelty.

James made his way to the closet and fetched a warm flannel before walking out into the hard, ice-like pellets of snow, neglecting to lock the door in his wake. For a brief moment, he stopped outside on the porch listening to the wind and watching the swaying oaks and jack pines.

All the leaves are finally down on that red oak, must have just happened. Funny, I would have never noticed something like that in the Cities before I came out here. Here, you actually notice the landscape and see it change and adapt with the seasons. I think one needs to live it, to experience it firsthand, to truly understand the pleasure it can give. There is something to seeing this in the first person.

It was election night, time for a minority of Americans to fulfill their civic duty. However, this election was different than most. Hard economic times, drought and uncertainty were the daily reality. This election would see a massive outpouring of participation, for real futures were on the line, and these days people instinctively looked toward their government and president thousands of miles away for the answers.

James still had not bothered unpacking his computer, so Cozy Pines was the closest point of contact to the outside world beyond his isolated kingdom. Tonight at Cozy he would find out who the next leader of the free world would be. And he knew his neighbors, his friends, would be there in the flesh as well.

The parking lot at Cozy Pines was crowded for a Tuesday night, filled with pickups and cars James did not recognize. He parked the Dodge between two Chevy trucks and walked inside, smelling the aroma of grease, cigarettes and alcohol immediately. Ray was working the bar and cooking while Ann waited on tables. *How do they keep doing it with only one part-time employee? They both gotta be in their sixties.*

"Hey, James is here," said Ray. "I'll set you up."

He immediately grabbed a glass, filled it with Leinenkugel's from the tap and slid it down the bar as James grabbed a stool and eyed those assembled here at the area's unofficial headquarters. Most people he did not recognize, but at least Martin was present. He was seated to James' right, staring intensely at the TV with a can of Old Milwaukee in his hand. The kids and Kate were absent. Martin was frantically denting the side of the can in a bizarre rhythm while he tapped it gently on the bar, and at first he didn't even acknowledge James' presence, so James decided to play along. He didn't bother to look in Martin's direction. But after several minutes Martin gave in.

"They have projected a winner," he growled.

"A winner in what?" said James, feigning ignorance.

"You know damn well what," said Martin, finally turning his head in James' direction. "It is what we expected. I mean, was there really any doubt?"

Both men trained their eyes up towards the TV. A dark blue background blanketed the screen, and a conspicuous red checkmark lay next to a picture of William Beecham, next President of the United States. Then the picture flashed to Beecham's ecstatic election night headquarters where balloons floated through the air, people screamed and hugs were exchanged. The campaign posters with the requisite catchy slogans decorated what the pretty newswoman said was the Radisson Ballroom in Washington, D.C. The man of the hour was nowhere to be found, but he would soon make his smiling appearance. He would proclaim the same platitudes and verbiage that he had so often repeated the past year, and the hearts of America would soar correspondingly, for the knight in shining armor was here to solve their problems. Here was the man who would ride into Washington, D.C.—two thousand-plus miles away from a lot of main streets in America—and make a change and difference for the better. Here was the man most people had never seen in person and had only heard about through the medium of television. They couldn't physically touch him, they couldn't really watch his actions and, despite technology's ability to shrink the globe, they couldn't really participate in most of his decisions that would affect them. And, yet, they put their faith in him. Martin could take no more.

"Goddamn it, Ray," he said. "Turn something else on, please. I mean, fuck, we all goddamn know what's going to happen. I'm going to get loaded."

To accentuate his command, he flung the beer onto the floor, causing the remnants of beverage to spill.

"Calm down, calm down," said Ray as he quickly reached for the remote.

James said nothing. But he wanted so much to question Martin, a man he saw filled with some sort of undefined rage—or conviction. However, Martin's protruding neck tendons and trembling lower lip persuaded James to introduce a lighter subject. Deer was always a good starting point.

"See any nice bucks?" asked James attempting to break the mood.

Martin swung around in the stool to face James. His eyes rolled up in contemplation. "Yeah, not as many as last year, though. I don't think there are as many deer out there as the goddamn DNR says, at least, not as many as in years past."

Martin's lip was trembling, and James was coming to realize that if this subject bothered him, any subject would bother him. *He's politicized about everything.*

"I'll tell ya," Martin said interrupting James' thought, "I don't know if people are going to keep on deer hunting in this country. They will probably ban it like everything else. I'll tell you, boy, it's the mentality, the fucked up neo-socialist mentality of the yuppies in this country today, James."

Martin's eyes grew wide, and the trembling in his lip reached a rapid tempo. "It manifests itself in the popularity of that wanna-be despot Beecham. People today want to have their lives pre-determined. They want all risk eliminated so they can feel safe as they go down and watch their kids play soccer in a fucking cute little SUV and return to some suburb somewhere built like every other fuckin' suburb."

He said the last sentence with slow, heavy emphasis, dragging out every word in venom-laced disdain.

"Sure, they are making a hundred grand a year with husband and wife both working eighty hours a week while the kids are raised by the TV or day care. That's the way they like it, I guess. Their useless lives are churned out year after year till they're tossed in some goddamn grave somewhere or their kids go ballistic and blow up a high school because they are not getting any attention paid to them. Its fucking ridiculous, I'll tell ya. And everybody is to blame. The whole country is fucked up with men who don't take responsibility and women who think they can do it all and let their kids suffer for it. People don't know their role, and on top of it all, they're willing to sacrifice liberty in the name of some perverse progressive ideas of equality, fairness and safety. I'll tell you this, James. Life is a fatal disease; life kills. You know these are all the same people that have a problem with hunting. If animals have a right to life, can a deer sue a pack of wolves for attempting to kill it? People and animals have been hunting for millions of years. Why? For food, yes, but there is also something else—something intangible—in the kill itself. To feel that blood on your hand, to hold the heart of the animal, that is how nature works, my friend, and the fucking suburbanites who just sit in their air-conditioned condos built on God knows how many animals' homes have no connection with nature, no connection at all with the animals that they supposedly want to save."

All the warning signs told James to leave early. He suspected Martin had been drinking rather heavily the last couple hours, and his latest rant only reinforced his assumption. Martin was looking for a fight not physical, but intellectually. *But he is not stupid. He can debate with the best of them.* It was too great a temptation for James to resist. His natural curiosity won again.

"But don't you think in these dangerous, unstable times it is necessary for us as a community, as a nation, perhaps even as a world, to concentrate on the common good, Martin," said James. "And, yes, that may require some change. The fact is, Martin, the world is changing fast. People are progressing and evolving. You can sit back and complain about it and be relegated to the role of dinosaur, or you can accept it and embrace it."

Martin grinned ear-to-ear and squinted his eyes. It was the look that told James he had accepted the challenge. But first he took a drag off his Marlboro and collected his thoughts.

"First of all, James," said Martin finally, "did you ever consider the possibility that thinking for the common good has lead to the events that we have today? What is the common good, how do you define it, how do you consider the common good without considering the individual? We have all these damn failed governmental programs that promote illegitimacy, favor one group over another and take my money and liberty in the process because some eggheads are thinking for the common good. The fact is that uncertainty and progress are not valid reasons to forsake our liberty, which springs from the natural laws of God. And as far as your talk of me being a dinosaur stuck back in some ancient age, well so be it. You've been brainwashed into thinking that change is automatically good, that tradition is bad, that standards are bad, that anything that roots the individual and places him in his proper context is bad and that committing treason against the laws of nature is something to be celebrated. Well, there is a price to pay for that. There is a price to pay. That is what is the matter with our society there, James."

James was not deterred. "But what about these environmental problems we see today, Martin. What about this drought? Don't you think that the greenhouse effect may be making it worse? And if that were so, it would require a change in people's ways and some sort of action for the good of all."

Martin didn't respond right away. But when he did, he spoke slowly and chose his words carefully. "You know, James, I think we are talking past each other. I mean, you are now talking about one thing, environmental destruction. And I'll agree partially that we may need to forsake some liberty and change our ways a little in that regard. But I do have my doubts about global warming being caused by humans. However, that is not really what I'm trying to get at. I'm talking about something else. I'm talking about our society being cut from its roots and traditions and thrown into some sea of change that people are celebrating but not really questioning where it is leading. However, let's not discount the role of perceptions. Perceptions are often wrong, you know, and our all-powerful media does little to help in this regard. Public perceptions about the world getting worse can be wrong as surely as perceptions about the good of change and progress. I think you'll generally agree with that, won't you?"

James nodded before Martin continued. "You just kind of have a little different take on things, James, but we're on the same track."

Martin dug into his flannel pocket for his cigarettes and handed one to James.

"Smoke?" he asked.

"No thanks," James replied.

"Why not? You should start. It is a great, filthy habit."

Martin quickly pulled the cigarette away from James and flung it behind the bar. "No, you are right James," he said. "I gotta stop smoking these fuckin' things. Sometimes, I tell ya, I wish the world would just go to hell. You know, a depression or something. Then I'd have to quit."

During the conversation, the two men didn't notice that a shadowy figure had sneaked up next to them from a darkened corner of the bar and grabbed a stool next to James. A grease-stained hat sat atop the figure's matted black hair. A stench of intermingled odors emanated from his person and he wore torn jeans, black combat boots and a green camouflage jacket His facial features were almost unrecognizable, obscured by a thick, dark beard. He was short with a wiry frame, but the veins protruding from his forearms indicated that he had grown accustomed to physical work.

"You two talk like you know the mind of God, like you have some sort of knowledge about the divine plan," the man said, his eyes darting back and forth between Martin and James. "If you really want to know what will happen, read the book. Read it, if you have the courage, for then you will see the consequences of God's wrath on a society that had turned its back on him"

The man then stared at James and ignored Martin completely James looked the man over as Martin smiled, crossed his arms and leaned back on his stool.

"It's all in Revelations, my friend," the man continued in his high-pitched, gravel-throated voice. "Beware, for these are the end times. All is unfolding as has been foretold. Can't you see?"

James was now only a few inches away from the man's face, and he didn't know how to react. The man drew even closer. "It is all in the book, I tell ya, boy. I'm ready with the book in my right hand and my AR-fifteen in my left. God will work through me. What about you?"

He suddenly reached for James' shirt, gripped it tightly and drew his foul smelling tobacco stained mouth as close as possible to James' face. "Prepare, for the kingdom of God is coming. Make straight his path, for soon man will have to answer for his sins. The hour is drawing near."

He then released James and headed straight for the door. A shocked James turned to Martin who anticipated the question. "No, James, the man was not kidding," Martin said. "You have just had your first contact with Mr. Larry Wesley. He lives in the trailer on the Larson's road. He's a loner, kind of an odd duck."

"Really, you think," replied James sarcastically.

Martin continued, "He's going to be one of those guys that walks into a McDonald's—well, we don't have any of those around here—and unloads on everybody."

"What does he do for a living?"

"You are not going to believe this," Martin said, "but Larry used to be a corporate account executive for some big software outfit out of Chicago. Guy had a six figure income, traveled the entire world and all."

"What the hell happened?"

"I'm not real sure. You know, he had the land where his trailer is for a while. Used to be a deer camp for him and his buddies. From what I can tell, he had some sort of a breakdown a few years ago. Just went crazy, you know. He quit his job and now has forsaken all, or most, worldly comforts. He lives like some sort of offbeat monk, with an AR-fifteen, of course."

"Does he really believe all that stuff about the end of the world?"

"As sure as he breathes."

"You two must get along pretty well then?"

Martin smiled.

* * *

The bell rang proudly as James entered Willy's Sports Shop on Monday, November eleventh. However, no one sprang to attention. The responsibility of customer service didn't weigh too heavily on the shoulders of Willy or Nancy, and James was pretty sure they never bothered to send out surveys to make sure their customers were "completely satisfied." However, eventually, the better half of the ownership team sauntered out from the storeroom. Her face was wrinkled and aged, but Nancy was full of vigor. It was the first time James had dealt with her.

"What do you need?" she asked with the same sort of annoyed growl as her husband.

"Just some ammo," replied James.

Nancy had the same routine down as her husband. She folded her arms and slumped down next to the register on the glass case. In a sing-song voice, she replied, "Well what kind of ammo do you need?"

James walked over to the glass counter and pointed to the boxes of 30-06 and twelve-gauge shells. He still had no idea which brand to choose, but now, at least, he thought he could converse with Nancy somewhat intelligently.

"Couple of each," he said.

Nancy dutifully picked up the boxes.

"Good thing you're buying these things now," she said. "Sounds like after that Beecham gets into office you're going to have to pay a lot more taxes on ammunition, you know. These politicians are going to turn hunting into a rich man's sport, if they don't ban it first. But what are you going to do, hum?"

She began punching away on the ancient register.

"Maybe you should fight it," answered James.

"Fight what?" sneered Nancy. "We the people elected those guys. What are we going to do, fight ourselves?"

"But did you vote for the bureaucracy that makes the laws that affect your business?"

"No, and it just keeps growing all the time, doesn't it? Tell me how people in Washington, D.C. and Madison know what is good for me? I thought here in America we were a democracy. Let's see, I need fifty-three, forty-two from you, guy."James reached into his pocket and fished out two twenties and a ten. At last count his savings and checking accounts still had nearly 7,000 dollars in them. Nonetheless, he realized he wasn't going to be able to live like this forever. *Expenses, medical and otherwise, are sure to crop up. The clock is ticking on my stay.*

"I need fifty-three, forty-two," said Nancy again in a louder voice, breaking James' train of thought. Embarrassed, he found four ones in his pocket and handed them over. He turned toward the door and nearly barreled into the stocky, bearded man who had just entered the shop. It was Ken Dresser.

"It's James, right?" asked Ken.

James extended his hand as Nancy looked on, a passive spectator behind the counter.

"Looks like you're getting ready for deer season there," noted Ken.

"I figure I may as well see what it's all about."

James looked outside to Ken's truck. The Newfoundland drooled back.

"Just look at that lazy fucker out there," Ken said as he took a pack of Top tobacco from his shirt pocket and rolled a cigarette, taking care to seal it with spit.

"Just getting done with work?" asked James.

Ken looked at his watch. "Hell, what a day. Everything went wrong. Bearing went down on a drive shaft. I couldn't wait till that clock said three. So, I figure I'd do some shooting tonight, or maybe stop by Lyle's and grab a beer for me and a burger for Butch."

James looked again out at Butch who was now resting his head on the truck bed rail and staring forlornly toward his owner.

"What do you hunt with?" asked James.

"Three-hundred mag. I make damn sure I do my part to keep the deer herd strong. When I hit them with the three hundred, believe you me boy, they ain't getting up."

"I bet," laughed James, not knowing what a three-hundred mag was. "What do you mean, though, by keeping the herd strong?"

Ken leaned up against a rack of fishing lures. "The way I see it, if that deer was smart, he would not have walked into my line of fire. By killing the weak and stupid ones, I make sure the deer herd is that much stronger. It is like they say, the strong will survive."

James thought for a few seconds before replying. "So by that rationale dropping a nuclear bomb on a forest would really keep the deer herd strong because the smart ones would have all run away, correct? I mean, where do you draw the line with human technology? We have the capability to destroy the world. Isn't there a point at which human intelligence supercedes natural selection, and we must act as wise stewards of the land and its resources but also participate in its processes?"

Ken looked amused. "Ok, ok, you got me," he said. "I know where you are coming from. Yeah, we need limits, but we still have to do something about the herd growth. We still have to do what is right."

He then looked at Nancy and nodded before he lit his cigarette taking a long draw before continuing. "You sound like you been hanging around Steiger too much with a comment like that. Remember, some things just are. You can look at 'em and understand that through common practical experience. Not everything needs to be verified by the politicians and scientists. Some things are just a-fuckin' meant to be, and, I'll tell you hunting is meant to be, just like that fuckin' chip mill. The logs are just meant to be processed, and I make sure they can."

Back at the cabin James walked down into the basement to fetch Kevin's weather-beaten 30-06 rifle. He hefted it and made his way outside to the small clearing beyond the pines where he had constructed a makeshift shooting range out of cans, bottles and an old picnic table.

Sitting down at the table, James lifted the gun up to his shoulders. *Heavy, but manageable,* he thought. The gun was a bolt-action with a three-by-nine Nikon scope. Looking through the optic device, he peered across the clearing into the forest, scanning for movement while trying to relax his posture. He then set the gun on the table and studied its action and safety lever on top of the bolt before loading five rounds into the enclosed magazine. Chambering one, he flipped the safety off. It was time.

It was yet another sixty-degree day, the sixth day of record warmth since the pathetic snowflakes of November fifth. Low, gray clouds hung over the landscape, making it seem a little cooler than it was. James raised the rifle up to his shoulder and brought the scope toward his right eye.

From his vantage point, James could clearly make out the red and white label of the Old Milwaukee bottle through the scope. He placed it squarely in the crosshairs. He was now shaking nervously. *I'm glad no one can see this,* he thought as a gust of wind drove crispy dead leaves against his body. Suddenly he flinched, pulling the rifle sharply down to his left before he regained his composure. Raising the gun again, he placed his index finger ever so softly against the trigger, and, just like he had been taught in one of Kevin's shooting books he was reading, he let out a slow, sustained breath. For a second it was as if the earth stood still. Then came the noise. He really wasn't even ready to shoot, or so he thought. It seemed as if the gun just went off like it was consciously releasing itself from the terrible suspense. The report echoed across the landscape, and the Old Mil bottle still stood.

The ringing in James' ears started immediately, and he chastised himself for not wearing earplugs. Quickly he pulled the bolt back, and smoke found its way out from the chamber, wafting skyward along with the hot spent shell casing, which fell onto the ground. James slid the well-oiled bolt back into place and loaded a new round. Once again, he raised the rifle.

This time he didn't watch his breath. He simply raised the weapon, found a bottle in the crosshairs and immediately fired. And this time the bullet hit its mark. James could see the glass explode. With caution in mind, he flipped the safety back on.

Smiling, he walked over to the bottles to view the damage. He didn't know where his first bullet had gone, but he beamed with inner pride at his success on the second shot, despite the fact it was from an easy distance. Deer season was only a few days away, and, little by little, he was beginning to understand the magic contained in those fall days. Still grinning, he looked skyward toward the gray, and a gust of wind brushed the face of a changing young man.

Chapter 8
Messenger Of The Divine

On November seventeenth something very strange happened in northern Wisconsin. The temperature dropped from a record high of seventy-two degrees to a high of thirty-one degrees in only eighteen hours. However, the next day temperatures were back in the sixties. Most people just shrugged off the erratic weather, and blamed the meteorologists for having no ability to forecast what the next day would bring. Nevertheless, despite the pleasant daytime temperatures, the shortening days provided a constant reminder that the long nights of winter should still lay ahead.

Deer season loomed during the last week of this month. Despite its falling popularity among the populace, deer hunting in northern Wisconsin in the twenty-first century was just as important as it had always been. It was one of the most important weeks of the year. The hunt was about family and friends, but so were Thanksgiving, Christmas and Easter. No, deer hunting was something different. It was ritual; it was life. Even in this enlightened age, children were let out of school. Businesses closed as the people flocked to the woods in the morning and returned to cabins and bars in the afternoon swapping stories—some true, most not—just like the way things had been in years past. In a world where nothing was sacred and everything was constructed by changing human forces, deer hunting was bedrock. Now James would be able to participate in the yearly ritual before it inevitably passed into history.

* * *

It was Friday evening, November twenty-first. James finished his dinner of cheap, canned beef stew and opened his nightly bottle of Leinenkugel's while nestled at the kitchen table. Darkness had long since descended on the landscape. Light snow, not predicted in the day's weather forecast, steadily fell down to the earth outside. James looked forlornly out the large sliding doors facing north across the lake. Not one single light could be detected on the desolate scene. Casually, he stood up and walked across the living room, aglow only by the dancing light of a roaring fire in the fireplace.

It wasn't the first time loneliness had taken hold of him, but this time it was more intense and knowable. His once-weekly telephone calls to his old co-workers Jim and Fred had trickled off to nothing. They really had nothing to talk about anymore. *Haven't even looked at job postings this week,* he thought. Then she returned.

For what seemed like hours he sat comatose by the fire. He closed his eyes and reluctantly remembered the nights they shared together. *How did I screw that up? Why? What the hell am I doing out here? I don't want to stay here, do I? There has to be some sort of resolution.*

Such was the course with his moods as of late, which seemingly changed like the weather. He would be content one minute and depressed the next. The same questions kept running through his head, building on one another, gathering together in an energizing force of frustration, a frustration that had to be directed somewhere.

With cat-like quickness, he sent the beer bottle toward the fireplace. The glass hit the burnt interior stone and broke into a thousand pieces, sending tiny, flaming-red embers rolling across the floor. James jumped to his feet and looked for his next victim. Grief had turned to anger and anger had now turned to rage. The rocking chair was the next to go, flung gleefully against the wall. Soon he was exorcising all the ghosts, destroying all objects in his path in a fit of hopeless wrath over the state of his life. But like a thunderstorm that blossoms suddenly on a hot summer afternoon, James quickly ran out of energy. And in his final gasp of energy he fell breathless on his back, staring up at the ceiling. *Useless. Useless.*

He so wanted to visit Cozy Pines, but tomorrow was deer opener and 5:00 AM would come awfully quick. Sitting up on the floor, he mentally got control of himself and tried to put his mind to the task looming in the morning. Since he didn't know the woods or the art of hunting enough to launch his own scouting exploration, he had decided to use the deer stand put up by Kevin years back that lay in an oak grove on the far side of the ravine formed by Mud Creek. Earlier in the day he had rooted out Kevin's tattered, musty blaze-orange clothing that was required for all hunters during gun season, along with as many layers of clothing as he could find. The gun was ready. The site was chosen. In less than ten hours he would descend into the dark forest to experience for the first time, and maybe the last, this barbaric and anachronistic practice known as hunting. He kicked some of the still-glowing embers back into the fire and ascended the staircase to try to sleep.

The digital alarm clock—recovered from the garage—read 4:02 AM as James threw the covers off his bed, sweating profusely. He immediately reached for his legs. *They are there.*

The last thing he recalled was entering a shadowy, lightless place completely devoid of sound. And it was so real. He could still feel the needles on the forest floor. True to course, the dream was progressing further and further along, but where he would eventually end up and what would eventually happen to him, was a total and complete mystery. *There had to be an end to it all.* He caught his breath after a few seconds and the terror subsided. He then double-checked to make sure the alarm was still set for 5:00.

The sound seemed to be far off like a distant church bell ringing its ghostly chime across the silent countryside. In one painfully ungraceful movement, James slammed the alarm clock off and rolled out of bed onto the hard floor.

"Damn it," he yelled out loud. "What a way to start."

He lumbered down the stairs to the kitchen table in the darkness, shivering in his long underwear. He thought about making a fire but, instead, decided to drink some milk with a bagel and get dressed quickly.

After his makeshift meal, he walked over to the clothes he had laid out in the living room. The wood floor felt ice cold on his bare feet as he shook off the foggy cobwebs of sleep. If it were any other day besides deer opener, he would have never dreamed of getting up so early. *It always felt cold in the morning, no matter what the actual temperature was.*

First he applied a second layer of long underwear, then a pair of sweat pants followed by two flannel shirts and two pair of wool socks over gym socks. He put on a snowmobile suit over the underlying layers. The temperature outside was thirty degrees, and he would be sitting still and motionless. He had heard from Martin and other people that the key to this activity was to only move your eyes and make as little sound as possible. Thus, one had to stay warm. Finally, James pinned his green hunter back tag on a lightweight blaze-orange jacket and put it on over his snowmobile suit, along with matching blaze-orange polyester pants. A blaze-orange wool cap and pair of orange mittens completed his getup.

Now, after he was dressed, he needed to gather his tools, which he had also laid on the floor: folding buck knife, book detailing how to gut a deer (because he would need some advising), string to attach the carcass tag, flashlight, pocket hand warmers and a plastic bag for the heart. James stuffed all these items into his pockets.

He then shook his head to fight off the lingering urges to sleep and loaded five rounds in the 30-06, taking care to make sure the safety was on. He placed ten more loose shells in his pocket. James stepped outside and saw that the snow had not abated overnight; in fact, it seemed to be falling even harder. A few inches of light puffy powder covered the yard. He flipped on the flashlight and trudged into the dark. Twenty minutes later he arrived at his destination.

James flashed his light at the stand. It was nothing more than a collection of two-by-fours and two-by-sixes slapped together fifteen feet up in an oak tree with a bench and a railing. He unloaded the rifle and tied it to a frayed nylon rope, which hung from the stand. Next, he climbed up the short two-by-fours nailed to the tree as steps and ducked under the railing. Slowly and steadily, he hoisted the gun up, breathing slowly. Once he held the gun, he cleaned the snow off the bench and sat down. He was now warm and sweating profusely, but in position. Now it was time to wait and watch in the darkness. He loaded the gun and chambered one round. *Patience.*

It seemed like an eternity as man and tree held their position on the ridge. The landscape was formless and alien in the dark. *I can see how movies play on the fears of people who have never been in a darkened forest,* thought James. He switched positions in the seat slowly and closed his eyes, hoping for a few winks. But he soon thought the better of it. *Don't need to fall out of the stand.*

Shivers came just as the forest soaked up the premature rays of morning light. Gradually, James reached into his pocket and unwrapped some hand warmers and slipped them into his mittens that were equipped with slots for fingers to fit through. With a determined, steady advance, the rays of light grew more numerous and fought off the obstinate darkness. Surprisingly, he wasn't as bored as he thought he would be. The anticipation and a keen sense of awareness, an experience he had never really known before, kept him alert and occupied.

The opposite ridge, though, was still steeped in shadow when James peered across the ravine to the stump. It was three feet off the forest floor and reflected a feeble light off two tiny mushrooms growing out from its bark. James held his gaze for two minutes, trying to discern the rest of its features. However, his sight began to blur, and he looked away for a minute. But when he tried to find the stump again, he found it was gone, nowhere to be had on the forest floor. Then his eyes spied a shadow skulk off the crest of the hill. It appeared to have a long tail and be smaller than a deer. Inexplicably, it evoked for a moment an irrational urge in James to follow.

He wasn't sure where the shot came from, but it sounded close. A few minutes passed, or maybe it was longer for time didn't seem to matter anymore to James, before another shot echoed across the landscape. Then, a moment later, another shot signaled early success. The shots quickened James' pulse and verified that there were indeed deer in the forest.

All of a sudden, he heard a muffled crunch, then silence. He froze, and the crunching noise started again. This time it was three distinct steps before quiet. He thought it was coming from behind him. *An animal, no doubt,* thought James. He began shaking and sweating again with anticipation. *Was this a deer already?*

The creature made five more steps before stopping. Begrudgingly, awkwardly James craned his neck around and flipped the rifle off safety as his heart thumped like a kettledrum. However, he could see nothing but trees, sky and snow. *It had to be something.* He looked down at the base of the tree and towards the creek. Still nothing. Soon the worries about moving were forgotten, and James stood up. Then he saw it.

The gray squirrel was foraging for acorns all by its lonesome. James relaxed and in simple amusement watched the squirrel go about his morning business noisily chattering, climbing up a dead birch tree, scurrying down again, running through the snow, disappearing under the snow, coming back out again and then finally disappearing into a log on the forest floor. Soon another squirrel, this one a smaller sized red squirrel, awoke from his slumber and went in search of breakfast. His day started by chattering in a spruce tree to James' left, no doubt annoyed to find an orange intruder at his front door.

Subtle, quiet realizations appeared. *This is the only time I've actually sat quietly and observed a forest, not as a hiker or a motorist driving by, but as a person who actually merges with the landscape. Yet I'm not just here to observe. I'm here to participate in the process. It is easy to disregard hunting as drunken slaughter among bloodthirsty killers. But what I think some people don't realize is the ... oh, I don't know ... the spirituality—is that the right word—of it all.*

The forest became even more alive as daylight advanced. More feisty red and gray squirrels bounded through the morning's welcoming mat of white as various birds flew skyward into the stripped, gray trees. Now the beat of their wings, usually inaudible from inside the confines of car or house, could be clearly discerned by the human on this glorious morning. A black and white chickadee landed on a small branch above James' head to push her curiosity to new bounds. Chirping in her own language, she eyed the large orange creature sharing her favorite tree. The bird tilted her head and in one fell swoop landed down on the barrel of James' rifle, thus presenting the essence of Nature herself—the beautiful juxtaposition of fragile innocence and violence. James was now a part of the tree as far as the chickadee was concerned. After eyeing the stranger and assuring herself that he was not a threat, the chickadee dashed off, her minute but hard-working wings beating a musical-like tune that disappeared into the surrounding woods. The activity in the forest delighted James' once-dulled senses. *It was as if the entire forest came alive with life at daybreak, like the entire thing was one living being.* And on the morning went, James merging with the forest's truths.

After some time the snow began to abate, degenerating into sporadic bursts of flurries. James guessed it was near mid-morning, and the initial onslaught of gunshots had given way to a relative peace. It lulled the inexperienced into complacency.

It was the movement, not necessarily the object, which caught his eye first. James tried to sit completely still as he peered straight ahead. *I'm sure I saw something move on the opposite slope.* He only moved his eyes, once again trying to mimic the techniques in Kevin's books. *Deer.*

He didn't need to raise his gun, for at this distance of seventy-five yards he could tell it was a doe, and seeing he had no hunter's choice tag that allows one to shoot an antlerless deer, he could only watch the animal go about her business. She walked stealthily, nose to the wind, eyes searching for the slightest hint of movement. Soon another doe arrived on the scene behind the one he was observing. It was as if the two appeared out of nowhere, magically conjured up by the forest herself.

The pair didn't see him at all, and they cautiously moved along the opposite ridge directly in front of him shadowing the creek. He could tell they were spooked and fearful. The lead doe would take a few steps, stop and sniff the wind. Occasional she would turn her head to face James with her ears radiated upwards, straining to pick up the slightest sound. However, after a few minutes of this awkward pacing, the does relaxed a bit and dropped their heads into the snow as if they were searching for food.

The lead doe then turned her head to face her companion, and, almost touching noses, communicated to her in a language humans will never understand. For almost five minutes the pair stayed put directly across the creek from James, pawing at the ground and walking in lazy circles until some important business called them. They looked ahead and trotted moderately fast across the ridge, disappearing to James' left.

At this point James could barely contain his excitement. He was now shivering more from exhilaration than the cold. Here in the snow and elements, James had experienced wildlife as it is, not as man wanted it to be in some zoo or aquarium. He smiled to himself and settled back into the comfortable confines of his oak castle. Time moved slowly.

But a few minutes later, James blinked, shook his head and rubbed his eyes. Something across the creek had caught his attention. Out of thin air appeared yet another brown body sticking out from the surrounding white. It seemed to be deliberately following the tracks laid by the does and loping along fairly quickly with its nose toward the ground. James raised his rifle quickly, and turned the scope up to its highest setting as he began to shake again.

There it was. The scope didn't lie. It was a buck, not a trophy, only a small six-pointer, but a buck nonetheless. Now the moment he had been preparing for arrived. His heart beat so fast his ears began to pound from the increased flow of blood. He flipped the safety off as the cortisone flowed into his veins creating a tightening knot in his stomach that made him feel sick and nauseous. Time was of the essence. This deer was not about to stop and dally in James' line of fire. He pulled the rifle butt back to his shoulder. What he saw, or more accurately, didn't see, horrified him.

His rapid, excited breathing had fogged up the scope, making it opaque and useless. Thinking quickly, he remembered the old 30-06 had open, iron sights. Saying a vague prayer, something James had not done for a long time, he put the rusted iron sights on the buck, keying in on his vital organs in the chest region. Reflexes took over, and as the buck passed directly in front of James, oblivious to his presence, he fired. Automatically he ejected the spent shell with the bolt and chambered another round, but the shot had hit its mark. The buck dropped to the ground, desperately kicking his rear legs in an attempt to escape. Again James fired, hitting the deer square in the chest. The kicking stopped.

The buck was dead. There was no long, drawn out process, no genetically engineered birth, no regular machine feedings of processed feed, no cramped four-by-six concrete pen, no trip in a trailer, no time spent in a line at an industrialized slaughterhouse. It was over in thirty seconds.

For a few minutes James sat on the cold bench stunned by the scene that had played itself out in front of him. He almost couldn't believe what he had done. James unloaded the remaining three bullets before slinging the rifle over his right shoulder and carefully climbing out of the oak tree. The snow had died off, and for the first time James could detect the fireball of the sun through breaks in the gray ceiling of clouds. The deer lay sixty yards away. It was plainly visible with its dark brown coat sticking out in contrast from the background of white snow now laced with tinges of red.

James approached the deer very cautiously. Its coal-black eyes were fixed blankly into space, an indication of the ultimate sacrifice. And as James drew closer he felt remorse, a sorrow even, for taking the creature's life.

He loomed over the broken body of his prey and studied the effects of his marksmanship. Blood was now collecting in crimson pools that melted away the surrounding pale snow. James nudged the animal with the rifle to make sure he was dead. Then he laid the gun against a sturdy birch tree and pondered the problem. *I've never field-dressed a deer before.*

In typical tenderfoot fashion, he fished out the old DNR field-dressing pamphlet from his pockets. He knew this was not going to be easy. His stomach for blood never did harden again after his junior high school days when he was forced to dissect frogs, salamanders, grasshoppers and assorted rodents. Regardless of the reservations, it was a job that had to be done lest the meat spoil and his work come to nothing. James grabbed the antlers of the buck. *Three points on either side, definitely not a trophy. He ain't going to break any records.* But it really didn't matter to him. He was now awash with the pride brought on by beginner's luck.

James positioned the head of the buck facing uphill and dug into his pockets for the folding knife. It was then he realized he had forgotten to tag the deer, which was supposed to be done immediately after the kill. He took off his back tag and removed a portion along a perforated edge before securing it to the deer's antlers with a string. "Now the fun part," he sighed.

He withdrew the knife from its sheath and opened the pamphlet to the proper page. Suddenly, James lifted his head and looked skyward. *My ears are not ringing at all. If I had been shooting in the yard with no ear protection, my ears would be bleeding. Must be the adrenaline.*

"Step one," said James to himself, "was to remove the genitals by cutting around the testicles and penis." He let out a half-disgusted sigh as he looked away from his prey. "That had to come first."

Overcoming his squeamishness, James made the required cuts and then read on, trying to let the printed word guide his knife. Grasping the skin below the rib cage, he cut back towards the anus, taking care only to cut the skin and not plunge the knife too deeply into the body cavity which would result in a smelly mess. His hands now ran red with warm sticky blood. The heat from the animal escaped from the open cavity giving the appearance of a spectral spirit cloud enveloping the scene. This was not some detached and impersonalized kill at a distant factory farm He turned the page, leaving his bloody fingerprint on the white paper, and continued to follow the directions as best he could, knowing full well this was no picture-perfect job.

The next cut was made through the belly muscle. Now the smell of the internal organs assaulted his nostrils, but James continued resolutely with his work. He reached his hand into the hot, steaming body of the animal and felt the stomach and intestines slip away from his protruding hands. Next he made a cut around the rectum on the outside and inside of the deer and pulled it into the body cavity. James flipped the animal over on his side. Reaching into the cavity, he pulled the stomach and digestive organs away from the body. They made a soft tearing noise as he used his knife to free them from their moorings. Soon the digestive system was lying on the ground, and James could begin work on the heart and the lungs. First, he had to cut through the diaphragm with his knife into the bloody darkness of the chest. He felt gingerly for the windpipe, which he quickly severed, and grabbed the powerful heart and lungs with his hands. They were pulled into the outside world. The job was done.

James cut the heart away from the lungs. He studied this, the very essence of the animal's life, intently and felt its tissue harden in the chill.

Good eating?" he questioned aloud as he placed it in the plastic bag. "We will see." He thought about keeping the liver as well, but the images of liver flukes from science class coerced him to leave it with the rest of the organs on the forest floor.

The walk back to his cabin was about half a mile, a tough task dragging a 135-pound field-dressed deer. He had heard many stories about old men dying from heart attacks under such exertion. *Another reason to start exercising.*

He walked back to the stand and untied the hoist rope. Then he fastened it around the animal's neck with a bulky, double square knot and ran it over his right shoulder. He leaned forward, and the animal barely budged at first. Yet slowly and surely, using his body weight, James was able to pull the buck through the snow up the ever-increasing steepness of the hill towards the cabin.

Once James reached the crest of the hill he stopped to catch his breath and reflect on the morning's occurrences. His breath came in fits and gasps, the ultimate result of his former lifestyle. He swallowed hard and for a second closed his eyes before turning back toward the gut pile. The sounds of the crows reached his ears even before his eyes fell on the scene. There were four of them, dark as night, noisily squawking at each other as they pecked through the entrails. Small flashes of white intermingled with the dark forms. They were chickadees joining the feast. It was life in graphic realism. *Nothing is wasted.*

For several minutes, James stood in silence, as if he was watching some Discovery Channel wildlife documentary. But this was very different. It wasn't experienced through a box in the living room. It wasn't sanitized for modern man's consumption as he sat eating chips. James had actually participated in the process instead of being a passive observer. This wasn't a false surreal world where transient human emotions and feelings were superimposed upon nature. This was nature in her eternal reality. And James, deer, birds, sky and trees were all threads of that one truth.

The sun shone ever brighter as its late morning rays fanned out across the forest floor, bathing it in the potential of the new day, a fitting corollary to the kill site, where the nutrients and organic material in the deer entrails were now fueling the continued life and potential of the chickadees and the crows.

Smiling, James started the final leg of his journey toward the pine plantation and home. He was changed. The experience meant something beyond just killing an animal and the limited scope of his own ego. *I would never have experienced this had I not been fired. Was there a reason?*

Back at the cabin, James sat down on a stump by the woodshed to rest. Sweat rolled off his forehead and dripped down onto his blood stained blaze-orange outfit. The traces of the early morning snow clouds had disappeared, and the day had exploded into brilliant blue sunshine agitating James' overheated body. He knew the sequence of events that now must be undertaken from his pre-hunt studies. It was time to hang the deer in the garage and begin the laborious task of butchering the carcass after first taking it to Willy's for registration. *I think I'll let him hang in the garage for a day or two first,* thought James as he pulled the deer by the rope past the cabin. He was so immersed in his task he didn't even bother to go inside to get a drink or some food. James then tied a sturdy, half-inch nylon rope to the buck's head. Next he hoisted the animal from the garage rafters with the help of a hook-and-pulley system used by Kevin for the same purpose. Blood trickled from the open body cavity onto the concrete floor, and James gathered some empty moving boxes to place under his hanging prey.

He stepped back to view his work, beaming a smile nobody, unfortunately, could see. The buck swayed slightly on the hook-and-pulley hoist, now tied off to an immobile workbench. His lifeless eyes met James', and a tinge of sadness once again fell over him.

He approached the deer and placed his hands on its soft hide. Then, without consciously thinking, he spoke. The words flowed from a place deep within never accessed until now. "Thank you," he whispered. "Thank you for sacrificing yourself for me. I'm sorry."

He turned away from the buck. *So be it.* There was work to be done. Hacksaws, knives, wrapping paper and, most importantly, information all had to be acquired. Now he decided to retreat to the cabin to rest up and feed his empty stomach. The day continued to grow warmer and brighter as the temperatures soared upwards into the forties and the cold morning air was all but forgotten, so typical of this autumn. The smile crept back over James' face. *This is the first real thing I ever did.*

Chapter 9
The Destroyer Of Worlds

For some individuals, that autumn brought the loveliest weather imaginable, weather that could only have been dreamed of in years past. Few New Yorkers complained of November temperatures that hit eighty degrees nine times. Besides, who really liked to break their backs shoveling snow in parkas or cover up the beautiful human body that was built through starvation and $100-a-month club memberships? Teenage queens, striving to emulate self-promoting celebrities, could strip down even more and strive to be the center of attention into the usual bleak winter months. People joked of melting polar caps and endless summer. Smiles abounded in these parts. But reality was far from being so rosy.

The fall harvest in the Midwest had been an unmitigated disaster, the victim of a second straight year of punishing drought. People around the world would no doubt feel the pinch as the price of bread crept skyward. Beef prices were following a similar pattern. The drought had scorched grazing land from Texas to Minnesota. If present trends continued, the quiet grumbling of the US consumer was going to erupt into a chorus of pocketbook pain. To make matters worse, the lack of rainfall had caused a severe drop in water levels on the Mississippi and Missouri Rivers. Trucking companies and railroads loved the situation, but the massive coal-burning power stations along those rivers needed barges to bring fuel. The coal could be shipped via rail, but it was more expensive. Amid all the uncertainty, there was one inalienable truth—in the end, the consumer would pay.

Yet, what made the current Midwest drought so disconcerting was that it was not the lone severe weather event to make recent world headlines. Strangely coordinated droughts were gripping other important food-growing regions. Ukraine was in the midst of its worst drought in 100 years, as were the cattle-producing areas of Argentina. In these hot, terrible places, people all asked the same question, "Where was the rain?"

They had only look at the TV to find out. India and Southeast Asia were inundated with monsoons that refused to let up after their traditional June-to-September season had passed. Whole regions seemed to be under water. Thousands drowned. Europe and even Great Britain had been beset with a rash of killer tornadoes, highly unusual events for this part of the world. Some produced winds of over 350 miles per hour. Curious weather was becoming the norm, but it didn't end there.

In the western Pacific Ocean, six unusually large typhoons had formed since late August. The Philippines fell victim to a strong storm in early October. Winds in excess of 180 miles per hour tore through Manila. And in the Caribbean, twelve category-five hurricanes had made this season the worst in memory, and, like the torrential rains afflicting Asia, the storm activity did not abate as the year drew to a close. Galveston, Texas lost fifty people to Hurricane Willard on December twelfth.

Despite the noise created by William Beecham's post-election rhetoric and promises, despite the usual parade of celebrity attention-grabbing antics, despite the meaningless sports stats and nightly homicides, the weather was making nightly headlines. So-called experts were called on to lay blame on everything from global warming to heightened news reporting of severe weather. Nevertheless, few could deny the odd weather was having a direct influence on the world and its economy. Storms at sea and low water levels on inland rivers were disrupting shipping. Prices for basic foodstuffs were rising because of the disastrous harvests. Drought situations were also exacerbating delicate political situations in some very unstable global hotspots.

However, the fact was people were jaded toward doomsday theories. They had been hearing the alarms of Chicken Littles all their lives. Had they not lived through threats of nuclear war, Y2K meltdown population growth holocaust and terrorist non-events in the past? People still had their lives to live. They still had to get those kids to soccer and plan tonight's meal in between those cell phone calls to the office.

The outer world continued to whirl around the sun as its fields burned and cities flooded, while in the secluded forests of northern Wisconsin, relatively untouched by the recent events, a young man continued to play out his part in a great epic. He rather liked his new friends and neighbors—all seemed to be very interesting people. And like the rest of mankind, he had yet to figure out the significance of it all.

* * *

The question was unanswered. It lay suspended in the air of James cabin like stale smoke. Two years worth of career sweat and savings were being squandered along with a college education and, despite the growing appeal of the alternative, James realized it would soon be time to leave this place. *But things are so uneasy,* he would often think, *strange weather, slow economy. Should I wait?*

James mulled over these thoughts on the morning of December tenth as he sat at the kitchen table. With deer hunting over and his prey neatly wrapped up in the freezer, his mind often focused on his uncertain future. However, it was not as if he was bored. He always had plenty of tinkering to do in the garage and house. But the conflict was tearing him apart—to stay or go. All the expectations of society dictated that he must return soon. He must work and be responsible. His heart, however, was often telling him something different, and the two forces were at constant odds with each other, which often drove him into depths of melancholy and begged him to ask the question. *Why am I here?*

He stood up resolutely from the kitchen table and looked outside. It was a balmy sixty-two degrees on this clear, sunny morning. Looking around the cabin, he made a mental checklist of items he would have to bring back to the Twin Cities when he chose to leave. *I got to find an apartment.*

James yawned and sat down again, stretching his back over the backrest of the chair while he closed his eyes. Last night had brought little rest. In the dream he had advanced deeper into the mysterious realm of trees. Even now, he could sense the chilled air and menace lurking within.

The day passed quietly enough. James took a brisk walk down his road and even read through some Twin City apartment listings from the Sunday edition of the Pioneer Press that he had bought in town a few days ago. However, he didn't place any calls to prospective landlords. At 4:30, somewhat winded from a second vigorous hike back to his deer stand and a quick round of splitting oak wood, James hopped into the Dodge for the trek to Cozy Pines. His extended family waited.

"Mr. Norris!" arose the yell as James entered the establishment.

He turned to see Paul, Mike and Aaron at the bar. All three had yelled simultaneously.

Ray smiled and added his own, "Hey James."

James made his way up to Paul. "You guys give up work or what?" he asked.

Ray had a Leinenkugel's on the bar before James sat down, and Mike extended his hand. "I thought that was your gig?" he laughed.

"Twelve-ounce curls are what we do best," added Aaron.

Paul chuckled half-heartedly. "Too fuckin' warm for the tenth," he said tapping his watch, "It is like September out there."

James looked up at the TV, which was tuned to some NFL report. "Kind of weird, all of it, huh?" he asked.

Paul shook his head. "Damn deer are still in rut I think. Bet they will not even yard up this winter. You see that storm that tore up the Philippines though? Horrible."

"How'd you guys do this year?" James asked. "Hunting, I mean." He pretended to hold a rifle in his hands.

Aaron smiled as he finished his beer and pointed at Mike. "Talk to him," he said.

"He got a nice eleven-pointer opening morning," added Paul.

"You getting it mounted?" asked James.

"You bet," said Mike. "It is at the taxidermist right now."

"All in all, we did alright," said Paul. "Mike got his, I shot a fork on Sunday, Aaron got two nice does and the wife shot a decent seven pointer."

"I shot a six opening morning," added James.

"Now did ya?" asked Paul rearing back on his stool as if he did not believe his new friend.

Mike butted in, "Now a six ain't bad, but I hear someone got a big eleven-pointer around here."

"Screw off," said Aaron.

Ray had been listening to the conversation intensely from behind the bar. He took a drag from his cigarette and spoke. "I'll tell you what, boy, I think that this weather is something big. People talk about the typhoons over there in the Philippines but, hell, it ain't nothing compared to what this drought is doing. Smoke from those forest fires in, what is it Guatemala or something, is choking the air in Mexico City. And you hear about those tornadoes in Oslo?"

No one jumped to attention.

"You see that, James?" he asked again in a louder voice.

James shook his head in the negative.

"Oslo ain't never had one before those," said Ray, his eyes

widening for effect.

"Yeah, who knows," Paul said. "It is really strange, sixty-two degrees here. Can you believe it? But we have been hearing this global warming garbage for years. I think part of it may be reporting, you know. You know they just didn't report about weather in the past like they do today so they may only be giving people the impression the weather is turning wild. If a guy were to go back hundred years, I bet the same stuff was happening."

"I am not so sure," said Ray. "Saw this thing last night on the weather channel where some guy was saying the global ocean currents could, like, flip-flop or something and change the entire global climate. Storms, big ones, would be one result." He clasped his hands together and turned them up and down in an attempt to dramatize the statement.

"Sounds like alarmist bullshit to me. Haven't we heard this all before?" said Paul. "Guys like that are always wrong."

"No, no, hear me out," persisted Ray. "I just wanted you to hear about this mechanism for disaster, and I'll let you decide whether or not it is bull. And I agree with you that people sometimes get too wrapped up in all these science-fiction doomsday scenarios. However, what I think is really important is what all this end of the world talk says about us. What does it represent? Why do we seem to long for it?

Paul rolled his eyes. "It sells, Ray. It gets people all excited."

"But these things could happen. The scientists say so," answered Ray. "Hell, I remember hearing about global warming over twenty years ago. I was watching a program on the Twin Cities news talking about carbon dioxide buildup and the greenhouse effect. The weatherman laughed it off. But look at what has happened since then. Everything they say could happen has come to pass. Look outside, Paul. We don't have winter anymore. You think that is just coincidence? I know correlation is not causation, but it sure as hell looks real in my book."

"We can't change the climate," said Paul. "How pretentious is it for us puny humans to think we have that kind of power. If something like that happens it is just God's will."

"God's will?" asked Ray. "What about free will? And we can change the climate. Remember CFCs and the ozone hole? People like you said the same things back then. But you were wrong. It was proven man caused the hole, and we acted. Now the hole is repairing itself. If we listened to people like you, we would all be dying of skin cancer."

"I think what Ray is trying to say," added James, "is that stewardship means we have to take responsibility for our actions. Our lifestyles and choices have consequences whether we like it or not. We can't just turn out eyes away. Like Ray said, we have free will."

"There is an order to the world," replied Ray. "I fear we may have disrupted it beyond repair."

"But, come on," said Mike. "Do you really think they can predict the weather ten years from now? Do you really think global warming is responsible for what we see on TV?"

"Who the hell knows?" said Ray. "I agree with you. The damn weathermen often get it wrong. But I'll tell you this. Just look outside. What is it, sixty some degrees in December? That just ain't right. Something is out of balance, out of order. That just ain't natural

"Do you know what restores order?" said Paul, turning serious and agreeable.

"What?" asked James.

"Violence," answered Paul. "Just like a thunderstorm on a hot day restores the balance in nature. Violence brings order back into the world."

"But, like I said," added Ray. "What is really important is what all this speculation represents."

"And what do you think that is?" asked James

"Man's longing for destruction."

All assembled grew silent, reflecting on Paul and Ray's words, thinking thoughts none dared to voice out loud.

Then, suddenly, as if to break the tension, Paul pushed the bill of his hat together and finished off the last sips of his Old Milwaukee. He looked at Mike and Allen in their tee shirts.

"You bastards ready?" he asked.

"We've been waiting for your slow ass," said Mike.

Paul shook his head as he put his hand on James' shoulder. "Gotta go," he said, "milking time."

James waved as the trio made their way to the door, which promptly flew open from the outside. A blonde woman barged into the establishment.

"Jeez, watch where you are going!" yelled Mike as Nicole Kaufmann nearly bowled him over.

She looked back at him as she made her way toward the bar. "Oh, it is just you," she laughed. "Cut me some slack. I'm late."

"What else is new?" said Mike as he left.

Ray glanced at the clock, shook his head and exited into the kitchen.

James looked nervously down at the floor. He had yet to really talk to her in all his previous forays here. Now here she stood only a few feet away. He feigned interest in the NFL report still on TV. Nicole tidied up behind the bar before pulling her hair back and running into the kitchen. James could hear her exchange laughs with Ann, and in a few seconds she returned to clean up some empty glasses. *What do I know about her? She is twenty-five, has a four-year-old old son and works here. Say something.*

"Late, uh?" was his ever-so-original question.

Nicole grabbed a napkin dispenser from behind the bar. She smiled immediately. "Yeah, got held up at Hawkin's."

"Hawkin's?" questioned James.

"That is my other job. I'm the secretary for Hawkin's Real Estate in Winter."

"Really, two jobs?"

"Unfortunately, yes. Gotta make money somehow. I'm saving up money to go back to school."

James set his empty beer can down, and Nicole grabbed him another on queue. "Thanks," he said.

"You are James Norris, Kevin's nephew, right?"

"That's the rumor," said a nervous James.

Nicole extended her hand. "I'm Nicole Kaufmann. I know I've seen you before, but I don't think we've ever talked."

"Nice to meet you," said James as he played with his hat. "How many hours do you work here?"

"Not as many as I used to. I've actual been cutting my hours back a little here. Right now I'm here maybe two nights a week."

She smiled constantly as she started to go about her business of cleaning and setting tables, keeping eye contact with James the entire time.

"Why you cutting back?" asked James.

"I want to spend more time with my son. He is four now. My mom helps take care of him, but with two jobs I don't get to see him as much as I would like. Saving for school may be my long-term goal; however, you have to have priorities."

"What is your boy's name?" asked James, already knowing the answer.

"Matt. He is my little man."

She ran into the kitchen but continued to carry on the conversation.

"Suppose he can be a handful when he wants to be," said James.

"You got that right," replied Nicole returning to the bar.

"What are you going back to school for?"

"I used to go to school at the University of Minnesota-Duluth. I was a history major until Matt came along. It was my junior year, and I could not afford to go to school and support him at the same time, so I moved back home. But I've always kept my love of learning. I read a lot, and someday, someday," she said shaking her finger at James, "I'm going to go back and finish that degree, probably be a teacher."

"Good for you," smiled James.

James was intrigued, and as was his nature, he decided to test the waters.

"So, if you're such a smarty pants about history," he said, "when has the world experienced weather like we are seeing today? We were just talking about how weird it is."

Nicole took a breath and curled her lower lip above her upper.

"James, I'm not sure," she said. "There is no doubt the weather has been strange all over as of late. But I think how the climate works is largely a mystery to science. However, I think some of the global warming we are seeing—especially in the Arctic—is man-made due to the burning of fossil fuels and release of carbon dioxide."

James nodded approvingly, listening to her every word.

"Nonetheless," Nicole continued, "the world has experienced rapid warming and cooling trends in the past without human intervention. It is cyclical, I think. Nature goes through periods of order broken by times of disorder and change."

"What are some examples?" asked James.

"Well, did you know that during the Viking Age in the Middle Ages the planet was warmer than it is now? That is how the Viking colonists eked out a living in Greenland. But then the planet cooled somehow and the Greenland colonists died off. By the seventeen and eighteen hundreds the Earth had chilled to a point that enabled the canals in Holland to freeze on a regular basis. They never do that now. People call that time period the little ice age."

"Is there any evidence civilizations have been affected by a changing climate? I mean, I think if the climate really changed fast the results would be destructive," said James.

"You bet," replied Nicole. "In the sixth century AD, Byzantine Emperor Justinian's attempts to recreate the past glories of the Roman Empire were cut short by a global cooling event that shortened growing seasons and may have contributed to the growth of Christianity at that troubled time. The Dark Ages soon followed. Cores of mud from the ocean floor indicate the world suffered another dramatic global cooling event around the year twenty-two hundred BC. By the year two thousand BC or so, the Old Kingdom of Egypt, Akkadian Empire and Hongsan culture in China all collapsed. Basically, all civilizations and cities from Greece to India to the Orient fell into disarray and disorder.

"You are saying these societies were destroyed by the weather?"

"That is what some people say, James. In fact, there are those who say that the flood myths that almost all cultures share throughout the world are the unconscious memory of a great destructive change in the climate back in our pre-history."

"Do you believe that?"

"I don't know. It makes for interesting conversation, but I think what we are seeing is just a temporary abnormality. I'm not losing any sleep over it. Besides, I'm sure our country and our world nowadays would have no problem adapting and surviving any long-term climate change."

She seems to really be enjoying herself, probably doesn't get a chance to share this knowledge with too many people.

"Gee, James, why are you asking me this stuff?" she said, confirming James' suspicion. "The only other person I can really talk history with is Martin, and usually that degenerates into a shouting match."

James just shrugged it off, and Nicole retreated back into the kitchen. Pots and pans clamored for a few minutes before she reemerged.

"How do you know all that stuff?" asked James.

Nicole laughed and took a step back from the bar. "Like I said before, I was a history major. I am not just a waitress, you know."

"I can see that."

Nicole started to aimlessly wipe the dark oak bar with a dirty dishrag.

"Where is Matt tonight?" asked James seeking to breath new life into the conversation.

Nicole obliged. "My mom is nice enough to watch him when I

work. She especially likes playing grandma since my dad passed away last year."

James nodded. "Is it difficult working, with a child to take care of?"

Nicole tilted her head and twisted her mouth into a half-smirk. "Now what kind of dumb question is that?" she said. "Of course it is. I have to sacrifice, or at least, put off my dreams for the good of my son."

She paused for a second, looking towards the slow moving ceiling fan, relentlessly pushing Ray and Anne's pirouetting cigarette smoke through the bar.

"But, you know, it is funny, I cannot image my life without him. If he were not here, I would probably still be out partying, hanging out at clubs and not growing up. Matt made me take stock of my life. I realized I couldn't have it all. There have to be sacrifices. That is a natural fact of life, and it is something I learned quicker than some of my girlfriends, I think."

James nodded as she continued.

"I could have taken the easy way out. I could have not taken responsibility for my actions like some of my friends urged me to do. It could have been all about me. But now I would not have it any other way."

Nicole's brown eyes flashed to the floor and then back to James. "James, I'm sorry to chew on your ear like this. Hell, I'm the bartender, you should be doing this to me," she said.

Crazy. How much do I really know about her? I think Martin said she was not seeing anyone. But remember Kim. Gotta stop meeting women in bars.

James looked at the fan, his beer and then played with his hat again. *Damn crazy. Oh, well ...*

"Do you want to go out sometime?" he said, looking sheepishly at Nicole who, for a second, had a shocked expression on her face. He almost didn't believe he had actually done it, and then thinking she may have misheard him, he asked again. "Do you want to go out sometime?"

His face flushed, and her winning smile was the only answer he needed.

Chapter 10
Redemption

The man had just passed through the guardians of the realm. The soft wind and rhythmic humming that had accompanied him earlier on his journey had faded away. Not even the slightest rays of light from the forlorn sky could penetrate the blanket hanging over his head. His initial fear was subsiding, somewhat, as his head turned cautiously from side to side, then behind, to make sure nothing was following him. *Why am I here?* he continued to ask himself. Some unseen presence was urging him further into that most recognizable yet unknown of places. *I've been here before. But when?*

Ahead lay the inner sanctum of the womb where a few rays of light managed to break through the protection provided by the guardians. The man stopped and listened, for the wind was picking up again and starting to grow more self-assured, as it often does when rushing thru a canopy much taller than the surrounding forest. *There was something up there.*

The air was still cold but did not contain the bone-chilling punch that had greeted the man at the realm's entrance. Here it was lighter, almost refreshing, accompanied by a sweet, crisp smell. The man pulled the few remaining guardians out of his way and stepped forward into the womb.

They were giants, arranged in a near-perfect circle. The man gazed skyward and watched the gentle swaying of their uppermost limbs. Walking over to an exceptionally large one, the man placed his hands on the ageless bark. It spoke back in a language he could feel but not comprehend.

The sound was barely perceivable at first, almost sounding like dull, distant thunder rolling over again and again, not unlike the humming the man heard before his entrance into the realm. But the man froze in recognition as the greatest feeling of sheer terror now swept over him. *Something is happening. Turn around.*

The man's back was turned to the thick forest beyond the womb, and the noise seemed to be coming from that direction. He mustered his courage and swallowed hard. *Just turn around, turn around.*

My God. A vaporous, ghostly fog was now emanating from the deep soul of the forest. It unfurled quickly and soon enveloped the entire womb. The man's heart started beating furiously, and his mouth grew dry and eyes widened. Then as the fog reached the man and began encircling his legs, his eyes lifted upward toward the point back in the forest where the fog originated. *No, it can't be.* A dark form in the midst of the fog was coming toward him. *Run ...*

* * *

It was Sunday, December eighteenth, and for the first time since deer season the weather actually felt a little like winter. James staggered down to the kitchen to get a drink of water, still shaking from his latest advance into nocturnal mystery. He checked the thermometer outside the kitchen window on this cloudy day. "Thirty degrees, not bad," he said.

The big day had come and gone. On Friday night James had met Nicole at her mom's modest ranch-style home and driven to Myran's Supper Club on the Chippewa Flowage Reservoir. During the week, James had run into Ken Dresser at the Marathon Station, and he had recommended it as a fine eating establishment between his added suggestions to "just take her to the Watering Hole for a damn burger." Some may have thought the comments were crude, but James was starting to really like Ken. *The man has an ability to bring humor into any circumstance, despite his frequent complaints about the sawmill. And he has no problem telling it like it is.* In fact, it was Ken who asked James to his face if he actually thought he had a chance with Nicole, seeing his employment at the current time was lacking. It only added fuel to the conflict. *To stay or go?*

James was rather proud of his planning, for the date went off without a hitch. Nonetheless, James could sense Nicole was being cautious, not like the first time they had talked at Cozy Pines. Conversation over New York porterhouse and grilled chicken stayed on safe subjects: weather, Matt and mutual acquaintances. After an obligatory peck on the cheek, Nicole had to return home. Her mom had agreed to watch Matt until her bridge group met at 10 PM.

But today was different. A slight cooling of the weather over the past week had finally brought a one to two inch layer of ice onto Mud Lake. It was early, good ice and totally transparent, which enabled the adventurer to look down into the depths. Also, it was the best time of the year to fish for crappie, according to Willy at the sport shop. Taking a shot in the dark, James had called Nicole yesterday to thank her for Friday and see if she knew anything about ice fishing. To James' total shock, she said she loved the activity. However, James was forced to reveal he knew almost nothing about it. Nicole chuckled over the phone and advised him to study up, which James had dutifully done the past day. Kevin had left behind no shortage of books.

Nicole would be over any minute. So James retreated into the cool basement to gather Kevin's ice fishing gear. But he soon grew frustrated. The fishing lines were a massive puzzle of tangled monofilament and nylon. *No time like the present,* he thought. And with that he sat down on a white plastic five-gallon bucket that was used to house the needed equipment when being carried onto the ice.

Done. After ten minutes of sheer hell and repeated line-cutting with a Swiss Army knife, James had succeeded in freeing the lines from their entangled prison. He laid the equipment neatly on the floor and laughed. "I'm actually preparing to ice fish," he said.

James was still not quite sure how to use the contraptions lying before him. One apparatus had thick, black nylon line, and James recognized it as a tip-up. The tip-up consisted of a metal rod, which ran through the middle of a rectangular piece of wood approximately a foot long. The metal rod was on an axle and could be folded up parallel to the wooden piece in a hollow portion or tilted to a perpendicular setting. A spool for line was attached to one end of the rod and a t-bar to the other. Placed on one end of the wooden piece was a flag on a shaft with a spring at its base. The flag could be bent down to fit under the t-bar. But if a hungry fish were to bite, the line would be pulled out, causing the spool to turn the metal rod, which would turn the t-bar and cause the flag to flip up alerting the hopefully sober fisherman dinner had arrived. James played with the tip-up and attempted to figure out its secrets. *Ingenious.*

He then set the tip-up down and picked up a jig pole. The jig pole could be used for larger game fish but was usually reserved for crappies and bluegills. Its design was simple: a wooden pole with monofilament line that could be wrapped around two small pegs, depending on the desired depth the fisherman wanted to fish. It came equipped with a metal pointer on one end that could be stuck into the ice. *Apparently Kevin never got into the whole sonar, new-fangled spinning reel thing like I've seen on TV.*

The hooks, the poles and the tip-ups were all a new world to James. He grabbed up everything he thought he needed and made his way up the creaking stairs. Halfway up, the thought hit him. *How do I get through the ice?* Setting the equipment by the door, he returned to the basement. While searching behind the wood stove, he hit pay dirt—a simple blue auger drill. It was hand-powered with six-inch, somewhat sharp blades. *It'll do.*

At exactly 9:30 AM a knock came to the door. James raced over to greet his guest, and Nicole bounded into the cabin clapping her leather glove-clad hands together.

"Ready?" she asked.

"Almost," replied James. "Just getting the rest of the stuff together."

Nicole was dressed the part. She wore a red-and-white Polaris snowmobile jacket and black snow pants. A blue wool headband covered her ears.

"You sure you got everything you need?" she asked.

James surveyed his pile of gear. "Tip-ups, jig poles, auger, got a couple of folding chairs in the garage–"

"You got shiners?"

"Shiners?"

"Yeah, minnows for the tip-ups. We are going to put in for northerns, aren't we?"

"I don't have any," replied James sheepishly.

"Well, today is your lucky day," said Nicole, "I just picked up a dozen at Willy's." On cue, she pushed open the screen door and returned with a Styrofoam bucket that shook with live minnows. "I even picked up some waxies for the crappies."

"Waxies?" questioned James again.

Nicole shook her head. "Don't tell me you do not know what waxies are?"

James answered in the negative.

"You really do need a fishing lesson," said Nicole as she reached into her pocket to retrieve a clear plastic box filled with squirming larvae-type creatures packed in sawdust. "Waxies," she said smiling at him. "We will put these on tear-drops for the crappies."

"Learn something new every day," replied James.

Nicole grabbed the minnows and the ice auger and bolted thru the door. "Let's go," she said.

The lake was glass, tinged black, yet clear. Across its once-liquefied surface lay two inches of solid ice. Pressure cracks crisscrossed the surface at irregular intervals.

"Looks like good ice," said James as he and Nicole reached the surface. Nicole, auger and minnows in hand, took a few steps back from the frozen shoreline and leaped onto the icy surface, sliding like an ice skater out onto the lake.

"Look, you can see right down to the bottom!" she said.

James shuffled behind her with the rest of the equipment and tried not to fall as he looked through the frozen prism to the bottom of the lake.

"You can even see the weeds down there," said James, "like some glass bottomed boat or something."

Nicole slid out a little further. "So, you know where the crappies are out here?"

James set down the five-gallon pail and folding Coleman chairs. "Ken Dresser said he and his dad used to do well straight across from the cabin off the far shore. There is a weed bed there about six feet deep that drops off to thirty feet quickly."

Nicole slid off in that direction. "Wow!" she hollered when she neared the opposite shore. "I can see fish."

James trundled over the slippery surface and peered thru the ice. She was right. Flashing amidst the weeds were slivery flashes of life.

"Looks like minnows or something," said James.

"This where we want to be?"

"It's the spot," replied James as he took the auger from Nicole and began to drill into the ice.

A few turns found the water gushing up through a hole. Nicole reached into the white pail. "You got a scooper?" she asked.

"Scooper?" questioned James once again realizing Nicole had probably caught him forgetting something.

"How are you going to clear the ice chunks out of the hole?" asked Nicole slyly as James looked down to see shavings from the auger blades floating like a thick broth.

James squatted down and removed his gloves. He used his bare hands to scoop the ice out.

Nicole laughed. "Very impressive. Cold enough for you?"

James held his hand up to his mouth and blew hot breath onto it. Nicole, meanwhile, picked out a tip-up and handed it to James with the Styrofoam minnow bucket.

"You think I should put a tip-up here?" asked James.

"Sure," said Nicole, "you can have three lines in the water at one time. May as well put two tip-ups in and then jig. Looks like you got a couple jig poles in the pail for me. I really don't care if I put a tip-up in though."

James studied the tip-up for a second and reached into the minnow bucket for a shiner.

"Are you going to test the depth?" asked Nicole.

This time Nicole didn't wait for the negative response. She produced a small, orange-colored weight with a clip on one end. "Take this here," she said as she clipped it onto the line above the large treble hook. "Let the weight take out line until you reach the bottom."

James did as instructed. He could feel the weight hit the bottom of the lake, and the line stop coming off the spool. Nicole now handed him a small red and white bobber.

"Pull the line roughly a foot off the bottom and mark how much line is left out by clipping on this bobber. If the bobber is gone when you have a flag, it means you have a fish that has taken out line, which is a good thing," she said.

"Why a foot off the bottom?"

"I'm just going on what my Dad used to do," answered Nicole. "He always brought the minnow a foot or so off the bottom when fishing for northern or walleye."

After setting the depth, James reached his hand into the minnow bucket and attempted to grab a shiner. The bucket rattled as the minnows, seemingly expecting their fate, raced to avoid his grasp. He finally caught one of the silvery-gray creatures after thirty exasperating seconds, but his first attempt at impaling the bait on the treble hook failed as the minnow suddenly escaped James's wet, slippery hand and flopped onto the ice. With determined bodily spasms the minnow floundered toward the open hole in the ice, and before James could reach his fugitive bait the shiner gleefully landed in the open hole, disappearing beneath the ice. To make matters worse, James had continued his forward thrust with the hook even after the minnow had escaped. The hook embedded itself straight into James left thumb, but the barb, luckily, had not pieced his skin. He quickly removed the hook from its fleshly prison and sucked the few drops of blood that oozed out.

Nicole slapped her knees. "Isn't this fun," she said.

"Great fun for the entire family," replied James.

James reached again into the minnow bucket. This time he successfully placed the shiner on the hook and lowered his dancing bait into the cold, dark depths. The shiner swam wildly around in circles as it sank down to the bottom. James then placed the wooden frame in position and lowered the flag onto the t-bar. Quickly forgetting any embarrassment, he moved on to another spot twenty yards down the shoreline and slightly deeper. His second tip-up installation went off without a hitch.

"You think on the edge of the weed bed for crappies?" asked Nicole.

James surveyed his two tip-ups. "I know that bed drops off fast. I could see that in the boat last fall. I don't know … ten feet is probably where we need to be."

He estimated a spot ten yards out from the two tip-ups and equidistant from both. He drilled two holes and Nicole checked the depth with a jig stick.

"Ten feet on the nose," she said as she tied a yellow and red teardrop on her line and baited it with a wax worm.

"How deep you fishing?" asked James.

"I'm staying about a foot off the bottom," answered Nicole. "But they could be suspended."

James grabbed a jig stick and set his depth. He marked his position with an orange cork bobber, split with a hole running through its center and held on the line by a toothpick. A waxie and teardrop were then sent back into the watery realm.

"Did you do the fishing chant?" asked Nicole. "Every fisherman has to do it to insure success."

"Huh?" asked James as he kept his eyes on the bobber and stuck the metal pointer of the jig stick into the ice.

Nicole did likewise and leaned back in the chair. "It goes like this," she said. "Fishy, fishy in the lake, if you're down there, would you bite my bait, please! And you have to say please. It is the most important part of the chant."

James shook his head. "You are strange," he laughed as he nestled into a perfect slouch.

The clouds made a feeble attempt to break as the two fishing friends sat on the frozen lake. A northwest wind picked up slightly, sending a few stray snowflakes across the landscape. James attempted to follow Nicole's lead by jigging the stick up and down to attract the wily and currently absent fish. Sometimes he'd raise it slowly a foot or two, jig it lightly and then let the bait fall back into position. For a few minutes no words were spoken and silence reigned supreme, but James felt strangely content staring into the ice hole like it was some sort of navel into the inner soul of the world. He didn't feel awkward in a way that demanded he start an immediate conversation with Nicole. The wind was enough for now, only broken by the familiar sound of a jet with its crystallized contrail appearing through gaps in the clouds.

It was Nicole who finally broke the peace as she stuck her jig pole back into the ice. "Wind is picking up," she said.

James quit his routine jigging action. "Maybe winter is finally here," he said.

Nicole clapped her hands together as if trying to stay warm and adjusted her headband. "So, what are you going to do with the cabin? You planning on staying here for the long term?"

James thought carefully before speaking. "Well, I'd like to but, hey I'm an accountant. I don't know if I could get a full-time job around here."

"Have you checked for jobs in the area?" asked Nicole.

"Little, mainly in that Northern Wisconsin Advertiser they have at the Marathon station in town."

Nicole put her hands on her knees and looked James in the eye as if seeking to read his body language. "But you do want to stay here if possible, not return to the Twin Cities, correct?"

She was forcing the conflict he could not resolve. "If at all possible," he answered.

"When you going to try to go back to school?" asked James attempting to change the subject.

"The way things are going right now, it'll be sometime next century," Nicole huffed. "It is not like school is real cheap, and I would like to stay out of debt as much as possible. Plus, with Matt . . . it is not easy." She glanced down at the ice before continuing. "I have to do what is best for him, no matter what I may want."

"That takes courage," James said.

Nicole gave James a thanking nod. "James, she said, "you know we live in a society today that tells someone like me that I have to go out and challenge the world and its stereotypes. In other words, basically be a man by driving to succeed economically and determining my worth by how much money I make. It is such bull. The stupid feminist establishment ridicules people like me. They say I'm caged, not progressive or liberated. Apparently I have not built new paradigms or smashed enough myths. It is hard sometimes for me to keep my head focused on what is right, but not necessarily popular, when our society doesn't even believe in a concept like right or wrong because it is supposedly just a man-made construction."

This was the Nicole James had met the first time they talked: competent, intelligent and mature. Here in the frozen element she was opening up again.

"Where is Matt's dad?" asked James.

"He lives in Duluth," said Nicole. "I met him my first year of college. He graduated two years ago and teaches at one of the public schools. I don't know. He is not really a bad guy. We were just too young, and I wasn't sure I wanted to stay with him the rest of my life. But he does do a good job with Matt. You know, a kid really needs a father, and he fulfills that role well enough. A family, of course, would be better. Sometimes, I think we could … "

Suddenly, she turned very stern. "Don't worry, James, I'm not looking for a father for my kid. He doesn't need revolving men in his life."

James had little time to ponder the remark, for his eyes caught a distinct red object flapping smartly in the northwest breeze.

"Flag," he yelled with childlike excitement. "It's up."

He and Nicole raced across the mirror-like surface, sliding, slipping and stumbling the entire way. Nicole's contagious laughter rose and fell in crescendos with each near miss at meeting the ice face first. She got to the tip-up first. "It's moving!"

James, hopelessly out of breath, arrived to see the t-bar on the rod spinning madly.

"He's running with it," said Nicole.

"Think I should take it now?" asked James.

"My dad always used to let the fish run until he stops. What the fish is doing is swimming with the minnow in his mouth. When he stops, that means he is trying to swallow the shiner and, hopefully, the hook. Then you can set the line and pull him in."

Almost immediately the t-bar stopped, and James swung into action. He lifted the tip-up off the hole and held the line in his now-gloveless right hand, doing his best to look professional for Nicole. James felt tension right away in the line, and with one swift stroke he pulled on it to set the hook. The fight began.

"He's on there," exclaimed James.

Nicole knelt down by the hole offering encouragement. "Keep tension on the line and let him run if he wants to."

James kept yanking the line up, but he still could not see his bobber. Suddenly, the fish made a violent run, and the line flew through James fingers. It was proving to be a worthy opponent in this timeless— and fading—struggle.

"Feisty one," muttered James.

But almost as soon as he started, the fish stopped his frantic charge and James was able to regain control of the situation. Soon he could see the bobber.

"Five feet to go," he said.

"I see him," said Nicole, "look!"

James peered through the clear ice to see the scene play out directly underneath him. He saw the tail of the fish first, moving aggressively amongst the weed growth. Then the fins and pointed head emerged of a sleek, green northern pike.

"Probably seven or eight pounds," Nicole said. "Not bad."

James almost had the pike to the hole when it made another desperate dive. Once again James let the line zing through his fingers before restarting his retrieval. When James got the fish directly under the hole, he tried to position the head for a quick exit from its watery home.

Nicole suggested otherwise. "Come on, be a man, reach in and grab 'em."

James gave her an "are you crazy?" look, expecting Nicole to acknowledge the joke.

"I'm not kidding," answered Nicole calmly.

Taking the glove off his left hand, James thrust it into the hole and grabbed the lake beast by the hard flaps that protected the gills. In one very inelegant motion, he heaved it onto the ice, wherein it began flopping spastically.

"All right!" yelled Nicole, "you did that like you knew what you were doing."

"Beginners' luck," said James as he squeezed the northern pike behind the gills and subdued its wild trashing.

The fish had chomped down hard on his prey and closed his toothy mouth shut on the hooks and shiner. He had no intention of giving up a hard-fought meal.

"You wanna hand me that spreaders?" asked James, referring to the device in the plastic tackle box that Nicole had been smart enough to bring over from the white pail.

James pushed the metal spreader into the pike's mouth. The powerful, spring-loaded device forced it open.

"Looks like he swallowed it pretty good," said James, stupidly poking his fingers into the gaping mouth.

"You wanna just cut it?" asked Nicole.

"You don't think I should keep him?"

"If you want, but in my opinion, those bony things are not worth filleting."

"Probably right. I remember Kevin really bitching when he cleaned them. They really don't taste that good anyway; crappies are a lot better."

Nicole handed him a pocketknife, and James cut the line. He placed the green fish head first into the hole. It disappeared with one mighty swish of its tail.

"High five," said Nicole slapping James' hand.

James tied on a new treble hook and skewered another shiner, setting the tip-up back into position.

"See, the chant works," said Nicole as she and James made their way back to the crappie location.

However, James realized something was amiss immediately. "My bobber is—"

He grabbed his jig pole and frantically began pulling the line. "Damn bobber was under," he said.

Within seconds a beautiful black and white crappie was flopping on the ice.

"Dinner is served," said James as he removed the teardrop from the paper-thin mouth. "I gotta go fishing with you more often."

Nicole was busy pulling in her line. "I just got a hit here too," she said, "he's still there."

In short order, she pulled a fat crappie through the hole. It was bigger than James'.

"Nice fish, Nicole," James said, "we keep getting these guys and we will have a meal for sure."

He reached for Nicole's crappie, which was lying surprising still on the ice, and removed the hook. He held it up next to his. "Yup, it is definitely bigger than mine."

Nicole laughed. "Sorry."

It must have been feeding time, for in a few minutes James and Nicole pulled nearly a dozen crappies through the ice. It was a flurry of activity as James moved as quickly as he could to remove fish and bait hooks. However, almost as soon as it started, the fish quit biting. The happy noise of sliding boots on hard ice and the accompanying laughter was replaced by the northwest wind once again.

"Pretty cool when that happens," said Nicole after some time had passed since the last bite. "Hopefully they will be back."

James nodded, still absorbed in trying to entice another crappie to bite by manically jigging the waxie up and down. But Nicole's next comment caught his attention. "You know, James, some girls would have been offended by that gesture."

James stuck the jig pole into the ice and looked at Nicole with a puzzled look. "What gesture?" he asked.

"Taking some of my fish off the hook," answered Nicole. "It is kind of like pushing in a gal's chair or opening a door for her. Some might say that sort of thing is an antiquated, oppressive action of an unreconstructed man in need of some training."

James was caught totally off guard. He could hardly even remember doing it. It had been almost a reflex reaction.

"And you subscribe to that thinking?" he asked with a hearty scoff, suddenly thinking his first impression of Nicole was horribly wrong.

"No, absolutely no. I'm saying I'm rather flattered you did that. It gave me renewed hope chivalry is not dead, not yet anyway."

James smiled. "Relationships nowadays are all about control, asserting one's ego, aren't they?"

"You bet. But you know, what is funny is that all those women who blab on for attention about how strong and independent they are sure do a good job keeping the twelve-step programs and drug companies in business."

James let out a howl of laughter that echoed across the near-winter landscape. "God, ain't that the truth," he said. "I've never heard it said better, or truer for that matter."

"It's all about gender deconstruction, James," continued Nicole. "The feminists want to create a one-sex human race, and they actually think that is possible because they believe society creates men and women, not nature. They spout out ridiculous jargon about gender being a social-political construct that can be changed. This perverted thinking is just so contrary to common sense. Yet they pawn it off like it is fact, and now it has infected our culture so deeply people don't even notice it when they see it. Furthermore, people are even more clueless on the philosophical underpinnings of this disease, which say truth and natural law do not exist because everything is relative. With this ideological foundation, the feminists go out to challenge just about any common-sense tradition, observation and fact. They say they are breaking stereotypes and building new paradigms. You can recognize their language a mile away."

"Don't you think," James added, "that if society celebrates women who act like men, it proves men are superior? Their attributes are being considered better, more prized."

"Exactly," said Nicole, "now the feminists will say that men's attributes are created by a particular society, but the fact is, and sometimes they have a real problem dealing with facts, each sex has its own unique attributes. God created two sexes because each one brings something different to the table. Of course there is a bell curve, everyone is an individual, but, generally, men are better at some things and women at others. It is just common sense; I don't need social science to prove it History and tradition prove the truth of my assertion. Personally, I don't find my nature a hindrance. To deny one's natural essence is to court the insanity of not knowing who you are or what is expected of you. We all have a role to play, and I'm proud to play it."

Nicole sighed and looked down into the ice hole as the sun began to sink early in the west with cascades of orange, yellow and red. It didn't matter to James if no more crappies came that day. Just being on the lake living the experience with Nicole was enough, for James had received something far grander than a fish fry could ever hope to give.

James Norris looked into the ice hole too and contemplated this amazing person who had taken her rightful place alongside Martin, Kate, Ken, Willy, Ray, Nancy, Ann, Paul, Dave and everyone else. His friends here were acting on him in ways he never thought possible, each with a little different angle, almost like they were working together. But still the conflict remained. *Stay or go. There has to be a reason for this. But what?*

James pulled his hood over his black stocking cap in an attempt to shield out the wind as wisps of white glided stealthily over the black ice. Soon the world took on the surreal beauty that can only come from winter twilight. Tonight would be reasonably cold, a marked change from the abnormally mild year. Yet, the forecast once again called for a warming trend this coming week. Christmas would more than likely be brown.

Chapter 11
Little Adventures

The air was poignant, telling. A strange anticipation was in the air even as elements of the population enjoyed the bizarre unnaturalness of it all. On December twenty-second, temperatures had soared as high as eighty-seven degrees on the Atlantic coast of the United States. The throngs of Christmas shoppers doing their yearly spending duties were delighted to fight the crowds at the malls while wearing t-shirts and shorts. However, it was a living hell for the poor Santa Claus dressed like winter still existed. A world lay asleep, intoxicated by its faith in linear progress and blind to its inevitable destiny. Change was on the way.

It was the wind that caught people's attention first, a hard, cruel wind straight out of the much-maligned Arctic, as if she was warning the warmth-loving human race that she had not completely submitted. Her time was not quite over, and mankind's dreams of an open sea passage across her melted, conquered kingdom would have to wait. Cold air was close behind the initial Arctic blast, suddenly shocking the late Christmas shoppers in those tee shirts and shorts back to reality. People soon realized December twenty-third would not be like the previous days or weeks. Something was changing, rather dramatically. The temperature in New York City dropped almost forty degrees, from sixty degrees F to twenty-one degrees F, in a matter of hours. Totally unforeseen by the pretty faces of the metrological profession, the wind bore down on North America, Europe and Asia with gusts reaching sixty miles per hour. By Christmas Eve snow had begun falling, lots of it, across Canada and the northern United States, and, coupled with the winds, it was producing a massive, dangerous blizzard. However, the storm was not just of a wintry persuasion. The occasional tornado formed in the white-out conditions, while ice three inches thick pelted the Carolinas. Ski resorts and those dependant on snow cheered, hoping the change would help their dire warming-induced financial decline.

The scientists sat in stunned silence, unable to gather an explanation for an event the likes of which had never been seen before. The storm was drawing plenty of moisture to add to the sustained Arctic winds, enabling snow to fall unabated. Furthermore, a furious clash of warm tropical air with the cold Arctic mass seemed to be taking place in the atmosphere, creating instability of almost unimaginable proportions. After only a few days, shipping in the North Atlantic was being disrupted, and transportation by truck and train in northern Canada, Scandinavia and Russia was virtually shut down. "When would it end?" the make-up wearing, surgery-enhanced TV meteorologists kept asking, off camera, of course.

In the tropical regions giant, strangely coordinated typhoons and hurricanes continued to blossom in the world's oceans. Shaken, storm-weary people from the Philippines to Japan to Bangladesh to Cuba held their breath.

The world was convulsing before man's eyes, and a few spoke in hushed tones of God's just vengeance. The rational reminded all who would listen that wind, cold and storms hardly constituted the end of the world. Yet their pleas and admonitions fell increasingly on deaf ears. And in the now-whitened woods of northern Wisconsin, average people took steps to protect themselves in the face of adversity, and a young man continued his journey separate from the larger community of mankind.

* * *

A sickening nausea built in the man's stomach, and the fog thickened. Quickly the dark form approached, advancing very deliberately and boldly but not in a full-fledged run. It was a living thing, silvery-gray in color mixed with wisps of black. The man could now see the form's eyes. They were deep-set, dark brown and bored into his soul. The eyes of wolves have that ability.

* * *

James was sitting up in bed before he realized what had happened. Then he jumped up to his feet and shivered violently in the bitter morning air, brought on by a fuel-depleted wood stove. He let the words tumble from his lips, whispering into the stillness. "Wolf ... the creature was a wolf."

He sat down on the bed to catch his breath, and in his thoughts he returned to the night years ago when he was lost. *Why wolves? And why is this dream progressing?* He had yet to see or hear one since he arrived here. Nonetheless, Martin and Paul assured him they were out there, lurking somewhere in the shadows beyond his field of conscious vision. *Must not have proved myself worthy to see one.*

Still shaken, James walked downstairs and slouched into a chair at the kitchen table. It was Saturday, December twenty-sixth, and the snow was falling for the fourth day in a row. Christmas had passed uneventfully enough. Nicole had gone to her grandparent's place in Green Bay, and Cozy was closed, so James had the pleasure of enjoying venison and beer by himself. Outside, the 30 miles per hour wind gusts whipped the snow into mini-tornadoes that twirled and danced merrily across the hushed landscape. Heavy snow covered the greenery of the red pines west of the cabin. Their boughs sagged wearily under the strain. In a few short days the world had been transformed, and now a solid four inches of ice covered Mud Lake. *So this is winter. Finally.*

James stood up suddenly and made his way over to a bookshelf in the first floor bedroom. He'd seen the book there before, and he began to run his fingers across the worn, loved bindings. The title soon leapt out at him, and he reached for it enthusiastically. It was called *The Story of the Wolf.*

Temporarily forgetting about restarting the wood stove, James flopped onto the loveseat and speed-read as best he could. A few particular lines caught his attention.

> *"Above all else the wolf is an animal. He needs to survive, and he kills to achieve those ends. He may keep a healthy balance in the deer herd in the process, but he knows no morality. He does not carry a stethoscope to check which deer are weak or sick. The fact that he kills the old, weak and sick is simple convenience. And the wolf may kill more than he needs at one time; such is the nature of the predator who is programmed to kill as much as possible when the opportunity arises, for the next meal may be days, or weeks, away. The wolf kills, lives and breeds in the realm of nature. She has her own cruel, beautiful laws lost on modern man who transposes his own attributes onto her."*

James thought back to Martin's comments about wolves, which, most definitely, painted the animal in a negative light. The book seemed to make more sense to James, however. *Somewhere between Martin and the environmentalists who canonize a creature they will never see lies the truth.*

James set the book down and made his way back to the refrigerator. He poured a glass of two-percent milk and stared out at the blizzard engulfing his cabin and world. He had kept in touch with the developing weather phenomenon mostly by radio, chuckling to himself as the weathermen grasped for some sort of explanation.

Idiots. Hell, I can look out the window and give a report that is just as accurate. It's snowing, it's winter and it has to stop sooner or later. James, like most people caught in the event, afforded himself the luxury of using the past as a guide for an uncertain future.

This place was becoming more like a real home to James every day. He considered his neighbors his friends and treasured their company at Cozy, not to mention Nicole. He really did enjoy her company and was planning on spending more time with her once she returned from Green Bay, but he suspected she wanted some assurance he had definite plans to stay here. James knew she was not one to throw her emotions into an impossible long-distance relationship. Yet, James himself wanted to move slowly with her, and he sensed that a relationship beyond mere friends was a ways away.

Soon, however, he'd have to make up his mind. His eyes moved to the red pines on the west side of the cabin. And once again, he pushed the thoughts aside as a deer made her way stealthily out of the pine curtain. She nibbled at the paired needles as the coarse snow settled on her hide and melted on her black nose. Surprisingly unafraid, she walked the neat line of planted pines before disappearing again into the stilled forest, occasionally pushing her snout into the snow. But the animal world was not done with its impromptu displays, for now the chickadees arrived to give James additional company. The tiny black and white birds fluttered to and from two thistle seed feeders as the stiff wind ruffled their tough feathers. They kicked up small whirlwinds of snow that evaporated into the gray with each flight from the feeder. James liked to watch their frantic activity. In fact, he had observed them so much he could identify the regulars individually as they went about the business of living, just like the pigeons he had grown to love at Litchfield.

Minutes passed and the old feeling began to creep back into

him. He hesitated to call it depression, but it was a weighed melancholy nonetheless. His thoughts returned to noisy, sex-drenched city club scenes *Maybe they were right. Maybe I am mere clay to be molded. This difficult soul searching is an anachronism. Why bother?*

James knew that to linger, to brood, would bring no relief. *There is something to be learned here, something to be won and overcome Action ... action is the cure ...*

Abruptly standing up, James quickly walked to the closet by the front door and grabbed a stocking hat, gloves and blue ski jacket. His food supply was low and the four-wheel drive worked.

It was almost painful to keep driving the Dodge truck. At ten miles a gallon it had a way of destroying James' dwindling budget. Yet, to James, it was a novelty, and James was willing to pay the price to indulge. The truck did not have automatic hubs, and James almost forgot to lock them into place before climbing into the cab. Such was the nature of the utilitarian truck, built for real work and off-road duties, not for comfort or status. He engaged the transfer case and was off, leaving deep tread marks in his wake.

Issac Stelsky had yet to plow James' road today, but the truck had no problem crawling through the ever-deepening snow. The 318 motor whined and the rusting hulk of the cab shook as James kept the transfer case in four-wheel drive low and the gas to the floor. Out on M, James shifted into four-wheel drive high and met Issac going north in the township's red snowplow. James slowed down and pulled over toward the shoulder to give Isaac room. The two exchanged friendly waves, Isaac looking rather important in his CAT hat and leather vest. James turned on the windshield wipers and flipped the defrost to its highest setting. On a good day it would take twenty minutes to reach town, but today, with blowing snow creating a layer of hard packed ice on the roads, it was at least a thirty-minute ride.

Rumbling into Loretta, James saw the town was quiet as usual. Four kids playfully tossed snowballs at each other in the city park, oblivious to the outside world. James watched them as he neared the Marathon station. He then looked at his gas gauge. It was not a pretty sight.

He pulled into the gas station and tried to avoid looking at the posted price of unleaded. But at six fifty-six a gallon, it was hard to ignore. Such are the joys and sorrows of supply and demand.

"Ninety-seven, sixty-four is your total," said the young, pimple-faced kid at the register after James had filled up the tank.

"You are kidding. Too much," answered James, grinning as if trying to renegotiate a new price.

"Sorry, pal, maybe you should ride a horse?" said the kid, smiling through his embarrassing excuse for a beard.

"It's coming to that, ain't it?" said James.

"I'll tell you what, man," the kid answered, pointing at James. "Just yesterday some guy rode one right through town, right up Main."

"No kidding," James said as he handed the kid a fifty and three twenties.

"Those swampy Minnesotans won't be able to afford their little weekend snowmobile excursions up here anymore," the kid replied with an evil laugh as he handed James his change.

After spending too much money on the sparse foodstuff at Freddy's and chatting ten minutes with Penny, James stopped at Willy's for a box of wax worms and additional 30-06 shells for his rifle. Willy himself was working the counter.

"Well, if it isn't Mr. James," he said as James entered the shop.

"Mr. Rosenbach, how are you?" replied James as he strode up to the counter.

Willy had taken a liking to the uninformed, green outdoorsman. His sarcastic berating was as strong as ever, but there was no doubt a friendship existed between them as James was beginning to figure out how to counter Willy's jibes tit-for-tat. Willy set his chewed cigar on the counter.

"What the hell you doing out in this stuff?" he asked.

"Need waxies and shells," said James, already reaching into his wallet.

Willy grabbed a clear, plastic box of the grubs from behind the counter. "You've been doing any good with the crappies lately?"

"Few on Mud, about ten to fifteen feet, but you didn't hear that from me." James gave Willy a nod.

"Of course not," snorted Willy. "One-eighties alright for the aught-six?"

"Works for me. You know, I got a six this year with those ones you sold me."

"Really, now ain't that the way. You come in not knowing your ass from a pineapple and get a buck. Nancy and I didn't hardly see anything. But she got a nice doe Tuesday, and the boy tagged a spike. It has been better."

"I just learn fast. Maybe I should take you out?"

Willy shook his head. "Twenty-five, seventy-six," he said as he picked up his cigar and began gently gnawing it with his teeth. "Heard you going out with that Kaufmann girl."

James was a little surprised. "How you hear about that?" he asked.

Willy looked disgusted. "Where do you think she bought the waxies when you guys went fishing together? I've known Nicole her entire life, nice girl."

"We've only gone out a couple times. Just kind of friends, you know."

"Ain't nothing wrong with that," said Willy as he turned and disappeared into the storeroom, leaving James by himself in the store.

Road conditions had grown worse by the time James made his homeward trip. They were so bad, in fact, he didn't see the Ford Bronco until he had already come upon it. It tilted precariously in the opposite ditch, buried in snow up over the passenger door. The windshield wipers still ran, along with the engine. A man in a black parka stood knee-deep in the snow beside the incapacitated vehicle, slowly shaking his head in obvious disgust. James eased the Dodge across the road and stopped.

"What happened?" he yelled above the grumbling engine as he rolled down the window.

The man pulled his parka hood down and squinted into the snow.

"It's James, right?" the man said. It was Dave Marquette.

"You bet," answered James, "I've not seen you since the day grouse hunting a while back. Looks like you got a little bit of a problem."

Dave fought through the piled snow to the Dodge window. "I just lost it, man," he said in his characteristically quiet voice. "My ass end swayed to the right and I overcompensated straight into the ditch."

James eyed the situation. "I don't have a chain with me otherwise I would try to get you out."

"That's okay," said Dave, "I've got a snap rope. I'm in there pretty good, but we can give it a shot, anyway."

"Sure thing," said James, happy to try something new. He'd never pulled anyone out of the ditch. When he was a teenager, he was usually on the receiving end of the rope or chain.

Dave opened the back of the Bronco II and removed the long, yellow strap designed to stretch and snap. The snapping action was supposed to exert maximum force on the stuck vehicle. To be used properly, the towing vehicle was to get a good run. James hopped in his truck and backed it up as close as possible to Dave's hapless vehicle. He left the motor running and hopped out of the cab. Dave wound the strap around the back bumper of James' Dodge, grimacing as the icy air stung his exposed fingers. He then ran the other end of the snap rope around his front bumper and frame.

"That bumper gonna hold?" yelled James above the howl of the wind.

"Should," replied Dave.

James got back in the truck and backed a little closer to the ditch in order to get slack in the rope. Other vehicles passed slowly, staring and eyeing the scene. A few smiled and waved. Dave climbed back into his Bronco and revved the engine. James craned his body around in the seat and gave Dave a thumbs up. It was returned.

The transfer case on James' truck made a sickening grinding noise as he eased it back into four-low and stood on the gas with all his weight. For a few seconds the earth stood still as the snap rope lost its slack. Then—

Wham. The rope snapped and straightened, with whiplash intent, throwing James' body forward in the cab. The truck stopped moving immediately, seemingly defeated by the buried Bronco, but James had no inclination to quit now. He continued to press down on the gas with all his might as the Dodge's tires spun through the packed snow to blacktop. Smoke curled up from the road amid the high-pitched whine of the engine. No longer was he looking back at Dave. He was optimistically looking forward out the front windshield, a silly grin on his face, fully confident in his ultimate destination.

And slowly the Bronco began to crawl ever so begrudgingly from its snowy moorings. Now James could smell the putrid stench of burned rubber as the rpm's of the Dodge hit redline. But final victory was no longer in doubt. The Bronco was almost up to the shoulder of M. After a forty-second tug-of-war, it was free.

James hopped out of the truck to help unhitch the snap rope. "Bumper still there?" he yelled to Dave.

Dave gave him another thumbs up and reached for his wallet as he walked up to James.

"Nah, don't worry about money," said James.

"You sure?"

"Absolutely," James replied, putting his elbows on the bed of the Dodge as if to rest after a strenuous workout.

"Thank you," Dave said quietly. "Say, this is probably not the best time to ask, but would you mind if I walked across your land to get onto Mud. Kevin used to let me chase around the early ice crappies."

"Be my guest, as long as you tell me where they are."

Dave just nodded and returned to his Bronco, waving one more time as he disappeared into the storm.

Only two vehicles were parked outside Cozy Pines. Ray had been in a hurry to clear the snow, and several small mountain ranges of white stuff crisscrossed the lot. James parked the Dodge next to Martin's F-250. As James stepped out of the truck, he saw, for the first time, the brown wooden box facing the road in the parking lot. He walked across the lot to investigate. Looking at the side of the box facing the road, James saw it was actually encased with a clear plastic window that could be removed. Behind the plastic he could see some tacked-up computer paper, and on the wooden box itself were the words "Williams Township Notices" in bold red letters. There were two pieces of paper hanging up. One was a hopelessly outdated burning ban from June, and the second was a notice for a town meeting in August.

"Somebody has got to change these," laughed James.

Yet he found the quaint postings somewhat reassuring in a world of electronic town halls and impersonal, distant communication. This old-fashioned—but reliable—system of spreading the community news and keeping the citizenry involved had not yet gone the way of the dinosaur.

Inside, Ann was behind the bar. She poured James a Leine's, and he seated himself next to Martin.

"What's new, stranger?" said James as Martin sat his Old Milwaukee down and acknowledged his neighbor.

"Same old shit, different day," Martin said.

"Haven't seen you for a while. What you been up to?" James replied, making himself comfortable.

"Little of this, a little of that, mainly shoveling snow," Martin grunted as he returned his gaze to the Bulls-Pacers game on the TV.

Ann had disappeared into the kitchen, and Martin reached for the remote left lying on the bar. "Let's see what else is on," he said, "no, no, no, no."

"Lots of stuff about this weather," he said, finally turning the TV off for good.

"How much snow you figure we got the past few days?" asked James.

Martin reached into his red and black flannel pocket for a Marlboro "I'd say probably two feet or so. Hard to say, it is blowing so damn much Boy, winter sure hit fast, I'll tell you. The only thing worse would be being one of those poor bastards drowning in that typhoon that hit Japan Can't believe the weather could change that fast. Well, at least, our savior President Beecham, will protect us." He then let out a loud scoff and returned his attention to his beer.

Ray had now appeared from the kitchen. Immediately he winked at James. "You hitting on my help, I hear," he said.

Martin suddenly turned to look at James. "What the hell does that mean?" he asked.

James looked down at the bar searching for the best way to avoid the attention and, hopefully, the question all-together. "I went to dinner and fished with Nicole," he said rather shyly. "But we are just friends."

Martin burst out laughing. "I can't believe that shit, Ray," he howled. "How many guys have asked her out the past two years? And she has shot down every damn one. She had her priorities, at least until you came along."

Ray looked at James. "He is right. You must be pretty special or something."

"We are just friends," replied James, truthfully, as he searched for a new subject and even flipped the muted TV back on. "Pretty scary stuff about the weather, hey guys?"

Ray handed Martin a fresh Old Milwaukee, and Martin seemed to savor the first sip, closing his eyes in pleasure. He unbuttoned his flannel and set his Mac Tool hat down on the bar while slowly combing his hair with his fingers. For a few minutes only the low muffled beat of the ceiling fan and the clang of silverware from Ann in the kitchen broke the quiet.

"A guy really doesn't know what is going to happen," Martin finally said. "You know, we are all Americans here. We are all supposed to be optimistic and progressive, thinking the best is yet to come. But I can't help feeling we are … "

He looked over at Ray. "Ray," he said. "How many times you plowed the lot the past week?"

Ray scratched his head. "Shit, I lost count."

"How much gas you use?" asked Martin.

"Too much," answered Ray.

Martin's eyes wandered upward toward the quieted TV screen. The images beamed into the eyes of the farmer, accountant and bar owner: storms, more storms, destruction and uncertainty. Martin shifted uncomfortably on his bar stool, then suddenly snapped to attention.

"So, it comes to this," he said in a monotone, yet fierce, voice.

"You mean with all this weird weather and all?" answered Ann, who had left the kitchen to take up position next to her husband.

Martin pointed at James, then Ray and Ann. "This weather stuff is just the beginning. I think something world-shaking is happening, and our new President, our celebrities, our reality TV stars, our governor and our CNN anchormen are not going to protect us. They will be completely impotent."

"It is not the end of the world," said James trying to calm his friend. "Heck, you were just watching an NBA game."

"Maybe, maybe not," Martin said calmly. "But you ever hear of the Fimbulvetr?"

James found the name familiar, but for the life of him he could not remember where he had heard it before. It was unattainable, back in the recesses of old dreams and memories, which were often hard to differentiate. "No," he finally said.

"The Fimbulvetr is the terrible winter that signals the end of the world in Scandinavian mythology. It foreshadows the time when the forces of disorder and chaos will finally destroy the ordered universe. I'm not saying this is it. But I am saying we need to defend ourselves. We need to organize, us here, all of the people in the area. I don't know what is going to happen, these are scary times, but we need to be vigilant and take action if necessary."

"Against what?" asked James, breaking off his attempt to reflect on banished memories.

Martin looked at him like he was stupid. "Against a breakdown of society," he answered quietly.

Ray, who had been listening intently, now chimed in. "You mean organize a meeting or what?"

"Exactly," Martin answered leaping off his stool and pointing at the TV. "If this situation continues, who knows what will happen? We could have more break-ins or robberies. What if older people, like the Fishers out by the creek, can't get into town? How are the roads going to get plowed? What if there are food shortages, power failures or worse? We need to organize and defend ourselves."

"The man does have a point," said Ray. "Ann and I were just talking about how we would heat this place if the LP can't be refilled."

"Nobody is going to protect us but us," Martin cut in. "What is wrong with being proactive?"

"We need a town meeting," said Ann. "Maybe more people will show up this time. I think that last one in August only brought in about ten people or so."

"Nobody cared then," said Martin.

"Yeah, I saw that township notice board for the first time tonight. Where do you meet, by the Marathon station in that red building?" asked James.

"No," Martin said, "that is for Loretta. We are Williams Township out here. We've got our own hall over by the Round Lake landing off of Mitchell's road."

James shook his head like he knew where that was. "You have like a town board or something?"

"I'm on it," said Martin, "with Ann here, Isaac Stelsky, Nancy Rosenbach and Paul Larson. You know Paul, right?"

"I know all of them," said James, proudly looking at Ann.

"Kyle Stevens is town chairman," said Martin.

"I don't think I've ever met him," answered James.

"Shit, he has been chairman for, what, probably fifteen years, at least," Martin replied, looking at Ray for assurance.

Ray shook his head. "Seems like he's been around forever. He lives over on Kelly's Lake on the dead end there on the north side."

Once again, James acted like he knew where that was.

"I'll tell Kyle we need a meeting soon," said Martin. "We need to discuss some sort of collective security arrangement so we can look out for each other."

"I ain't joining no militia. That kind of ran its course in the nineties," laughed James, winking at Ray.

"What the hell does that mean?" Martin yelled, turning in his stool to face James. "There is nothing wrong, or illegal for that matter, with arming ourselves if we need to. Have you ever looked at the Constitution? This country was built on the principles of self-government, liberty and localism, every day people taking charge of their own destiny and their own communities. If this is a militia, so be it. The term has been poisoned by the ignorant media and the lazy, modern populace that thinks freedom means watching the latest episode of some Thursday night sitcom on a big-screen TV and driving a Hummer to McDonald's for a value meal."

James shook his head. "You are right, Martin, you are right."

"You think I'm crazy?" asked Martin.

James set his beer down, now somewhat annoyed. "Of course not—"

"Maybe I am. You want to see fuckin' crazy, do you?"

Martin pointed at James while Ray and Ann exchanged glances Then he stood up. "You are going to think I'm absolutely insane. Come with me." He headed for the door.

James dutifully stood up as well and looked at Ray and Ann for advice.

"Better follow the man," said Ann, pointing toward the door.

James obliged her.

Martin was already in his truck, madly revving the engine, when James entered the parking lot. Martin rolled down his window and slammed the truck into reverse.

"Follow me to the farm," he hollered.

Kate was shoveling snow as Martin pulled in his driveway with his young friend in tow. Martin's farm was unassuming, about what one would expect of such an enterprise. His two-story, sturdy white home was bedecked with black trim, slightly faded. Two giant white oak trees sheltered the family abode set amidst the northern woods. The barn, which stood behind the home, was an original, one of the rustic red ones that once dotted the countryside of America. And like many of its brethren, it too needed work. It was listing badly to one side. Martin's herd was out in the pasture that lay to the west and north of the house and buildings. A small pasture sat across M to the east as well. Deep trails cut into the snow attested to the favorite routes the cows took to and from their indoor shelter.

Rusted hulks of machinery sat idly in the yard. If Martin lived in Richfield, his home would not have won any accolades, hushed criticism and whispered denigration perhaps. Furthermore, those whose lives revolved around the showing off of their status with their miserably tidied homes and lawns would find the omnipotent smell of farm in the air most unpleasant.

James pulled the Dodge next to the F-250. *What was Martin up to?   In reality, how much do I really know about this guy?* He found himself quickly analyzing every word Martin had ever said to him.

Martin first walked over to Kate and embraced her as James exited his vehicle and followed.

"Second time today doing this," said Kate, leaning on her shovel. I got some chicken for dinner."

"Great," said Martin, looking at James. "We just butchered those babies yesterday. Where are the kids?"

"Marie came home and then decided to visit Laurie for some unknown reason. Steve took off fishing with Chris and Tony," said Kate.

Martin looked concerned. "He's coming back, ain't he?"

"I told him you needed him for chores," replied Kate, "But you never know."

It was only then she acknowledged James. "You following Martin like a puppy or what?" she laughed.

Martin jumped in. "I've got to show him something."

Kate replied with a solemn, "Ok," and picked up her shovel with no further questions. James followed Martin inside.

The inside of the Steiger home was sparse with few of the knick-knacks one would expect in a country house. The visitor first entered a living room with the typical sofa and chairs clustered around a TV. A hallway ran to the right and led to the bathroom and two bedrooms. Beyond the living room lay the kitchen, a victim of some yellowish linoleum that transported one back into the 1970s. Martin walked into this room and opened a door on the right wall that led to the musty, unfinished basement. James purged thoughts of entering an Ed Gein-type lair.

The basement was a mess, not unlike Kevin's, filled with tools and clothes. A monstrous, jet-black wood-burning stove, complete with heat ducts leading to the various rooms, sat in one corner next to a large supply of tinder-dry burning wood. The basement was ten degrees warmer than the rest of the home, thanks to Kate's raging fire. Martin, however, already was at the opposite side of the basement, away from the stove, where a massive safe sat on the concrete floor. It had a combo lock built into it and an engraving of a man hunting with a dog on its door. James knew immediately the object of Martin's show-and-tell was inside. Martin spun the lock in accordance to a memorized combination and looked at James.

"I trust you, otherwise I would not be doing this, ok?" he said.

James just shook his head with childish excitement.

Martin flung the door open, revealing a stockpile of twenty firearms complete with various magazines and cleaning supplies. James now realized ammunition boxes were stacked neatly around the outside of the cabinet. Most of the firearms appeared to be typical scoped hunting rifles and shotguns with a few large-caliber, stainless handguns. However James could immediately see Martin also had the guns of a more politically incorrect persuasion. At least two AK-47s were interspersed among the weaponry with an AR-15 and what looked like a replica of a Thompson submachine gun.

Martin casually reached into the cabinet and grabbed an AK-47, slapping in a forty-round banana-type magazine. "I started buying these in the early nineties because of all those Clinton gun laws."

James didn't know what to say.

Martin's brow furrowed under the weight of conviction. "I know what you are thinking. 'He is a gun nut, paranoid, some Tim McVeigh type.' Well, your uncle knew the truth all too well."

Martin picked up a folding chair that was leaning against the wall and handed it to James. He sat down in another and laid the gun across his lap, making sure the muzzle was pointed away from James.

"Your uncle knew the importance of an armed populace. He was like me, what you see here." He pointed toward the cabinet. "James, I'm not kidding when I say we need to protect ourselves. Of course, I am telling you this now because of the storm, but, in reality, what you see here goes to the very heart of a belief system. I want my neighbors to be on the same page as me, if you know what I mean?"

James sat back in the chair. "I don't care if you own guns, Martin.

I mean, I own a few of Kevin's now myself."

Martin set the gun down on the floor. "But do you see the need for preparedness, preparedness among ourselves."

"Martin," James said, "I know you think the world is going to hell in a hand basket, but I don't think playing soldier is the answer."

Surprisingly, Martin did not get angry. Instead, he stood up and made his way to a refrigerator next to the gun cabinet. He opened the door and came away with two Old Milwaukees.

"James, I don't think you understand," he said, handing James a beer. "I'm not saying we need to play soldier—God that sounds stupid. I just think it would not hurt if all of us here were familiar with the means to protect our lives and liberty in the event the shit hits the fan, so to speak. Who else do you expect to protect you?"

Martin didn't let James answer before continuing. "Real power, real security, does not lie in Washington D.C. or rest in the hallowed halls of Madison. It rests here, among us, locally. We should be responsible for our own security and take care of ourselves, not let some far off bureaucracy run our lives. The people nearest the problem, the little platoon of neighbors and friends, are the ones best able to handle it."

"What about the police?" asked James.

"You see a lot of cops here?" answered Martin. "Besides, they have no obligation to protect you, and what are they going to do that you can't do for yourself?"

James set his beer down. "Sounds almost like vigilantism, Martin."

"If defending my home, family and liberty is vigilantism, then so be it."

James rubbed his eyes, immersed in thought. "You sure believe in the Second Amendment, hey, Martin?"

"Damn right. The right to bear arms is as practical and necessary today as it was in 1791. The Founders believed liberty was inherent in the very laws of God. In other words, it is in man's nature to desire liberty, and rights are what must be secured so man can fulfill that nature. But governments, by their very existence, can be a threat to those rights, so their power must be checked. Enter the Second Amendment. You see, it is a natural right for a man to defend himself and his liberty. The citizen soldier with his personal firearm is a check against the potential abuse of governmental power. In other words, the cartridge box guarantees the ballot box. No armed population can ever be subjugated, even in this day and age of laser-guided bombs and Predator drone planes. It would be impossible. It is called guerilla warfare, and it works."

"But isn't the Second Amendment really just about protecting the collective right of a state to form a militia. I remember back in college some professor saying that the first phrase of the Amendment, 'A well regulated Militia being necessary for the security of a free state,' limits 'the right of the people to keep and bear arms' to just state militias, which today would be the National Guard."

Martin let out a howl that would wake the dead. He was only able to regain his composure after several false starts. "And you believed all those lies, lies and more lies?" he asked. "Listen, James, the fact is that there is not one shred of evidence the Founders believed the Second Amendment to be anything but an individual right. Why in a document —The Bill of Rights—that secures natural, individual rights, would they stick in an odd collective right? It makes no sense, but, hell, read what the Founders said, especially James Madison, since he was the primary author of the amendment. There is no doubt what they meant. This stupid collective right theory is not even mentioned in American jurisprudence until after the Civil War. And if you know anything about eighteenth century language, the term 'well regulated' means well-trained, not regulated by government. Besides, the opening phrase does not inhibit the plain language of the next phrase, 'the right of the people', which is the same language as the other amendments in the Bill of Rights. We've got to learn to stand up for the truth, no matter how politically incorrect it may be."

His lip was trembling again.

"But things change, Martin. Don't you think our Constitution would be meaningless if it was stuck in the eighteenth century? We are evolving—changing—as a society. Shouldn't the Constitution reflect that reality?"

Martin sighed deeply, not with resignation, but with faith. "Oh, James," he said dramatically. "Haven't we been down this road before? You speak of an evolving Constitution; you speak of the idea that our traditions, our principles, are mere roadblocks on the way toward some progressive utopian reality, do you not? Or perhaps you have no clear idea of a utopian reality and worship progress for progress' sake. Are you like these people who say we no longer can speak the truth because it is the twenty-first century?"

"No, I didn't mean—

"Yes, you did mean that. That is what you just said. Now, let me ask you this. If our country and world are changing, then who makes the decisions when our laws should be rewritten to reflect society's new morals, ideals and values?"

"Well, I would imagine we would vote," said James.

"Wrong. This idea of an evolving Constitution undermines voting and democracy because we are left at the mercy of judges who reinterpret laws according to their perverse progressive ideas."

"So what are you saying?"

"I'm saying that your talk of an evolving Constitution is bunk. We need to interpret the Constitution by looking at the exact wording of the document and what the Framers meant to say at the time of its creation. The fact is, James, the great strength of the Constitution is that the principles contained in that amazing document are inherent in the very laws of nature. Liberty herself is conformance to the laws of nature. Our Framers, writing in a very unique period of history, tried to create a society that is in accordance with these laws, but now that once-fine conception has decayed to the point where people think that breaking the laws of nature in the name of some perverted progress should be celebrated."

"Martin, I hear you, but still I don't see how your belief system would sanction a society were everyone gets a gun and does their own thing. Don't we need some sort of common glue or worldview instilled in our populace so they abide by the laws of nature, as you say? Isn't responsibility the prerequisite of liberty?"

"Correct, James, very good. Now I admit we have been severed from our traditions and shared beliefs. And I will allow you the idea that liberty and responsibility are inseparable. However, I am not willing to simply toss out the Constitution and throw up my arms in defeat. James, I would accept some gun control if the damn government would admit that the Second Amendment means what it plainly says and acknowledge the importance of the citizen soldier by creating some sort of militia out of the body of the people like they did back in the seventeen hundreds. Maybe countries like Switzerland have the right idea. Also, our children need to be taught the principles behind our founding documents in school and encouraged to live free but responsible with firearms and everything else. However, primarily, this is the duty of family, and today many families are asleep at the wheel."

James shook his head in agreement as Martin leaned toward him with his patented, knowing smile. He'd seen it before and knew what it meant.

"Let me ask you a question there, James," said Martin. "Do you think we are free?"

"What do you mean?"

"Are we free?" asked Martin again. "I mean that is what makes this country great, right? We hear all this verbiage about how we spread freedom around the world. But did you ever stop to think that maybe all that is mere noise to divert our attention from the fact that freedom here at home does not exist anymore. It is very easy to eliminate some Middle Eastern nation's pitiful sixties-era army in the name of freedom; it is very difficult to root out and change the forces at work at home that are turning true freedom into mere words and propaganda."

"But we can choose our own leaders and speak freely."

"We can? Then let me ask you this. Do you vote for the judges that reinterpret laws to advance some asinine idea or agenda?"

"No,"

"And let me ask you this, if you ran your own company, could you hire anyone you wanted even if all your employees supposedly looked the same?"

James laughed. "No. I'd probably be sued."

"But I thought we are free?"

"But, but—".

"Now, James, I recently got my property tax bill for the past year. This is money I owe the state and school district for my house and my land. Do you know what I owe this year?"

James shrugged.

"Almost three grand," snarled Martin. "I pay three grand just in property taxes to rent land I supposedly own, and it don't make a god damn bit of difference if I actually made any money. Every fuckin' year it goes up around twenty percent. They just demand more and more. Honestly, I don't know how I'm going to afford it this year. Is that freedom?"

"Sounds unjust, Martin."

"It is unjust," Martin yelled back. "Now let me ask you this. Are we free when the government steals our money in the form of taxes to socially engineer some idiotic programs and mandates in the name of equality and fairness that are in direct violation of common sense?"

"No. I guess not."

"And are we free?" Martin continued, "when we are silenced for speaking the truth because someone's—or some group's—feelings are hurt? Am I free when I cannot profess my faith and praise God in a public place for fear of offending someone? Are we free when the very idea of there being an objective truth in freedom derived from the very foundations of creation is under constant assault in our universities and governmental institutions?"

James could not answer, and Martin was rolling, now standing up from his chair and pointing down at James. "Do you think you are free when you wake up at five AM and fight rush-hour traffic to go to some job you hate, some job where if you say the wrong thing or hang up the wrong poster, you may get fired? Are you free when you are forced to work for that damn company because you owe three quarters of a million on your house, two SUVs and riding lawn mower? Are you free when you leave that job at the end of the day to pick up your kids from soccer, make dinner clean the house and fall in front of the TV to watch commercials saying you have to buy this product or wear this perfume or live this way in order to have a worthy existence?"

Then Martin relaxed his body and dropped his arms to his side James kept quiet, meditating on Martin's words and his personality *Although many people would not agree with Martin, there was one thing nobody could deny, Martin was intelligent and informed, even though he did not have a degree from some prestigious college. Some people may call him ignorant because of his occupation, but he wasn't, he wasn't at all.*

Martin sat down, and once again spoke, more subdued, but no less angry.

"We are not free, Mr. Norris. We are fed the lie that freedom means cheap gas, free porn, strip malls, big-screen TVs, Hollywood movie stars and some degraded idea of equality in results instead of equality before God. All this bullshit is a mere diversion; it does not nurture the soul's longing for freedom. For freedom cannot be packaged, it cannot be sold, it cannot be hoarded and it cannot be created or legislated by government. Freedom is living your life in accordance to God's will and fulfilling your role in the world. Freedom is living in accordance with the natural law, and government only gets in the way of this natural tendency and longing. And when man can no longer live this way, when he is no longer in harmony with his nature and separated from the natural law, he is not free. We are only free when we know God, and we no longer even acknowledge His existence in this glorious twenty-first century, James. No, Mr. Norris, we are not free.

far from it, we are mere slaves."

Martin flung an empty beer can against the basement wall, and Kate's footsteps upstairs could be heard as she entered the kitchen. Martin then laughed as if trying to lighten up the conversation. "Listen," he said, "I'm really not a gun nut. I have no unrealistic, glorious fantasies, just like to see conviction in the people I choose as friends. And you can tell a lot about a man from the friends he chooses. God knows what is going on. If nothing else, at least take care of yourself."

With that said, Martin led the way out of the basement back to the kitchen where the wonderful smell of fresh chicken teased the nostrils. Kate appeared holding a dinner plate stacked with neatly sliced bird, mashed potatoes, green beans and bread. She smiled at James and Martin.

"Dinner sure looks good, Kate," Martin said as he raced over to the kitchen table close on Kate's heels. "I'm sure gonna enjoy this. Hell, if this weather keeps up, we will all be stuck here living off squirrels and boiled tree bark."

Kate laid out the feast and silverware as Martin loaded his plate, looking like a kid cut loose in Toys-R-Us.

"Kate has been putting in a lot of hours as of late," Martin said. "A dinner like this is a real treat." He flashed his wife a coy smile. "Sometimes she treats me right."

"Got plenty for you, James," said Kate with her mouth already half full.

"No thanks," James answered putting his land on his stomach. "Got to watch my girlish figure."

"Sure?" persisted Kate, "bachelor like you probably does not eat too good."

"I do alright," said James not letting Kate know his real reason for not eating, namely, not wanting to intrude on the couple's time together.

Martin, in between gulps of food, tapped Kate on the shoulder. "Showed James the collection," he said.

"Really," said Kate standing up. "Bet he didn't see this one."

Martin laughed as Kate left the table and opened up a kitchen cabinet drawer. She pulled out a .38 snub-nose revolver.

"This is in case Martin complains about dinner," she laughed setting the gun back down into the drawer.

"She ain't too bad a shot," said Martin, reaching for more potatoes.

James looked at Kate. "Remind me not to rob you guys," he said, making his way slowly toward the door.

"Sure you don't want dinner?" called Kate again.

"No, thanks," James said as he stepped out into the elements.

Outside, the sun had set on the hushed, bleak landscape, drawn into premature slumber by the shortened days of the winter season. The security lights of the Steiger home betrayed a steady blanket of snow continuing to fall, and the wind was unabated. James began to shiver immediately in the chill and jogged out to his truck. The starter turned and plugs fired, causing the ageless engine to roar to life. For a fifteen-year-old vehicle, the truck started like a dream; rarely did it disappoint.

He now faced the prospect of returning to an empty, cold house, in a snowstorm, no less, on one of the shortest days of the year. For a few seconds he watched the snow fall through the headlights of the truck as he sat in the Steiger's driveway, losing track of time in their hypnotic dance to the ground.

He thought back to the day's events: the recurrence of the dream, visiting town, pulling Dave out of the ditch, talking to Ray, Martin and Ann at the bar, taking part in organizing a town meeting and, finally, Martin putting his trust in him as a friend and neighbor. To some it may have been a trivial day wasted doing errands in bad weather and meeting simple, unassuming folk. Yet—and it was not the first time this awareness had come to him—James realized today had given him the opportunity to learn and, more importantly, experience activities, ideas and beliefs he knew very little about. The day had been a giant, open-air classroom, and he was the student. He began to feel better. The prospect of returning to his usual state out here, alone, no longer seemed so discouraging. He smiled and pulled the truck away from the house, taking care on the snow-covered road. It was the final act in a day of little, yet meaningful, adventures.

Chapter 12
To Slay Thou Shalt

The wolf continued to advance with a determined gait. Its eyes were fixated forward, and its fur flowed wave-like through the fog. It knew its ultimate destination. Yet its teeth were concealed and it made no noise. In search of mere prey it was not.

The man's mind raced. *Was this creature going to attack me, or worse?* Now only twenty yards away, the wolf gathered speed and broke into a run. The man could hold his pose no more.

He turned from the creature and sprinted into the soup of the omnipresent fog. Headlong he charged, not knowing which direction he was running or where he was going. He tripped over a rotten tree on the forest floor but quickly got on his feet again and turned his head to see if the creature was there. It was.

* * *

It was Tuesday evening January third, and it had been three days since James last saw Nicole at the small but festive New Year celebration at Cozy Pines. He thought about dropping by her house for an impromptu visit the next night, but thought the better of it. He didn't want to push the relationship. There were simply too many unanswered questions at the present time. At least that was what his conscious mechanism told him. So, Nicole Kaufmann was a friend, and, for now, she would remain such in James' conflicted life, an anchor unattached, a potential unfilled.

A New Year's Day respite from the snow had been suddenly shattered the next evening, and now the new year was continuing the ways of the old. The past twenty-four hours had witnessed an additional eight inches of snow accumulation. James spent the day, after shaking off the fatigue brought on by the reappearance of the nocturnal canine, trying to figure out how to replace a broken brake line on the truck. At first he was rather proud of himself for deducing what the problem was. Removing the corroded line was easy enough. However, the nightmare began after James returned from his slippery trek to Freddy's and tried to install the new one. For the life of him he could not figure out how to bleed the air pockets out of the line. Just when he thought the job was done, he would pump the brakes and shake his head with despair as the pedal sank down softly to the floorboards. By 5:00 PM, his frustration knew no bounds, and he was resigned to the fact he would have to call Martin for help. Besides, his guest would be arriving shortly on her night off.

It was Nicole who had suggested they get together, forcing James to think of something for them to do on a dark winter evening. He had toyed with the idea of cooking her dinner, but he figured she would not be real impressed with burnt meat. Knowing full well the local social places they could frequent in the snowstorm were rather limited, James did the unthinkable—he rummaged through the garage and found Kevin's old TV. The modern world had arrived at James' cabin.

Granted, he could only get three channels. Yet the dust-encrusted box could be used with an ancient DVD player, and he had put forth the effort of fishing out his movie collection, which mainly consisted of tired twenty and thirty-year-old comedies. Thinking all girls loved to watch movies on the couch, he had set the TV and DVD player up next to the fireplace.

At 6:30 James heard her footsteps coming up the porch stairs.

"Sorry I'm late," said Nicole as James opened the door. "Roads are terrible."

"Isaac's been out all day," replied James, "M was half-way clear when I went into town at 11:30 and was nearly impassable when I came back."

"Why'd you go to town?" asked Nicole, sitting down at the kitchen table.

"Working on the truck brakes."

Nicole immediately saw the TV. "Unreal," she said teasingly "you got a TV. What is going on here?"

"Figured it is about time I dug it out."

Nicole stood up and opened the refrigerator. "Little sparse. I was expecting a three-course dinner."

James suddenly felt self-conscious. "You mean you have not eaten?"

"No," laughed Nicole looking at him rather accusatorily. "And all you got is beer and venison."

"Sorry," said James meekly as he took up a chair, "I had a little snack earlier."

Nicole was now rooting through the cabinets talking to herself. "Salt, pepper, tomato sauce … um … James, I think I may be able to do something here."

"You mean dinner?"

"Of course, silly. You got hamburger. I can whip up a few sloppy joes. They are my specialty. You'll love them, or, at least, you better."

"Need any help?" said James jumping up, not really believing he had tomato sauce buried in the cabinet somewhere.

"Not sure if you'll be too much assistance there, James," she laughed.

The dry red oak was crackling and exploding in the fireplace, sending flickering showers of reddish orange throughout the cabin. James had started the blaze while Nicole made her sloppy joes. Now the two sat at the kitchen table thoroughly filled. She had not been lying about the joes. James had to admit they were the best he'd ever tasted. The north wind howled outside across Mud Lake and rattled the north-facing cabin windows like a banshee announcing impending doom.

"Listen to it," said James, looking toward the ceiling. "Is it ever going to end?"

"Heard there is going to be a Williams Township meeting," Nicole said as she stood up and walked into the living room.

"Martin is pushing the idea," said James. "He is really worried about us here being prepared in the event of some social collapse."

Nicole sat down on the rocking chair. "He may be right. Looks like this weather has some sort of strange coordination to it all over the world. Northern Canada is cut off from the outside world; roads are shut down all over the place. Who knows how long the roads will be open around here, not to mention the power grid? I guess Green Bay lost power today. The wind snapped a bunch of snow-covered power lines. Could be days till they are up again, and I'm sure they are not the only ones who have lost power in the country. Really, I'm amazed it has not happened here yet."

Nicole's revelation made James feel isolated and shut off from the rest of the global community here in his retreat. The loss of power in some areas was news to him. And for the first time since the storm began, he started to really worry. *I'm alone out here. What if things got worse? Could I cope?*

Nicole looked forlornly out the window into the dark nothing, and James could sense a hint of blue surrounding the vibrancy that was her life. James never considered himself a good reader of body language, and he never felt the need to validate feelings. But there was no doubt something was weighing on Nicole.

James slid a kitchen table chair into the living room next to Nicole.

She didn't acknowledge him at first.

"You alright?" James asked, purposely trying not to sound too sensitive. Nicole continued to look outside for a few seconds before she finally turned her head to face James. She spoke haltingly, as if she was not on familiar ground.

"Talked to my friend Becky the other day," she said.

"Really," James said feigning knowledge of the mysterious woman.

"You don't know her," said Nicole. "She was my best friend in high school, went on to college in Madison and will soon be finishing law school in Houston. Seems she has already gotten three job offers, with some pretty prestigious firms too, all on the East Coast in New York, Washington, places like that. Guess she has always been a go-getter, smart, you know? She will probably be a partner in record time."

"You were good friends, then," said James, now beginning to see where the conversation was heading.

"Best," replied Nicole. "Anyway, she was asking about me, what I'm doing or what I'm trying to do, and what can I say? I can't measure myself against her. I'm a waitress and secretary. I take care of my mom and child, and the fact is I have no idea when I'll be able to return to school. She just makes me feel so ... "

"Inadequate," answered James.

Nicole sighed, "Maybe I should have been like her."

James was not a natural comforter. But here was a person he respected and liked made to feel less worthy by the dragons of modernity for following her natural nobility. She was not asking for help, but she was asking for reassurance. However, it was territory beyond the boundaries of James' marginalized existence. It was all too fast and too soon. He remained hesitant, but events had forced themselves upon him, like all the other events of his life the past few months. It was a challenge demanding a response. He had to act; he had to speak.

"You think that she was talking down to you?" asked James.

"No," replied Nicole, sounding not too sure of herself, "at least not intentionally."

James fixed his gaze at his friend. "I think you can be proud of who you are and the responsibilities you have taken."

Nicole smiled, somewhat half-heartedly, but it was a smile nonetheless.

"You have not chosen glamour. You have not chosen what is popular or apt to bring you attention and accolades. But you have chosen what is right and true and just. And for that you can be proud," he said.

Nicole blushed intensely and looked down at the table. But she was not half as embarrassed as James, who castigated himself after realizing just how preachy and sanctimonious he'd just been. Nicole suddenly bounded up to her feet and went to the refrigerator. She opened the door and reached for an Old Milwaukee.

"Didn't know you liked Old Swill," said James.

"Then you don't know me well enough," replied Nicole.

Unbeknownst to James, an unseen weight had been lifted off her.

"Man, listen to the wind against those windows," Nicole said as she settled down in the rocking chair again.

James rubbed his eyes and stretched his back over the chair.

"You look tired," said Nicole.

"I am tired."

"Why, you have a real tough day at work?" teased Nicole.

"Yep, it is tough on the nine to five grind," replied James. Then, suddenly, he changed. "No, seriously I ... "

He was debating how much he should tell. Even now, in his conscious state, he could see the wolf's eyes. "Been having problems sleeping lately," he said finally.

Nicole looked genuinely concerned. "You've always been like that?"

James shook his head. "Been having nightmares, started a few months ago."

"About what?" asked Nicole with a quizzical look on her bright face.

James' eyes flashed down to the cold maple floor as he collected his thoughts. Slowly he lifted his gaze to Nicole's questioning eyes. His expression was somber, almost sad, with a hint of worry. "Wolves."

Nicole didn't answer right away, leaving James in limbo.

"Every night?" she asked finally.

"Comes and goes. It is more or less the same dream, but it is progressing, like a scene playing out. Now a wolf is chasing me. I don't know. It is all kind of weird, I guess."

"Weird is right," Nicole said.

"Suppose I am just strange," replied James, now wanting to change the subject. "Maybe it is telling me I need to get a dog or something."

"Dreams mean things, James, especially repeating dreams. They are a doorway into the unconscious."

"Do you really believe that? Sounds like you've been reading up on your Freud with a comment like that."

"I am not real sure, James. I've never had a reoccurring dream. I guess to tell you the truth, I think most modern psychologists think they are essentially meaningless."

"Meaningless, meaningless," said James shaking his head and lowering his voice, "signifying nothing like everything else. Well . . . so be it."

It was now Nicole's turn.

"So when are we going fishing again?" she asked.

The odd glow of the TV never did light the cabin that night. Through the evening the friends talked as the snow piled up in a grand crystalline mass, driven by the kiss of the north, a poignant sign the winters of old had not faded into history. Well into the evening they conversed, like two travelers thrown together in an isolated lodge by forces beyond their control. The subjects were varied and diverse, the laughter common. James carefully stayed away from further talk of wolves; to not do so would have crossed a barrier within him, yet another aspect of the conflict raging inside. *Isolation or responsibility. But responsibility to do what?*

And there she sat across the table like some forbidden fruit, and at the end of the night she would walk into the snow with only a gentle hug. But James had given her something far more lasting. Never again would she doubt the decisions she had made in her life. James' heartfelt praise had seen to that. Furthermore, the slaying of the corrupt world's dragons liberates not only the ones held captive by the expectations of a sick society but the slayer himself. For James had extended his concern beyond himself, overcoming his selfishness in the process. He was part of something beyond himself, more so than he knew.

Chapter 13
That Most Precious Of Attributes

Buffalo was the first major city to go. New York and Boston followed shortly. It happened on January twenty-third. The entire power grid failed as winds reached gusts of fifty-five miles per hour and the temperature plummeted to minus forty-seven degrees below zero, without even figuring the wind chill. A state of emergency was called as snow-choked streets became impassible for all but the sturdiest of snowplows. The unfortunate homeless froze to death on steam vents as frightened residents bundled up in their $2000-dollar-a-month apartments. Luckily, power was restored after the winds abated the next day, but nerves still remained frayed. However, even with the power flowing again, businesses were losing immeasurable amounts of money, and the entire economic engine of the country was being held captive by the awesome display of nature.

President Beecham was dutifully sworn in one day after the major power outage. His grand platitudes so often repeated on the campaign trail were all but forgotten by a population dazed by the terrible weather. Nevertheless, Americans still instinctively looked toward their Washington for answers. Beecham did his best to say the right things for the benefit of people's feelings. The National Guard was called out in major cities, and an emergency federal disaster assistance program was started. Ironically, the more northern parts of the country were faring a little better than areas further south that lacked the equipment to deal with more snow than they had ever seen before. Traffic fatalities were frighteningly high in once-balmy locales as drivers, content their SUVs could conquer the laws of physics, lost control on snow-packed interstates and highways. The imminent shutting down of the gasoline distribution system would soon end that particular calamity.

The entire world was grinding to an alarming halt. Shipping was at a standstill, and most rail and truck traffic from North America to Europe to Asia was stagnant. Populations of countries and continents were in danger of starvation and exposure if the present situation continued. Armed conflicts between countries and peoples ceased as personal survival became paramount. Energies directed toward goals besides simple living were energies wasted. Mother Nature had accomplished what a thousand peace conferences, mediators and treaties could never do. Even the religious zealots, who in a former time prayed for the annihilation of infidels, quieted their tongues as God's fury visited them with cruel winds out of Siberia and dwindling food supplies. It is easy to believe God is on your side and speak of loving martyrdom until one realizes Nature is deaf to such cries of righteousness. All are humbled before her, and the zeal of the believer cools in her power.

Multiple swirling masses of cyclonic destruction continued to form and reform, leveling entire regions and turning once-serene warm-weather getaways into ghastly places of ruin and death. Torrential rains washed away parts of Africa, south Asia and Australia. And there seemed to be no end in sight. The appetite of the storm could not be whetted. As one hurricane blew itself out or one blizzard died, another rose to take its lost comrade's place, as if the event was deriving its power from an other worldly source, the trial of Noah visited upon modern man.

The educated bureaucrats of the United Nations called an emergency session, attempting to somehow deal with the growing catastrophe. However, many of the chosen delegates could not make it to New York because of the weather. The storm had hit too hard and too fast.

The Twin Cities of Minnesota had not lost power yet. Its population used to experience winter before the realties of global warming came home to roost, but they had not seen anything like this even back in the old days. They went about their business the best they could. However, the great mall was frequented less and less. The young professionals had trouble reaching their Minneapolis office spaces, and the loud dance clubs saw their patrons disappear with nightly temperatures of minus forty degrees. Trains and trucks were having increasing difficulties bringing necessities into the city. And what was unspoken among the inhabitants, but known all too well, was that in a few weeks, if the situation continued, hunger would set in. Stores were already running low on basic foodstuffs. The Mississippi River was frozen over three feet deep in some places. Areas of northern Minnesota had already received 140 inches of snow, and people were beginning to speculate what would happen when it finally melted. If it happened quickly, the Mississippi would swell to levels never witnessed. But, for now, most people concentrated on staying warm and fed. And above St. Paul, the lights of the cathedral still shined into the dim winter night, bringing some comfort to the masses below. The Twin Cities were no New York, yet they were experiencing the same trials and tribulations as the other great population centers of the world. They were civilization itself.

* * *

Township chairman Kyle Stevens and the rest of the town board did a good job of getting the news out about the town meeting. Everyone in Williams Township had been called via telephone—the service still worked—and a new notice, finally, placed in the half-dozen township bulletin boards scattered throughout the countryside served to reinforce the initial phone call. The notices detailed the main topics that were to be discussed: road maintenance and plowing, transportation and aid for the elderly, potential depots of food and fuel, and Martin's favorite—security. When Martin first conceived of the idea a few weeks back, some people in the township scoffed at the idea of holding an emergency meeting. Few clung to that belief now. The rapidly deteriorating situation was beginning to shock even the most optimistic out of their complacency. Something would have to be done, for the sake of survival itself. The meeting was set for Thursday night, January twenty-fourth.

* * *

James arrived a little late, having taken extra time on the treacherous four miles of back roads to the town hall. The hall was a modest brown aluminum-sided building, forty feet by twenty feet. It lay in a grove of aged poplar trees a short distance from the public boat landing on sixty-acre Round Lake. The headlights of the Dodge cut a swath through the torrents of snow to show the small parking lot was overfilled, and people had begun parking their vehicles along the road. Several people had ridden snowmobiles. With the road shoulders piled high with snow, the result was that the vehicles were actually parked in the middle of the road. Cars and trucks parked on the left side of the road almost touched doors with the ones parked on the opposite side.

The amount of white stuff piled up by Isaac's plow was truly amazing. It gave the driver the impression he was traversing a canyon carved through the heart of a miniature mountain range. James parked the Dodge as close as he could to the hall and followed the pale light flickering out through its windows to the front door.

The place was packed inside, standing room only. A dense cloud of cigarette smoke floated smog-like and stealthy above the crowd. Some sat in the folding chairs hastily placed on the concrete floor while others stood against the walls. Immediately James ran into Ken.

"Uh, no, here is trouble," Ken said extending his hand.

"What are you doing out on a night like this?" asked James.

"Good question. A guy should be truckin' up to Cozy to get just a-fuckin' shitfaced instead."

"Where is Butch?"

"Right there," said Ken pointing toward the far wall. And there he was all right, joyfully reveling in the attention focused on him by big Mrs. Stelsky. She waved at James.

"See your woman is here with the kid and old lady," said Ken.

"What woman?" asked James.

Ken motioned toward Nicole, who was seated in the front row with Matt and Betty. Matt was big for a four-year-old. His big, bright eyes and high cheekbones clearly gave away where his genes came from. Nicole turned around briefly and saw James. She smiled and waved, as did Betty, but quickly turned to face the table set up in the front of the room. All the seats next to her were taken. James would have to stand by Ken.

Kyle Stevens' 400-pound frame occupied the center of the front table. It was the first time James had seen him. His suspenders barely contained his stomach, and he often took out a handkerchief to wipe sweat off his meaty, deeply-wrinkled brow. He wore thick glasses and a red and black boony hat with the flaps down over his large, hairy ears. To his right sat Martin, Ann, and Paul, while Nancy and Isaac sat to his left. James eyed the rest of the room. Several faces were familiar. He waved at Aaron and Mike Larson sitting next to their grim-looking mother. Dave and Jessica Marquette sat in the second row next to Willy Rosenbach, doing his best to advertise the business by wearing a Willy's Sport Shop stocking hat. Ray stood by the far wall, where he gave James an arching two finger wave upon noticing him. Next to him stood Kate, Marie and Steve Steiger. Even Penny from the grocery store was present. And there was one other short man with a dirty green flannel and thick black beard James had seen before. He was standing by the back wall not too far from James. James nudged Ken.

"You know that guy?" he asked.

Ken turned his head. "What guy?"

"The guy in the green flannel."

Ken let out a laugh. "That's Larry."

James shook his head. "Now I remember."

Big Kyle struggled to his feet to call the meeting to order. The assembled quieted almost immediately. Kyle breathed a few deep, heavy breaths before speaking.

"Hi everyone," he finally said. "Glad you all could brave the weather to make it here tonight. Before we get started I just wanted to say that you were able to get here because a certain individual has been working extremely hard the past few weeks. He doesn't get paid as much as he should for all the work he does, so I think it may be a good time to show our appreciation for Mr. Isaac Stelsky."

Kyle started clapping, and in a few seconds the rest of the crowd joined in. Isaac just smiled as Kyle continued.

"Now don't shower too much praise on 'ole Isaac because later we will be talking about how to get him some help. He has been putting in hundred hour weeks, so if anyone here has ever wanted to drive snowplow, now may be your chance to give it a shot."

A few laughs echoed across the room before an older man in the front row stood up and pointed at Isaac. "If I could drive that thing I sure as hell wouldn't have taken out my mailbox like you did yesterday."

Isaac shrugged his shoulders. "Sorry Jim," he said, "I've been telling you to get a swinging box the past ten years."

The older man sat down and shook his finger mockingly at Isaac. They were obviously friends.

Kyle took a drink of Diet Dr. Pepper before continuing. "A few weeks ago, when Martin approached me about having a town meeting, I looked at him like he was crazy. Well, I still think he is crazy, but the meeting was a good idea."

Again laughter erupted in the hall, and Kyle waited a few seconds.

"Frankly, folks, I'm probably just as scared and perplexed as all of you. I don't know what is going on, and by watching the news, those damn politicians and scientists have no clue either. I do know this, however, no matter what happens, no matter how long this storm continues and no matter how horrible the global situation may seem to be, I have faith that the people in this room and community can pull together and see all of our friends and neighbors through this trial."

Jim, the man who had teased Isaac, now spoke again. "Seen on one of the city channels that they are already talking about food shortages."

Kyle shook his head. "I saw that too, and that is why I'm glad all of you showed up. Those are the problems we want to avoid and solve here amongst ourselves as much as possible. So, tonight we are going to talk about what we need to do to get around and make sure we all stay safe, warm and fed. But before we get rolling, I just wanted to tell you all a story."

Kyle grabbed his handkerchief out of his pocket and once again wiped his sweating brow, as if public speaking was more than equal to the exertion required in a long distance run or aerobics session.

"My Grandfather lived through the Great Depression about two miles from this hall. He told me quite a few stories about those times, like poaching deer for food and traveling to find work. But what he impressed upon me the most was how the people that lived in this area stuck together to help each other out. One of the earliest stories I remember as a youngster was the story of old Mrs. Arbuckle, who used to run an illegal bar by the Lanstrom's place. Well, people knew it was there, but they kept quiet. And you know what? Every year during those bleak times everyone in the township had their property taxes paid for them. I think you all know who did it. The bottom line is we took care of each other even if the higher ups in the world didn't like it.

My grandfather never told me one story about someone going hungry or forgotten by his neighbors during those tough years. Now, I don't know if this damn weather is going to get worse or better, but I do know that together we can see this through no matter what happens. I'm relying on all of you here. It is in our hands. Our buddies in Madison and Washington are not going to protect us."

James felt something heavy leaning up against his legs. He looked down to see Butch pressing against him with all his weight in an all-out attempt to knock him over.

"Gotta pet him," laughed Ken, "cause he don't take no for an answer."

James scratched behind the Newfoundland's massive ears. "Looks like I've got a friend for life," he said.

Isaac stood up in front of the room next after Kyle plopped his massive frame back onto his folding steel chair and finished off his Diet Dr. Pepper.

"All in all it has been going pretty good out there plowing," said Isaac. "I think you can see, though, that the shoulders of the roads are really getting pretty well piled high. I guess what I want to say is just be careful when you are out there and please try to give me some extra room if you could. Also, Kyle and the rest of the board have given me the okay to start training someone else in because I'm getting pretty near wore out. Sometimes I think Meg doesn't even know who I am."

"That is a good thing!" yelled Meg.

Isaac winked at his wife before continuing. "Anyway, the board will pay an extra driver for his time, so if anyone of you are interested, come and see me after the meeting."

He then pointed to Ken. "You could drive the plow couldn't you, Ken? You drive that damn loader all over the yard there at the mill, and you told me you have a CDL, right?"

Ken shook his head. "Damn it, Isaac, I was hoping you wouldn't find out about that."

"So, you'll help drive?" asked Isaac as all the eyes of the room turned to face Ken and his dog.

"How could I say no?" he laughed.

He turned to look at James. "Drafted."

Kyle once again struggled to his feet. "I'm sure you have all heard about the rumors of food and fuel shortages across the country as the weather worsens. Now, I don't want to scare anyone, but I think we should be ready for that eventuality. Also, I think there is a real possibility we will continue to suffer power outages and phone service interruptions. Why, two nights ago my cousin Frank, who lives over there east of Park Falls on the old High Line Road, said he lost phone service for almost eight hours. And from what I've seen on the news, some parts of northern Minnesota have been without power for almost a week."

"Anyway," Kyle continued, "I've been talking to Ann, Martin, Isaac and Nancy, and we are going to set up an emergency depot at Cozy Pines and at the garage here out back. We are asking people to donate canned food, venison or whatever they can so we can begin stockpiling it for future use. It is purely voluntary. There may be some people who have more than enough food who may want to give some to their neighbors. This is all precautionary, of course."

"When are we going to be able to start shooting deer?" asked a serious Ray.

Kyle looked over at him. "Don't ask, don't tell," he said. "Cozy Pines is going to be an unofficial headquarters. If anyone wants information on anything we are doing, call or stop in over there. Also, feel free to call me, assuming the friggin' phones still work. By the way, is anyone still getting cell coverage?"

Nobody in the room raised a hand as neighbors looked at each other.

"Have not gotten a signal for two weeks," said Jim from the first row.

"Gasoline may be another concern," Kyle said. "I know Marathon in town is not gouging anyone intentionally, but it is starting to get expensive. What is it now?"

"Seven-oh-eight, I think," said a woman from the second row. "I was talking to the kid that works there though, and he was saying he did not know when they would get refilled. The ships and trucks just can't go anywhere."

"So, they are going to run out?" asked Willy Rosenbach.

"Not sure," answered the woman.

"Where you going to get gas for the plow, Kyle?" asked Willy. "If Isaac can't run the plow, how we going to get anywhere?"

"I think we got a couple hundred gallons in the tanks behind the garage," said Kyle. "What we may have to do is use some of Ann and Ray's old, corroded tanks that were dug up when they stopped selling gas years ago." He looked over at Ann. "You guys still got those, right?"

"Sure do," said Ann. "They have been rusting away for years."

"What we could do," said Kyle, "is load them up in the plow, and Isaac could make a run to Spooner or Park Falls to fill them up. We could also use the gas for private vehicles in the event of an emergency."

"You talking about putting the tanks at Cozy?" asked Willy.

"Seems like a logical place," answered Kyle. "You know, Martin and I have been talking about keeping a truck and snowmobile gassed and ready to be used as an emergency vehicle or ambulance."

Martin now chimed in. "I'm going to be keeping my new Arctic Cat at the town garage for emergency use. But I would encourage everyone to use as little gas as possible and drive snowmobiles instead of trucks."

"Good point, Martin," said Kyle. "I know most people here burn wood, but for those that do not, watch your LP levels. I've spoken to Frank from Meyer's petroleum and he is completely out. So, once again, be careful. If you get into trouble, please tell us so we can help you out anyway we can. I would gladly take people into my home if need be, and I think most people here tonight would do the same."

Most everyone nodded.

Kenny slapped James on the chest to get his attention. "You got a sled?" he asked.

"No," James answered, "I'll tell you what, though, I kinda wish I had one now."

"I bought a new Polaris five years ago," Ken said. "That winter was actually pretty snowy, but the fuckin' warm winters convinced me to sell it. I think I lost like two grand on the deal. Now I sure wish I had kept the damn thing. A lot of guys have sold 'em because we weren't getting the snow. Now it is like a new ice age. It's the way it goes, I guess. Just can't win."

Kyle took a big swig of a fresh Diet Dr. Pepper and sat down.

Martin now stood up. "Thanks, Kyle," he said. "There is something else I wanted to address tonight. First, I wanted to let you all know about what happened to Cheryl Vagnais and her daughter Brittany last night. To tell the truth, I didn't know a thing about this until Kyle told me right before the meeting, and it only makes me more glad all of you showed up. Some of you may know Cheryl. She is that divorced teacher that lives over on Ham Lake. Anyway, last night someone broke into her home and robbed her at gunpoint."

A hushed silence fell over the crowed.

"She all right?" asked Jim from the front row.

"She is fine, I guess," answered Martin. "We've spoke to Sheriff Thurnstrom, and he has no idea who these people are or if they are still around. It is hard to say, but I'd wager a guess they are taking advantage of the weather. I would not be surprised to see this again."

Martin continued. "I think with the current situation being what it is, we all have to be a little more vigilant. The cops are not going to protect us. We are witnessing an event that is shaking our world to its foundations, an event most of us here would have thought to only be possible in movies and preacher's sermons. That is why I thought we needed this meeting. And I know we have not talked, or will talk, about everything tonight, but I hope we've taken some steps to be proactive on some major issues. In light of the recent robbery, I think it may be a good idea to just be more wary for the sake of yourselves and your neighbors. Don't be afraid to report suspicious people, and watch out for other's houses and property too. I hope this kind of robbery does not become a trend, but if people are hungry, who knows what will happen? We are also toying with the idea of organizing some sort of citizen patrol if the situation warrants."

"You mean we get to be vigilantes and shoot people!" yelled Willy.

"I hope to God it does not come to that, but we must be prepared," replied a serious Martin.

"Would you do it?" asked Ken.

"Do what?" asked James.

"Volunteer for Martin's militia."

James pressed his lips together and nodded his head before speaking. "Would be kind of my duty, wouldn't you say?"

The meeting then flowed on to a variety of topics, with Kyle and the board answering questions. The neighbors also talked amongst themselves as well, causing the volume of conversation inside to increase. After an hour, the main business had been accomplished, the official duties done, but nobody seemed ready to leave. A free flow of ideas and news now spread throughout the hall. Friends laughed with each other and people crossed the room to shake hands.

James scanned the room for Nicole after the meeting lost its formal structure. She was no longer sitting in the front row of seats. There was no sign of her, Betty or Matt, leaving James with the disappointing conclusion she had left. *Must have been in a hurry,* he rationalized.

A year ago this would have been an impossible scenario for the young Richfield accountant, but life had cast him into an adventure that was challenging him in ways he never thought possible. And the people gathered together here in the hall were influencing him in profound ways. However, despite being in a room full of people, in many respects he had never been more alone. There would be nobody at the cabin when he returned except his thoughts, the spectral creature of his nightmares and the nagging question. Tonight he did not want to leave the hall; he didn't want to face the struggle.

The friends and neighbors obliged, talking and planning well into the bitter evening. It was almost as if they too did not want to face the harsh weather outside, instead wishing to enjoy the warmth of camaraderie. James stayed, content to talk and learn from those assembled here, the average backbone of the country possessing that most precious attribute lacking in the enlightened elites who attempt to speak for all—common sense.

Chapter 14
Of Man And Beast

It was the smoke that first caught James' attention on this Friday morning. For weeks now he had become accustomed to gazing out to view a landscape of trees, blowing snow and frozen lake. No man-made objects had interrupted that most perfect of vistas. But something was different now. On the frozen expanse of Mud Lake sat a small shack structure. He got dressed immediately.

James stepped outside to partial sunshine. For the first time in almost two weeks it was showing its face on the chilled, whitened landscape. The mercury had even climbed into the low twenties. But dark, laden clouds forming on the northern horizon betrayed the transience of the thaw.

Walking crisply through the knee-deep snow, James felt physically healthy as he breathed the winter air. He had slept well the night before. No wolves had emerged within his quieted, rested brain, the first such absence in days. But, nonetheless, the trudge through the snow was tiring, and James soon realized his walk would have been much easier had he retrieved the snowshoes hanging in the garage.

The shack had been dragged from the west by snowmobile across James' land. Deep tracks pressed into the accumulated snow were plainly visible across the frozen expanse. As James drew closer, he saw a pile of split wood that was keeping the wood stove inside the structure well fed. The mailbox stickers on the door of the shack read "Dave Marquette." James knocked.

"Come in," hollered Dave.

James opened the door into sauna-like warmth. Dave was seated in a tee shirt next to the radiating warmth of the wood fire. The sweet smell of a Swisher intermingled with the smoke leaking out of the ancient stove. Utensils, matches and a few empty pop cans lined the shelves mounted to the shack's walls. A folding card table was placed in the far corner, and a portable radio on the wood floor squawked incessantly. The floor had a one-foot-by-one-foot opening cut into it so a hole could be drilled into the ice. Dave hunched over that hole, sitting on an empty five-gallon bucket. A few nice crappies lay by his side.

"Got a few," said James.

"Kind of slow now, though," answered Dave. "Had a good bite about thirty minutes ago. Then they just stopped."

"No tip-ups?"

"No."

"How long you been out?"

"Been out since six. Hell, can't really work, you know, everything is shut down. Figured I'd take my mind off the worry by going fishing. Don't tell me you are just waking up?"

"Of course not," replied James, acting offended.

James opened up a folding chair and sat across from Dave. "You put this together?" he asked eyeing the workmanship of the shack.

"Sure did," answered Dave. "I wanted a portable shack but not one of those mass-produced glorified tents. There is just no room in those. With this I can stand up, walk around, not to mention the wood stove gets this place fifty times warmer than an LP sunflower."

"Sure looks nice," said James, "I'll have to get me one of these some day. Why didn't you just come on at the cabin?"

"Can I?"

"Sure. Next time just take your sled down the road and come through my front yard. Probably would be easier for you."

"Cigar?" asked Dave, handing James a neatly wrapped Swisher Sweet.

"Thanks," James replied. He lit it with Dave's lighter, and let the smoke drift into his mouth. An emergency statement on the radio ended, and the Stones' *Under My Thumb* came on, lightening the atmosphere a little.

"Looks like the weather may be breaking a little," James finally said after listening to the first few verses.

"Don't count on it," answered Dave. "Radio says wind and snow is picking up in Canada again, heading this way."

"Amazing," James said.

Dave shook his head. "You got that right."

Suddenly James coughed as smoke billowed out of his nose and mouth. He had tried inhaling the cigar, to embarrassing effect.

"I don't inhale the damn things either," said Dave. "But I'll tell you what, they just seem to go with ice fishing."

"What you think of the town meeting?" asked James.

Dave shrugged. "Went pretty well, I guess. Yeah, I suppose with the current situation being what it is we'd better prepare for anything."

"I don't think I had a chance to talk to you there," said James.

Dave jigged the pole violently a few times.

"Got one?" asked James.

"There was one there, but I missed 'em. No, James, I left pretty early, had stuff to do at home, you know."

"So, you keeping the snow off your driveway there, Dave?" asked James, changing the subject.

"Damn near a full time job. But I'll tell you what I'm really gonna have to do is get the snow off my roof."

"Why?" asked James.

"All that weight, man, it is liable to collapse it, you know. Don't tell me you have not shoveled yours?"

James shook his head.

"You are lucky, but I'd do it fast, especially since you could get ice dams."

"What are ice dams?"

"That is what happens when the heat radiating up from your house melts a thin layer of snow near the shingles of your roof. The water trickles down to your gutters and freezes thus forming a dam, which then holds back more melt water that then drips through your roof. Not a good thing."

"I see," said James, feeling an urge to run back to the cabin.

"You hear about that cabin over on big Kennzington?" asked Dave.

"No."

"Well, there is a big house, mansion really, on the north end of the lake by the boat landing. Some people from St. Paul own it. Anyway, guess the whole roof caved in the other day from the weight of the snow. Imagine having a half-a-million-dollar cabin and seeing the entire thing damn near demolished by snow. Bet it will not be the first time it happens if the weather keeps up. I'm just waiting for the Gannon's place to give way. I don't think they have been up for a year."

"Who are they?"

"They are a couple from Chicago that own the million-dollar cabin up there on M a few miles north of your road. They bought the land a few years back and tore down the cabin that was there. Now they come up like two weekends a year. Kind of a waste if you ask me."

The wheels in James' mind spun; memories percolated. *That must have been where I was that night ...*

"Didn't an old man named Shawn live there?" asked James.

"Yes," answered Dave, sounding surprised. "Did you know him?"

"I met him one time visiting my uncle when I was little," said James, not wanting to reveal the particulars of the story.

"He was a neat old guy," said Dave. "Man, he had some stories to tell."

"What happened to him?"

"He passed away a few years ago. Not really sure what from."

James suddenly felt very sad, and the intensity of the feeling perplexed him. *Why? I only met him the one time.*

James looked across the ice hole at Dave after finally throwing the cigar out the front door of the shack. The question just blurted out like it was not even the product of conscious thought.

"Are you Indian?" asked James.

Dave stopped his jigging and stared at his companion. For a few awkward moments James worried a taboo subject had been broached. But soon Dave smiled. "What do you think?" he laughed. "Of course I am, Ojibway."

"Well, I … I … don't know."

"Don't worry about it. Just lighten up, like I care."

"You get along with everyone here, I mean, is there much racism?"

"Some. There are some real rednecks. I will not mention any names."

"Why is there animosity towards Indians here?"

"Why is there animosity toward any ethnic group?" scoffed Dave. "I don't know; it is as old as mankind. But I think around here some bad feelings were made worse in the late-eighties when the courts granted Indians off-reservation hunting and fishing rights, including spear fishing for spawning walleyes. That really ticked a lot of people off. Seems to have gotten better with time, however. For the most part we can get along here. Live and let live, right? I mean, does it really matter if you are best buddies with people of supposed different races as long as you respect each other? I find nothing more annoying than people who brag about how they have a black friend or Asian friend. It is like they pick their friends solely on what sort of political benefits they can derive from them. I pick the people I want to associate with by their individual qualities. Every group has its assholes. There are Indians I would not associate with, and there are whites I would not associate with. I hope people would understand that above all else I am a man, not a representative of some government-constructed group."

"You knocking diversity? It is group identification that matters now in the twenty-first century."

"Now that whole concept is a crock," answered Dave with unusual passion. "Diversity. Now what the hell does that mean?"

"It means our country is diverse, I guess."

"You probably had that fad pounded into your head like gospel with Litchfield Accounting."

"Oh, yeah," laughed James trying not to remember the mandatory diversity re-education.

"Diversity," Dave continued, "as it is defined by the powers that promulgate it, consists of race, ethnicity, sex and handicapped status. Now these groups, except sex, are not even inherent in nature. Government bureaucrats dream them up. The problem is that this country was based on the ideals of individual liberty and equality before God. In other words, there is a universal truth or natural state of man. The entire diversity pantheon is such a threat to our country because it undermines those ideals and instead says what matters is the individual human as a representative of some victimized group. Thus, truth and just about everything else is relative to a person's group identification."

"You know what I find funny, Dave, is that, if you really think about it, real diversity can be defined in as many ways as there are individuals."

"Exactly," said Dave, "but that would be too complicated for the diversity crowd. It would require them to look upon every person as an individual, which would prove their idiotic theory is just that. Why couldn't education make a person diverse? What about geography and family background? I suppose it is much easier to say diversity means skin color—easier, anyway, on the brains of human resource professionals. And why does it all matter? Give me one scrap of evidence, beyond the propaganda, that having diversity, however you define it, makes for a better or more efficient company or organization."

James didn't answer at first, content to let the truth of the statement sink in. "Do you think our society is more diverse today than in years past?" he finally said.

"I really don't think so," answered Dave. "I mean, go back to the Iron Range in Minnesota a hundred years ago. You had immigrants speaking perhaps a dozen languages while at work in the mines. Do you think they had diversity training back then so the Italian miners could get along with the Czech miners? And let's not forget that hundreds of Indian languages used to be spoken. Now English pretty much dominates as a language, except in the Southwest. So, in terms of language, I think you could make an argument the country has become less diverse. Also, our culture and economic system swallow up regional variety the world over."

"Hundreds of Indian languages?"

"Hum?"

"Oh, you said that there used to be hundreds of Indian languages."

"Correct," Dave said, "the simplistic diversity religion lumps Indians into one broad category of Native Americans, but it neglects to acknowledge the vast differences and variety within that category. Indians never looked at each other as a common race, even though some may now. Indians had, and have, different cultures, languages and religions. Anthropology even suggests different Indian groups came to the Americas at different times, and some may have even come from Europe eons ago. They were by no means united; wars were common. Some tribes were imperialistic while others were passive. That is the complexity, and truth, of history. The fact is it is much easier to paint history as a contest between victor and victim than acknowledge its often-murky reality. For example, how often do you hear about the Crow and Arikara Indians who scouted for Custer and died alongside him at Little Bighorn?"

"Never," answered a wiser James.

"Here they come again," laughed Dave as he pulled a deliciously plump crappie through the ice. "This one is a keeper."

James Norris leaned back in his chair and prepared to spend some more time in the comfortable ice shack on that cold day, once again in awe of the capacity of his neighbors and friends to reveal truths once obscured. And in his mind, below that layer which makes itself readily available, a realization of a definite plan and purpose began to reveal itself.

* * *

All the man could manage to do was tumble headlong into the unknown that lay beyond the inner sanctum of the womb. The humming sound continued to cascade and rise again in rhythmic repetition. Then a hole was torn in the gray sky, and grotesque, disjointed scenes played out above him. He saw a grand and splendid place on a high hill dominated by a cathedral of gold. Its bells were ringing. And there were multitudes gathered there, holding hands with faces full of awe, all staring skyward beyond the gold dome. They stood in water, water that was almost waist-high on some. It was getting deeper, and some began swimming to escape its creep.

Now, hopelessly lost, but still running as fast as he possibly could, the man turned his head to see if the tormentor was there. He saw only the surrounding gloom, which caused him to collapse immediately on a moist blanket of moss in exhaustion and tepid relief. And now the forest grew quiet. The hum was gone, and the bells died away. A great, blinding light streamed into the realm from the east.

* * *

A knocking at the door woke James up. There was no time to even try to assess the meaning of the latest scene. Hastily he tossed on some jeans and a flannel and jogged down the steps to see Martin and Kate outside on the porch. It was snowing again.

"Sleeping?" Martin asked as James opened the door.

His smile betrayed the truth.

"I knew it!" laughed Martin as he and Kate stepped inside.

He placed his hand on James' shoulder. "Well, my friend, are you ready for a little responsibility?" he asked.

James didn't understand.

"Now how are you expecting to get around?" Kate said. "Gas is getting pretty scarce."

James still did not understand, but his gaze now wandered outside to the large black animal standing in the yard. Its short, slick fur was jet black, and its mane and long tail were tossed softly by the wind. A small identifying white blotch stuck out on the right side of its protruding snout. The realization began to sink in.

"Guys," James said, "now, I appreciate—"

"We are not going to listen to that crap. I don't care if you don't know a horse from a salamander, we are going to help you," said Martin.

"Feed?" asked James.

"We will bring the hay wagon down," answered Martin smugly.

"I've never ridden—"

"That is why we are here to show you," said Kate. "We've raised horses all our lives. We've got six of them, so why not let our neighbor, and friend, use one in this time of emergency."

"James," Martin said, "Kyle says Marathon in town has no more gas."

"Do you want to be bound up in the cabin for God knows how long?" asked Kate. "How you going to see Nicole?"

James didn't find the comment amusing; he had not heard from her in days. His eyes fell on the splendid, muscular beast, its black fur highlighting the snowflakes collecting on his back. It was looking back at him.

"What is his name?" asked James as he shivered in the open doorway.

"Blazer," replied Martin.

James smiled and shook his head. "I better not regret this."

Five minutes later James returned from the loft fully dressed for the elements.

"Phones still all right at your place?" he asked Martin and Kate.

"Far as we know," said Kate, "but who knows for how long?"

The trio slogged through the 160-plus inches of snow toward the clearing beyond the pines to the west of the cabin.

"Kevin's fence is still up around this little field?" asked Martin.

"Yeah," James said, "I guess he was really good at that, huh?"

Kate and Martin jumped over the fence first with Blazer. It was almost completely buried in drifted snow thanks to the relentless wind.

"You think he will stay in here?" asked James.

"That depends on whether or not you are a good master," said Kate.

James eyed the fence. "He didn't seem to have too much of a problem getting over that."

Neither Martin nor Kate replied.

"How long you had him?" asked James as they stood in the middle of the field.

"He's three years old," Kate said. "He was born on the farm."

James ran his hand down the polished fur of the animal, slowly coming to the realization this was the first time he had ever touched a horse. It turned to look at him as if acknowledging that he was his new master, not minding the icicles forming around his nostrils in the sub-zero air.

"Now, how long does it take for this horse to be mine, you know? How long does it take a horse to become comfortable with a new owner?" asked James

"Depends on the animal," said Martin, adjusting a worn leather saddle on Blazer's back. "Some take easier to new owners than others. A few can have a rather independent spirit, if you know what I mean."

"And how is this guy?" asked James, wondering if he could even climb into the saddle.

"He is a softy, aren't you?" said Kate, petting his snout.

The wind seemed to be picking up, driving the snow hard. James squinted and pulled the hood on his brown Carhartt jacket over his head. The field was whipped clean of snow in some places, revealing bare, brown grass. Sporadic cyclones of snow danced mischievously across the tundra-like landscape.

"Does he move alright in the deep snow?" asked James above a louder-than-normal gust.

"No problem," said Kate. "Better than any snowmobile. You ready to give it a shot?"

James looked at her, then Blazer, then back to her. Without warning, in a horribly clumsy display, James placed his foot in a stirrup and heaved his frame onto the beast. To his dismay he almost fell off the other side. Kate and Martin found it amusing.

"Easy there, tiger," said Martin, steadying Blazer, who only stamped his feet a little anxiously.

"Part one accomplished," yelled James, seeking to right himself. "Now what commands do I need to know?"

"'Whoa' means to slow down," Kate said. "Pull back on the reins to do that. To get him to speed up, just yell 'Yah' and slap the reins on his back. But I'm sure you will develop your own style."

"Sounds just like the movies," said James.

"Really almost is," said Kate. "And remember, always expect the unexpected."

"Great," said James, rolling back his eyes. "Let's give it a try, shall we?"

And with that being said, James slapped the reins. Blazer immediately broke free from Martin's grasp on the saddle and galloped proudly ahead. James hung on for dear life as he approached the opposite tree line.

"How do I get him to right or left?" screamed James above the wind.

"Lean into him," yelled Martin as the trees approached. "Pull the reins in the direction you want to go."

James did as he was told and coaxed Blazer to the right.

His confidence grew, and James gently persuaded Blazer back toward a rather proud-looking Martin and Kate.

"Look like a goddamn pro," remarked Martin as James rode past now heading north.

Almost without noticing it, James felt himself speaking to his companion, urging him to speed up or slow down, thanking him or reassuring him. Blazer seemed to respond in kind, like a natural extension of James. Upon reaching the north side of the field, James carefully, yet firmly, turned Blazer back toward the south.

"You ready?" he whispered into Blazer's ears as if he actually expected a response.

He proceeded to ride Blazer into a full-fledged gallop past a now absolutely stunned Kate and Martin, the massive muscular heart of the horse powering the running machine. Exhilaration and terror swept over James at the same time.

Blazer was not the Dodge. The abstraction of the steel and plastic had been replaced by a flesh-and-blood mode of transportation. In the time James spent with Blazer that morning, he could feel a friendship growing. Blazer had taken to his new owner right away, as if they had always known each other, and the bond that can only be forged between man and animal had been born again at the Norris cabin. It was a bond communicated in language unspoken yet deeply understood by the parties. As the morning wore on, James thought he could sense Blazer anticipate his thoughts and commands, answering with action instead of words.

Kate and Martin stood stalwart in the snow and wind, warmed by the feeling of being matchmakers of sorts, and watched the new friends ride up and down the beaten field. Their waves good-bye escaped James' attention. He was now focused solely on mastering the art of riding. The date was February thirteenth.

Chapter 15
Chasing Shadows

February usually holds the promise of warm days soon to come. Its lengthening days and intense sun invite the seasonal recreators to enjoy some of winter's finest days. Even if the proverbial rodent sees his shadow, spring is only six or seven weeks away, a mere flicker of time in the busy, modern world. In years gone by, golfers would fish out their clubs and convention centers would fill with throngs of eager cabin fever-suffering outdoorsmen checking out the latest models of boats or booking summer trips to Canadian fishing destinations. By month's end, sub-zero temps were a thing of the past and the ice's stranglehold on area waterways was numbered. In spring, "hope springs eternal," the saying goes. Those were the ways of the past.

The ways of the present, the ways of reality, painted a much more melancholy story. There was no letup in the storm. In Minnesota and Wisconsin snow depths were upwards of 300 inches. On February fourteenth the mercury dropped to negative fifty-five degrees in the Twin Cities. It was the coldest night since a negative fifty-one degrees January twenty-second. Most of the northern hemisphere was shut down completely by the early part of the month, and by mid-month the nightmare scenario was unfolding. Phone service, electricity and most other forms of communication and transportation ceased to exist. Families in city and country huddled together in hastily designated government shelters or tried to stay warm burning what they could. What batteries could be found powered the radios that crackled into the night, tuned in to the latest government emergency information. Sunken, grit-stained faces stared through the frosted windows to a world transformed at a speed nobody thought possible.

Death crept swiftly across the world. Not since the plague, and maybe not even then, had mankind witnessed such a catastrophe. Those who could foraged for whatever food and necessities they could find. The specter of mass starvation, once the quaint demon of times long past and foolhardy explorers, came to rest among the masses stuck in those once-clean homes set amidst those once-perfect golf course like lawns.

And what of the future? Was it a possibility? The reconstruction would approach a scale never attempted in the catalogues of man's endeavors. These were the questions that tormented the minds of those living through these times, cut off and isolated within their neighborhoods and family units. The uncertainty over the fate of civilization rivaled the physical deprivation as the chief source of pain. Not even that great, benevolent protector known as the United States Federal Government could ease the suffering. The new president, Congress and bureaucracy sat in Washington D.C., powerless and incapable.

It had to end sometime. Sometime. It seemed so remote, so distant. The energy driving the cataclysm would eventually run out. At least these were the beliefs promoted by the educated and learned that passed through the airwaves into the homes of the survivors. But none of these professionals dared speak of the events now witnessed as being a prelude, an opening act, of something else. Years of faith in the linear progress of mankind for progress' sake had dulled man's recognition of decay and other not-so-subtle elemental truths. Yet, God did not stop the flood after fifteen or twenty days because man felt the rains could no longer continue. The rains fell for forty days until the desired result had been obtained.

* * *

James was sweating despite the minus-fifteen degree chill as he tossed another armload of freshly split red oak into the basement through the drop box. The oak was not cut in neat sixteen inch lengths usually associated with "proper" firewood. Instead it took on all sorts of lengths and sizes. The absence of gas for Kevin's ancient, but well-maintained, chainsaw necessitated the use of an ax to harvest wood for the insatiable appetite of the stove. Keeping warm was becoming a full-time job. James was amazed how quickly the stove ate wood in this Arctic weather. What was once a hobby was now taking on the appearance of drudgery. James had to spend one to two hours a day with ax in hand hacking away at whatever he could find. He was now truly in awe of the tough lumberjacks who felled the pine forests of the state over 100 years ago with tandem saws and axes. But the fire never quit. It required constant attention, constant nourishment, like some spoiled little child. It was never satisfied.

James went around to the front door of the cabin and walked down into the basement to stack the wood he had just dropped. Once there, he took two logs in his hands and opened the doors of the furnace. No flames greeted him, only hot coals, and it had been a mere two hours since he had last loaded the stove.

"Gotta start burning oak only," he muttered as he tossed the logs into the placid hell.

They immediately started to fizzle and pop as the water contained in their until-recently living core was brought to a boil. Soon a sweet aroma drifted through the basement.

Electricity was gone. It went out for good on February twenty-first, and all gas and fuel in the township were nearly spent, rendering James' Coleman fuel-powered lantern and stove useless. Now on March first, James was forced to acclimate his body to a more natural rhythm, rising with the sun and sleeping at sundown. The few candles in the cabin did little to illuminate the premature night.

The past few weeks a true isolation had set in. The phone could not ring, rendered obsolete by the storm. He never heard from Nicole; she could have been dead for all he knew. It was the same with David, Ken and the rest. There were no trips to Cozy and no visitors to the cabin. Such were the blessings of the catastrophe. His only real contact was with Martin, who came down on a horse-drawn hay wagon to drop off feed for Blazer and bring the latest neighborhood news. Given the circumstances, the township had done an excellent job of maintaining communication. Every day someone would ride a horse to almost all the residences to check in and make sure everyone was well.

Food. It was becoming a pressing concern for all. Neighbors more fortunate were helping those who were hungry, and those fortunes depended on the gun. Ammunition was becoming more valuable than gold. All animals in the forest were legitimate targets. A tribal network of sorts was being created in the community, with freshly killed game redistributed to those who needed nourishment. But the deer, the squirrels and the grouse were all suffering as well, for their food was hard to come by when it was buried under so much snow. The winterkill of deer would be astronomical. Yet, despite the ferocity of the weather, despite the horror, all in all Williams Township was surviving, drawn together by the forces at play.

James placed a frying pan on top of the wood stove, which now did double duty as a cooking range. He then unwrapped a package of venison that had thawed on the floor and placed its now-warmed contents into the pan.

Despite the situation, James felt no real sense of physical deprivation. He was not cold, the constant work saw to that, but the loneliness, the uncertainty and the doubt were what really bothered him.

When would all this be over? he thought. And once again the conflict emerged. In spite of the catastrophe engulfing the world, in spite

242

of the utter impossibility of actually getting there, he could not shake a feeling he should return to the Twin Cities and take his rightful place in the modern community.

He tried to purge the thoughts, which persistently lingered nonetheless, until they were replaced, replaced by the wolf. Here again answers eluded him. He had not had a dream since the night before Martin and Kate arrived with Blazer. That one had ended in the vision of a cathedral surrounded by multitudes of people in water and the disappearance of his pursuer.

James reached onto the stove to flip the smoking venison. Then he withdrew within himself again, for there he could sense something. The feeling first began to manifest itself the day on the ice with Dave. *The storm, the dream, my life, my being here now in this place with these people has happened for a reason ... destiny?*

There was much work to be done the rest of the day. Wood had to be chopped, ice had to be cut and melted for water and five dead squirrels in the garage had to be skinned out. James was actually developing a taste for the furry critters. Tonight, however, after the work was done, he resigned himself to take Blazer to Cozy Pines and re-establish contact with the world. James could not even get the government radio broadcasts anymore. His batteries had died long ago. *Riding a few miles in the dark can't be that hard.*

The sky was perfectly clear that evening—the snow for the day had disappeared by noon—and a fat full moon cast the landscape in a bluish glow that made vision amazingly clear. However, the conditions were perfect for extreme cold. By late afternoon the temperature was negative forty degrees.

At 5:00 PM James dressed in four layers before venturing outside. The air felt like a smack in the face, and the cold blast froze his nostrils momentarily shut. His lungs ached as he breathed deeply in the frosted air. Sharp sounds of water freezing in the surrounding trees shot through the woods.

Once out in the field, Blazer seemed to lunge at James as if expecting to be brought into a stable. James did worry about Blazer in such weather, yet Martin assured him the horse was tough and would be fine unless he was covered in freezing rain and ice. "I'm going to put you in the garage tonight when we get home," James whispered into Blazer's ear.

The familiar vehicles were absent. No F-250s or Chevy half-tons greeted James as he approached Cozy Pines along the emptiness of snow-covered M. But the storm could not completely defeat the comforting environs of the bar, for James could detect a faint glow emanating from the windows. Two horses were tied up outside. James recognized them immediately as belonging to Martin and Kate. Quickly, he dismounted and tied Blazer up to a large maple tree, remembering the place as it was not so long ago. He opened the front door.

Martin, Kate, Ray and Ann turned to face James, looking like cave dwellers huddled around a primitive fire in the stone fireplace. They were all bundled up in snowmobile suits, and their faces were dirty with grime and soot. Wool hats were pulled down firmly over their ears, and they stared at him as if he was some sort of intruder in their camp, a hostile invader from the dangerous, alien world that lay outside the door.

Then out of the forlorn group, Ray stood to greet James. "You finally came down here on a night like this," he said.

"At least it is not snowing. How much kerosene you got left?" James asked pointing to the lamps hanging from the ceiling.

"Not enough," replied Ann, standing up to throw two birch logs onto the fire.

"How's Blazer treating you?" asked Martin.

"He is a blessing," answered James.

"I'll tell you Martin here always had a way with horses," said Ray, returning to his chair next to the inviting fire.

"Where are Steve and Marie?" James asked Kate.

"At home," she replied, "we never leave the house unattended."

"Why?" asked James.

"Ever see a chimney fire?" Martin chimed. "The way we are burning wood right now causes a lot of creosote to build up. That stuff can catch on fire pretty damn easy."

James' mind raced back an hour ago when he placed four giant oak logs onto the fire. His worried look caught Kate's attention.

"Don't worry," she said. "It is not like it happens all the time."

"Any news?" James asked.

"We all seem to be getting by," Ray said after a pause.

"We think old Bill Turnbull out on the narrow gauge had a slight heart attack though," said Kate.

"He live alone?" asked James.

"Yeah," Kate said, "Kyle went to check on him two days ago, and he seemed to be really sick. So I rode out with Martin yesterday. He doesn't look good. The Moens' daughter is staying with him now."

"You kind of in demand?" asked James, referring to Kate's nurse status.

"Surprisingly not," she answered in a near whisper.

"By the way, James," said Martin suddenly. "We are having a town meeting again, weather permitting. Kyle will get the word out when we set a definite date."

"You still get radio?" James asked Ray.

"Use it sparingly," he answered. "Not sure how they are doing those emergency broadcasts, but we get the updates on seven-eighty AM out of Park Falls. Nearest I can tell, nothing is running. They are trying like hell to organize emergency shelters and food drop offs in major cities, but it has got to be damn near impossible to get anything through on the highways. Looks like the South is suffering just as bad. Said the other day Houston got another ten inches of snow after two inches of ice built up on everything."

"What about the rest of the world?" asked James.

Ray lit up a cigarette, not even the seeming end of civilization could stop his love of the smoke. "Sounds like Europe and Asia are in the same weather pattern as us, but the reports from some regions are sketchy, at best. Most communication is just gone. Africa, South America and Australia have missed most of the snow, but floods have all but obliterated some areas. South Asia is pretty much under water.

"Where can the storms be drawing their energy from?" James questioned.

Ray shook his head. "Who knows?"

"Who knows?" came the echo from across the small gathering.

James looked at Martin. But he had not uttered a word. It was only then that James noticed a fifth person gathered around the warming firelight. He was sitting outside the circle in the surrounding darkness and was barely perceivable except for his eyes. They flashed in the darkness like an animal's. The man slid closer to the fire and reached for the forked metal fire poker. He thrust it into the flames, causing an explosion of small sparks. His black beard was dense, shaggy and covered his entire face. It was Larry Wesley.

"Who knows?" Larry asked again, continuing to play with the fire, which cast his face in a nightmarish glow. "I know."

Martin and Kate tried to ignore him, as if they knew where this was heading. But Ray, who seemed perfectly content to let Larry have free run of the fire, rose to the task. "What do you mean, Larry?" he asked.

Larry took the fire poker out of the coals. It was now glowing red. He pointed it at James, Martin, Kate, Ann and Ray in succession as if he was a teacher and it was his pointing stick. "The wrath of God," he said in his raspy voice. "God is punishing all for their indiscretions. You think this is all an accident? You think this can be explained away with some science about ocean currents and climate change? No. It is a cleansing."

"A cleansing for what?" asked James, almost on instinct.

"A cleansing for violating the laws of God," yelled Larry as he pointed the poker back at James. "A world that spends a thousand dollars on a pair of shoes while it kills babies, that elects fornicators to the highest office, that plunders and poisons the earth, that rewards the greed of corporate thieves, that turns its back on God's commandments, will not be allowed to stand. The Lord is coming."

Larry then drew quiet and thrust the poker back into the fire.

However, a fanatically religious man holding a glowing fire poker could not squelch James' natural curiosity, now tempered and honed with a delight in debate thanks to Martin.

"But why am I, or Martin here, or you even forced to suffer the same lot as the sinners?" asked James. "What kind of a God punishes all for the sins of the few? If that is the God you speak of, then I want no part of Him."

Out of the corner of his eye James saw Kate cringe. Unlike Martin, who loved to argue yet was rational, Larry was cast by others in the area to be completely irrational. To argue with him was futile and potentially dangerous. James had just committed the cardinal sin when dealing with Larry—never challenge his faith.

Everyone sat silent, expecting an outburst. But none came. Larry just sat in his chair staring back at James with a smirk on his face. James held firm, throwing caution to the wind. He would not retract his statement, and Larry blinked first. "You don't believe in God?" he asked.

"I don't believe in a God that arbitrarily destroys all his creation because some choose to break his laws," answered James.

He closed his eyes and thought back to his Catholic upbringing and religious instruction for light and fire were beginning to burn again in ways he never expected. "Are you a Christian?" he asked Larry, turning the tables and going on the offensive.

"I am," Larry answered quietly.

"Did not Jesus die for the atonement of Man's original sin, and did not Jesus teach the forgiveness of sin?" asked James. "God became flesh and died for our sake, so we could be set right with him. Jesus contradicted the vengeful God of the Old Testament."

"Perhaps you have not read what Jesus actually said," answered Larry. "Now, let me ask you a question. When was the last time you read the Gospels?"

James didn't lie. "I really don't recall."

"Fair enough," Larry said, still amazing Martin, Kate, Ann and Ray with his civility. "I think you are sadly mistaken in your belief that Jesus' teachings on forgiveness can excuse man's ultimate destiny."

"What do you mean?" asked James.

"You think that Jesus preached peace on earth?" said Larry.

James nodded his head.

"Well, I suggest you read the Gospel and listen to what Jesus had to say upon his entry into Jerusalem."

Larry stood up and held his hands, tightly balled into fists, above his head. He closed his eyes and slowly opened his mouth, letting his lower jaw quake before speaking.

"And as he went out from the temple, one of his disciples said, 'Behold, how it is adorned with goodly stones.' And Jesus said, 'As for these things, behold, the day will come; there shall not be left one stone upon another, all shall be thrown down.' And they asked him, 'Master, but when shall these things be? And what sign shall there be?' And Jesus sighed deep in his spirit, and said, 'Why do you seek a sign? Verily, I say to you, there shall be no sign. When ye see a cloud rise out of the west, ye say, there comes rain, and so it is. And when ye see the south wind blow, ye say there will be heat, and so it comes. Ye can read the signs of the sky and earth. How is it ye cannot read the signs of this time?'"

Larry opened his eyes and turned to look at James. He recited the passage like one possessed.

"'Suppose ye that I come to give peace on earth? I tell you NO, but rather division. There shall be houses divided. Son against father, and father against son. And ye shall hear of wars and rumors of wars; for all these things must come to pass; but the end is not yet. For nation shall rise against nation, and kingdom against kingdom; and there shall be famines and pestilences, and earthquakes. All these are the beginning of sorrows O Jerusalem, Jerusalem, ye kill the prophets and stone them which are sent to thee. I would have gathered thy children together, and ye would not! Behold, your house shall be left desolate. And ye shall not see me, until the time comes when ye shall say, Blessed is he that cometh in the name of the Lord. Take ye heed! Behold, I have foretold you all things. And in those days, after that tribulation, the sun shall be darkened, and the moon shall not give her light. The stars of heaven shall fall, and then shall they see the Son of Man coming in clouds with glory, and a great sound of a trumpet.'"

Larry sat down before continuing. "You see, Jesus came to level the world as it was known, and in the process fulfill the teaching of the Prophets. It was his purpose to clear a path for man's union with that which created him, for is that not the ultimate fulfillment of man's life and natural state—to know him who created us? So, in a sense, you are correct to say Jesus was sent to set us right with God. But what you fail to understand is that we are set right with the Lord through destruction of the corrupt order. All people, all societies, must surrender to the divine will in the end and die to themselves, only to be born again."

"And that is why we must suffer?" asked James. "Because we do not surrender to the will of Jesus who is God?"

"We suffer because our souls are not in accordance with the divine,' answered Larry. "When man strays from the divine truth, his soul rots. You see, James, God not only is up there or out there doing his work.' He pointed toward the ceiling and floor. "God is in here," he continued, pointing at his heart, "and in you, Martin, Ann, everyone, and you are free to accept or reject his grace. But, mind you, if you reject, a schism will develop between your soul and the divine Lord. The ultimate cause of the misery in our life, all this war, torment and suffering we call history, is a separation from God. This suffering can only be alleviated when the soul is brought back into accordance with the divine will.

It is the duty of society to bring its laws into accordance with the divine as well. Our society did this at one point in time, but it strayed. Now it will face its inevitable death. Such is the way of the world. God's laws are not arbitrary; God's laws don't change with the progression, or what I would call decay, of society or the enlightenment of the mind. God's laws are not a reflection of a society's particular time and place. They are eternal and exist for a reason. You see, James, some of us, like I did one fine day when I was selling software and working a hundred hours a week, see the decay, corruption and decadence of modern society. We sense the dissociation between its sickness and our own souls that remain in accordance with the truth. However, we know we are powerless to prevent the inevitable decline. We retreat to our caves and redoubts and extinguish ourselves rather than participate in evil. You see, James, the source of our discontent and the cause of mankind's destruction are in you, not out there some place. And you thought destruction would come by some bearded foreign guy wearing a turban or green beings in flying saucers from outer space or some world dictator with the number six, six, six stamped on his forehead who creates a hell on earth while the chosen ones are swept off to heaven. The real source of our discontent, the real source of the apocalypse, is here." Larry reached out to James, tapping him on his chest. "It is here, a schism in the soul."

Larry grew quiet, and James lost himself in thought, not knowing he was the first person in Williams' Township memory to bring out this side of Larry. He thought back to the night so long ago when he was lost and the man he met that night, Shawn. James closed his eyes, Larry's words causing seeds to blossom after years of mental denial. *What did he say?*

The clock crawled forward on its inevitable march toward the witching hour. Like explorers wandering through an unknown, hostile wilderness, the little group clung together around the fire and occasionally peered through the frost-covered windows into the shadows beyond. No one dared leave the comfort found here, even Larry, who seemed restless. But when he looked toward the door he would begin talking to keep the gathering going. However, all good things must end, and after some time, James prepared to leave.

"Sure you don't want to spend the night?" asked Ray. "We could set you up with a cot."

James' mind, however, was on the unattended fire back home. He stood up and looked at his friends as he pulled his hat over his ears. "No thanks, Ray," he said.

"Be careful," Kate yelled as he opened the door into the blast furnace of cold. "You got a flashlight?"

James reached into his pocket to reveal a Mag Light. "Don't leave home without it," he said, "just got to conserve the batteries."

The sky seemed to be even clearer than earlier in the evening, not even a wisp of a cloud broke the expanse of stars, and the moon directly overhead lit up the landscape like a great floodlight. The snow sparkled in the blue luminosity.

Blazer turned his head to face James, seemingly pleading with his master to take him home. James placed his hands on his friend's snout. "Garage tonight," he said as he climbed into the saddle and began the journey home.

Blazer kept a remarkably steady gait through the incredibly deep snow that rendered County Road M impassable for anything but tracked vehicles. The moon illuminated Blazer's tracks from earlier in the evening, and James kept his head slowly turning to the left and right, talking calmly to Blazer in the stillness.

"Easy, guy," he said brushing Blazer's mane. He tried to purge his mind of any irrational fears. However, he kept imagining himself as Ichabod Crane with the forest pressing in around him and the Headless Horseman drawing closer, the hot breath of his ghostly steed at his heels.

In the radiant moonlight, the landscape turned as bizarre as another world. Strange sounds crept through the air from places unknown and forgotten. At one point James swore he heard the far-off wail of a train whistle. Yet, the nearest operational tracks were over thirty miles away, and, as far as he knew, the storm had shut down all the railroads. There had been tracks in Loretta at one point in time, but that was over eighty years ago when the logging era was ending.

A mile down the road James passed the remains of an old country schoolhouse on the left side of the road. He had never noticed it before. The brick walls of the building were still in fairly good shape, but the windows had long since been broken out. Small trees grew in the once-cleared yard. A red sign out front read "Spring Lake School 1920-1962."

James halted Blazer and closed his eyes. The vision of laughing children carrying their books to school on a spring day sprang to life on this terrible winter night. He could hear the school bell echoing across the countryside, the sounds and sights steamrolled by progress. Then he opened his eyes. The ghosts of the past were just that.

A gust of wind, cold and raw, arose out of the north and sent the trees into a slow, melancholy waltz. James slapped the reins on Blazer but then stopped him immediately. It was a flickering reflection that caught his attention. He snapped his neck to the right and focused his gaze toward what he thought was a logging path in Paul Larson's woods. And there stood an animal, its eyes clearly shining in the radiance of the moon. *A dog? Or a ...*

It stood in the shadows cast by a grove of oaks. James held a frozen stance on the back of Blazer, and the creature stared back at him, unmoving as well. The gray fur of the creature caught the moonlight, and its eyes shone like the crystals of snow upon the forest floor. A large, broad head with two distinguishable ears was silhouetted against the backdrop of the surrounding snow pack.

Blazer began to stomp nervously, and James shifted in the saddle to get a better look at the creature. Yet, the more he tried to focus on the apparition, the less he could make it out. Slowly the body of the creature faded into the dark, but James could still make out the eyes. It was then James realized the creature was retreating into the woods. James closed his eyes, rubbed them vigorously and reopened them. The creature was still there, inviting James into its world.

The dream flashed through James' mind, the demon's presence lingering in his frosted breath. Again Blazer stomped, this time more aggressively. A decision had to be made. He scanned the surrounding woods and the logging trail.

"Yah," James commanded into the night. His voice shattered the air like the death of a thousand crystal plates.

He wielded Blazer to the right and charged headlong down the logging trail in the waist-deep snow, throwing up a cloud of crystalline, jewel-like snowflakes that seemed to suspend indefinitely in the light. The chase was on.

At first the creature refused to move as James drew closer on Blazer in full gallop. Then, just as it seemed James would catch up to it, the creature turned tail and ran deeper into the woods along the trail. James continued in hot pursuit, pushing Blazer to reckless speeds. Branches came dangerously close to clipping him and sending him on a fateful journey to the ground. Yet the harder James pushed Blazer and the faster he went, the more elusive the creature became. It remained just out of clear sight and refused to reveal its true identity.

James slowed Blazer to a stop and scanned his surroundings. He had no idea where he was and could only assume he was on Paul Larson's land somewhere. He looked at the logging trail ahead, which grew narrower and narrower before it curved off to the right and disappeared.

James no longer felt any fear or apprehension. But for an instant he seemed to have lost his quarry. He turned frantically in the saddle from side to side, and then, out of nowhere, he caught a glimpse of a tail in the moonbeams. The creature was 100 yards away, but now it stood off the logging trail in the depths of the forest herself. James could see the animal take a few steps toward him, stop, turn tail and then retreat further into the woods, turning its head backwards as if it was challenging James to follow. He obliged.

Throwing all caution to the wind, James rode Blazer off the trail toward the apparition in a maniacal, almost suicidal charge. The creature now broke into a full-fledged run itself. An aspen branch smacked James' face, and a tiny trickle of warm blood oozed down his cheek. But he was powerless to stop his night ride. He dashed onward, determined to reveal the identity of the specter.

The chase continued until the union of forest canopy and sky disintegrated, and James arrived at a tiny clearing in the forest. James could make out the shadowy creature streaking across the open expanse and disappearing into dense spruce trees. But soon his attention was also directed to the northern horizon. Blazer stopped this time without the command, his eyes guided, like James', toward one of Nature's most spell binding displays—the Northern Lights.

Cloud-like wisps of light conducted a bizarre, fiery dance across the heavens. They would gather together into a mass then suddenly separate into greenish-silvery curtains of colors. To James they were nothing but mesmerizing and magical, and he sat in the saddle spellbound by the display like some modern day child staring at the artificial light of the television while his favorite program beamed into his mind. But this was a show of a more natural persuasion, a gathering of spirits in the ballroom of the northern sky. He momentarily forgot his bleeding cheek, the cold and the object of his pursuit.

It was Blazer, stamping his feet rhythmically in the snow, who brought James back from his dream state. James dropped his gaze back to earth and climbed off Blazer to look across the clearing to the place where the spruce grew so tightly together.

Massive white pines swayed in the background. *Why here?* He took a few steps toward the pine grove, the hard snow crunching under his weight. *Such a strange place, almost like ... womb?*

Connections were being drawn in the terribly frigid air. "This is it," he whispered aloud. "This is the place I have been dreaming about these past months. And is this not where I heard the wolves howl on that night?"

Once again he took a few cautious steps toward the grove as an insidious fear began to crawl into his mind. He channeled his gaze and entire being toward that place. The odd sounds of the forest on that winter night called out to him, urging him onward. *Just walk in,* he told himself. *There is nothing to fear. The dream is just that—a dream.*

A war waged inside his head, yet all his rational insisting could not win the argument. He held back as an odd feeling of unworthiness mingled with the fear, telling him this place was a prize to be won and the trials and knowledge needed to capture it had not yet been conquered and discovered.

James' eyes watered in the northern wind; his raw face was chapped and vividly red. Blazer stepped up behind James, and his hot breath warmed the back of his master's neck. James reached behind to pat his snout. It was then that he noticed Blazer's hoof prints cutting a clear, distinct path across the snowy clearing. And James' own boot prints in the snow from the point he hopped off Blazer were impossible to miss as well in the moonlight. But he could not see any other tracks.

James began to feel dizzy. He ran behind a confused Blazer and scanned the hoof prints coming from the opposite forest intently. Then he dashed to his left for twenty yards and scanned the clearing. No tracks. He ran the same distance in the opposite direction. No tracks. He looked again toward the pine grove. No tracks broke its threshold.

James hopped onto Blazer faster than he ever thought possible. In his mind he could hear the rhythmic humming so often heard in his recurring dream. *This can't be. There was something there.* He dug his heels into Blazer and headed in the direction of home.

Overhead the northern lights continued their entrancing dance across the sky. The apparition James had been following seemingly had been transformed into that awesome display of Nature herself, which spoke in a language James was almost ready to comprehend.

Chapter 16
End Of Trials

It was time to awake. Something strange happened on March twelfth. An eerie, unsettling quiet descended upon the ravaged globe. The rain and snows slowed and hurricanes blew a final gasp. And for the first time in months, which felt like eons to the survivors, the welcoming sun sent the mercury soaring. People ventured out into a world forever changed. Mountains of snow had obliterated man's fabrications and constructions. Like shell-shocked, starved veterans from the trenches of The Great War's apocalypse, they cautiously trudged through the collected depths to find neighbors and family.

On March thirteenth the temperature rose to sixty degrees in the Twin Cities. Yet there was little cause to celebrate. Travel was still impossible, for there was no fuel, food, law or working government. The infrastructure of civilization was wiped clean by the convulsions of nature. Those left were charged with the monumental task of rebuilding. So they stumbled out into the world, squinting in the sun, unable to speak.

The temperature hit seventy degrees a day later, and the snow, some 400 inches of it, began to melt in earnest. Melt water congregated in deep pools before flowing in haphazard torrents towards the natural watersheds of the land. Creeks and rivers swelled, and their crisp flow became ever more powerful further downstream, especially as the ice began to lose its chokehold on the waterways.

By March eighteenth, with temperatures holding in the low sixties, rivers were rising to levels never witnessed before, and there were still hundreds of inches more snow to melt, assuming the storm really was over and the warming trend was not just a teasing intermission before a final act. The unspoken words of anticipation were etched on the faces of the surviving masses—"What next?"

* * *

It was the first day of spring, and it sure felt that way at James Norris' cabin. He stood outside on the porch this Friday morning, sweating, having just spent the past two hours shoveling off the deck floor. There were a few remaining snow patches; however, James was confident they would soon melt and turn into isolated puddles. He had also opened up all the windows in an attempt to let the fresh air whisk out the stuffiness that had crept into the shut-up dwelling over the past few months. It was the first step in any true spring-cleaning.

The temperature today was in the low forties, slightly cooler than it had been the past week. James still kept a fire going at night, and today, with the air turning slightly cooler, James had opted to keep it burning all day. A torrent of water reminiscent of a May rainstorm was running off the cabin's eves. In the surrounding forest a few patches of bare ground poked through the snow pack, and birds chirped joyously in the warmth as they searched for food. A low blanket of clouds roofed the landscape, and a fog floated through the woods, brought on by the moisture of the melting snow. A hint of possible rain, or wet snow, was present and discernable.

James had not spoken to another living soul, except Martin on his hay wagon trips, since his night ride to Cozy. But his days were full nonetheless. There was always wood to cut, and two days ago he shot a nice doe that wandered into the yard during the evening twilight. The next day was spent cutting up the carcass and packing the meat in boxes and coolers. He placed these in the garage and hoped there they would stay somewhat fresh.

His time alone had pushed him to new depths of contemplation and self-examination. Every night he gazed into the glow of the wood stove, amazed he was living through the greatest catastrophe in man's history. Yet the work required in just staying alive kept him from bemoaning the state of the world. The devastation brought on by the storm was not the source of the conflict within him. It resulted from internal, more mysterious, origins.

James walked into the cabin and removed his boots. The town meeting was scheduled for today, and James was looking forward to it. He yearned to see the people he had come to know here. He was not necessarily worried about them, but he missed the talking, laughing, arguing and, above all, the learning. These were the people he considered his friends in this great worldwide upheaval: the Steiger's, the Larson's, Ray and Ann, Dave, Willy and Nancy, Ken, Larry and the others. Not to mention Nicole. A developing relationship with her was cut short by the storm. He felt like he was a part of their small community beyond the larger world, if only on the periphery.

James sat down in the rocking chair and looked out on the lake. It now had a slight ring of open water along the shoreline. Suddenly, he sprang to his feet and ran to the sliding doors, for out on the lake was a dark form. James slid the doors open and walked barefoot onto the deck. The black form soared skyward. It was a crow, not a wolf.

So it had been for James since his ride home from Cozy. He still stubbornly insisted he had followed something flesh-and-blood that night. However, he had not dared return to the grove. And there was another problem. *Do I belong here? Ridiculous. The question should be—is there even a Twin Cities left? The logistics are impossible even if I want to go back.*

"Ridiculous thoughts," he said aloud while looking down at the deck. "I should just feel lucky I'm alive." With that he retreated inside to gather up a wool flannel and blaze orange stocking cap for the ride to the town hall. He then threw another large white oak log into the sizzling wood stove downstairs before venturing out to the clearing for Blazer.

Once there, he turned back to face his cabin. Smoke was rising lazily out the Metalasbestos-coated chimney.

"Home," he said.

It took almost an hour to reach the town hall across the still snow-choked country roads. The sky overhead looked as if it could snow or rain at any moment. Yet, on James' journey nothing fell.

Only a few snowmobiles were parked at the hall. But twelve horses, some with sleighs or wagons in tow, stood outside. James lashed Blazer up to a large aspen in front of the building next to a gray-brown steed he thought might belong to Paul Larson. The two horses looked at each other tepidly and exchanged a guarded greeting.

Upon opening the door, James could tell instantly the meeting was in progress. The hall was packed, even more so than the first meeting. However, one thing had noticeably changed. There was no cigarette smoke. Tobacco had fallen victim to nature's fury. Kyle was speaking in the front of the room, and the loyal town board sat on either side of him. James had just enough room to stand by the door, next to a couple he didn't recognize. He smiled at them, and they returned the favor. The male partner patted James on the shoulder and nodded his head. All human life, seen less and less by those isolated in the storm, triggered a recognition and camaraderie. Strangers became instant friends.

And there they had assembled. These were the people James had come to know and respect. These were his friends. Ann Bakke sat at the front table doing her civic duty as town councilperson, along with Isaac Stelsky, Nancy Rosenbach and Martin. Ray sat in the front row, looking his usual solemn self. Paul and Angela Larson and their loyal sons, Mike and Aaron, sat to his right. Big Willy Rosenbach was a few rows back; his belly looked a little reduced these days. Larry was there, standing by the far wall with a buffer zone of empty space around him. James tried to get Ken's attention, but he was chatting with Meg Stelsky. Kate, Steve and Marie were all sitting in the second row with their backs to James. Dave and Jessica were standing toward the back of the room, almost within talking distance from James. James could have yelled a hello to them, but he chose not to make a scene.

Then, finally, his eyes fell on her. She was up near the front, on the right side of the room. Next to her on her left was Betty. On Nicole's right was a man James did not recognize, and to his immediate right sat Matt. He was holding the man's hand like a son would.

James knew the truth without being told. *Nicole was back together with Matt's father. Now what ...*

In that brief flicker of time, everything changed. An anchor holding James here in this place was gone, a casualty of the storm. Strangely, however, James felt no real sense of regret for not acting more aggressively. Destiny often has a beautiful soft-spoken voice that resonates powerfully in the soul. *Didn't I know all along it would be like this? In the end, perhaps, it is the best for all, especially Matt.*

As James looked again at the assembled neighbors, he began to feel like an outsider, like he never really did fit in here. *Maybe that is part of the plan. Yes, I was destined to meet them and have them change me, but I was never meant to live among them forever. They are messengers. But why?*

James was now silently thanking them, remembering each person's specific contribution. He looked at Martin first and then Kate, seated back in the crowd.

Before meeting them, I was ignorant. I never thought about what liberty, or freedom for that matter, meant. To me, the Constitution was but a piece of old paper. It really didn't mean much in an evolving society. I think until now I had been exposed to words and clichés and symbols but little substance.

But Martin has taught me that the individual rights and liberties that used to underpin a common American belief system are inherent in man's very nature; they are part of the natural law and spring from the creator, not from government. Thus, the goodness of laws built upon this underlying premise does not evolve or progress or change with the times. To say so would be to cut off man from who he is.

Martin is also a very eloquent ambassador for the idea that problems are best solved by those closest to them, and those people, usually, are up to the task, unlike the self-appointed experts with the entitled power to dictate from afar. The ultimate truth of his belief is evidenced here in the hall today.

Finally, Martin and Kate showed me how a marriage can work when natural roles are fulfilled. Kate was just as intelligent as Martin, but she played her role without the psychobabble of partnership, fulfillment or validation. And to nobody's surprise, except perhaps those who get paid to sit in universities and attack such arrangements, it has worked.

Next, James looked to Ken, with his black Jackson Timber jacket proudly on display.

He loved his work and hated it all the same. Yet, every day, week, month and year he showed up. Thousands of Kens, and Pennys, across the country kept thousands of factories, plants, stores, schools and offices in operation. He was the nameless, faceless yet vital employee, struggling day in and day out. Modern society holds the celebrity, the one who sells the pop movies or music, up as the hero. They are the ones children are told to emulate in all their false glamour. They are the ones asked to comment about issues of the day, and in times of crisis people looked to these fictitious Gods as saviors, especially through the fake world of the infernal TV.

Such a culture exalts those who achieve wealth, fame and fortune. It ridicules those who don't, those common sawmill mechanics. But it is an unwritten law that people like Ken make the world work. You can feel that truth written on your heart. Like he said the day at Willy's—some things just are. Only the storm could stop Ken and now give him his just reprieve.

Right now Ken was scratching big Butch's ears. He then turned in his chair to adjust the dog's collar. James could see the profile of his face from the back of the room. He was smiling.

There is Dave. He is the messenger on race, which in today's world springs from the agendas of ignorant bureaucrats instead of nature. Dave, and the others here too, have exposed the lies and hypocrisy of all those great champions of the diversity religion. How many proponents of diversity would consider hiring one of these people here to increase so-called diversity? The people who preach such ideas probably wouldn't even consider lowering themselves to talk to such supposedly unenlightened folk, despite what they could bring to the table. Yet, the truth is, a man's ideas, background, family and personal life makes him diverse in his own way. Of course, the diversity devotees would never consider so many variables of diversity, to treat each man as an individual would be admitting their idiotic ideas are just that, as Dave had said.

But Dave is just one person, one person who makes sense. The sad fact is the diversity religion that holds group identity paramount and seeks to tell history from the standpoint of victimized group narratives is the ruling ethos of the country. The country's original ideals founded on natural law and the idea that each man is an individual before the eyes of God have passed into history themselves. Until now, there was no hope of renewal, but the storm has changed everything.

Look at Larry over there, the religious pariah of the community. Yes, he was possessed with fanatical religious fervor. However, if one looks past the appearance, one finds a man with legitimate concerns and powerful ideas. I think Larry is right when he says God rests in everyone's heart, and each man has the free will to accept or reject his grace. Also, Larry does have a point when he says so many problems are because people turn away from that truth within them.

There are individuals amongst us who walk a fine line between genius and madness. In a dying society those who make the most sense sometimes stand in the dim corners on the outskirts of the civilized world. Perhaps he was saner than most. However, Larry felt no desire to change what he saw in the world. He had essentially committed suicide.

He saw Ann, Ray, the Larson's, Isaac, Meg, Penny, Kyle, Willy and Nancy. *Like Sisyphus doomed by the Gods to forever push the terrible rock up the hill only to see it roll back down before the moment of triumph, these proud people had defied the Gods of modernity and took stoic joys in the struggles itself. They had, willing or not, introduced me to a new way of looking at the world, life even. They have taught me self-reliance, the value of tradition, common sense and, indirectly, faith in a power beyond myself. They introduced me to hunting, inviting me to participate in the reality of nature and her laws. I was estranged from the truth, but now I see the animals not as economic units to be manipulated but messengers from above who sustain life through their sacrifice.*

Finally, he looked at Nicole. *She'd get attention and praise if she flew an airplane, became a CEO or played some sport. If she does the right thing and takes responsibility, she is ignored. I hope in some small way I've influenced her and freed her from the expectations of this system. I am grateful I've met her. I think now, perhaps, a marriage can work if natural roles are fulfilled. There is hope if one can see through the emptiness and sexual obsessions of modernity and see the truth, the truth revealed by her.*

So there they were. Each and every one had played a specific role in the transformation of James Norris. In his ostensibly routine conversations with these people, James had opened his ears and heart to their wisdom. These people took an ignorant representative of modern culture and transformed him into something extraordinary. And, in a small way, James acted on them as well. All were guides on James' journey, ancillary actors on this quest inward and away from the larger community of the Twin Cities. Taken together, their messages could be said to represent a worldview.

However, there was one person missing, the person who had more effect on James than all the others. He was the one who helped a young man discover his psychological center on a warm June night thirteen years ago, albeit James did not know it at the time.

"Shawn," he whispered to himself as memories rose up to the surface of consciousness. "He told me something that night. What did he say?"

Then in his mind, as if jealous of the time allotted to Shawn's memory, the old conflict reared its head yet again. *To stay or go.*

It was all too much. He needed time to think. This was a decision and task he must face alone, and those assembled here had already fulfilled their role. James looked at them one last time.

Outside, the sky had finally made good on its threat. Huge, wet spring-type snowflakes were falling softly toward earth. They were few in number but fell steadily, melting instantly on whatever they touched. James untied and mounted Blazer. Then man and beast disappeared into the shroud of snow.

James followed the Round Lake road to M and headed north as the snowflakes grew larger and more numerous. Blazer loped along, head down, as his master lost himself in thought, almost oblivious to the landscape.

Two miles down M, James passed a chunk of Sawyer County public land on the east side of the rode, clearly designated by a green and white sign. A narrow trail led off into the forest. He remembered Paul Larson saying that not too far in the woods was a small lake that was home to a fair share of crappies. James halted Blazer. He was in no hurry to get home.

The forest was hushed, completely silent. Here and there a few snowflakes clung to the low limbs of the fir and tamarack that lined the trail. James reached the lake in mere minutes.

It was a most beautiful little body of water, completely surrounded by balsam fir. Their bright green needles stood out gaily against the pale backdrop of the hardwoods. By virtue of the surrounding forest being public, there were no houses. James watched the flakes fall delicately across the frozen waters. Some of them now stuck to his orange stocking cap and flannel, and soon a cold dampness began to sink into his core and cause him to shiver.

"I want to stay," he said out loud. "But why do I feel this obligation?" Then he sat silent for a few moments as welcome thoughts of food, warmth and shelter, those necessities so often taken for granted, now took their rightful place. He turned Blazer and headed back toward M, looking over his shoulder at the idyllic lake.

It was when he passed Martin's that his gaze fell to the northeast, pulled toward the horizon by the dark fog that was drifting upward into the bleak sky. He stopped Blazer and took a closer look. It was not fog.

An ominous, threatening plume of smoke was billowing skyward like some industrial smokestack. It lingered for a while above the treetops before lazily drifting away to the south. James thought the origin of the smoke to be about a mile or two down the gravel road that led to the east past Martin's.

James kicked Blazer into a full sprint and turned down his road. He hung on for dear life up and down the hills and across the creek. The gray-black smoke filled up his entire view to the east, and he could smell the horrible, putrid odor of burning dreams. "No!" he screamed. "No, not this!"

He and Blazer flew up the snow-covered driveway as a red and orange glow reflected on his face, and an incredible heat melted away any remaining snowflakes on his body.

A most sickening sight met his eyes. The cabin was consumed in flame, which had spread to the garage as well. Fire had already done its most damaging work. Sounds of glass shattering in the inferno reverberated through the air, sounding like so many tortured souls of hell. The cabin roof had collapsed, and as James watched, one entire wall caved in, sending an army of sparks showering up to the heavens. Demonic tongues of flame lapped devilishly out toward James as if taking some wicked delight in their destruction of his home. All that remained would be ruins and ash.

Dazed, as if not believing the scene to be real, James hopped off Blazer.

"How?" he asked himself again and again.

But the reason for the catastrophe did not matter. The fact was that fate had intervened on James' behalf. His second anchor was cast off, reduced to rubble. No longer could he skirt his responsibilities. The hour had arrived, the trials were over and revelations must now follow. There was no more conflict.

Chapter 17
Revelations

The sun was setting in the west as James stumbled around the scene like some survivor of a nuclear blast. He would sometimes step too close to the inferno and recoil back from the intense heat. Blazer, however, seemed unaffected by the event and trotted out nonchalantly to rest in his field. On some level he knew when he would be needed again. James, unable to speak, looked toward the advancing darkness. It was now very clear where he must go. The time had come.

Overhead, a sliver of a moon was rising, casting a faint silver shadow across Mud Lake. James shivered in the twilight and walked to the edge of the pine plantation. As he crossed the field and the woods beyond, low clouds blanketed what little there was of a moon. Guided by an unseen hand that pulled him effortlessly through the dark, James ventured around the west side of the lake. Across its frozen water he gazed back at the place where his cabin once stood. Embers from the blaze glittered over the treetops. They cast the surrounding environs in an eerie light, like the glow of an enemy encampment beyond the walls of civilization.

James continued walking. He was sure of the way, knowing that the key to his existence lay ahead in the forest. The snow seeped into his boots and chilled his already wet feet as a whispering wind arose in this primal cathedral to sing a soft chorus. Soon he arrived at the break in the forest.

His eyes fell across the clearing to the place where the guardian spruce grew so tightly together. A slight fog emanated from the inner womb of that most sacred place. In a trance-like state, James crossed the clearing and stood outside the entrance. *Who am I?* he thought. It was time to find out. He swallowed hard and entered the grove.

The temperature in the grove was cooler than the surrounding forest, and James began to shiver even more violently as he walked silently through the guardians of the realm into a complete abyss of darkness. Then the tunnel opened into a small, circular clearing surrounded by an old growth stand of giant white pines. *Just like I remember.*

James stood still in the circle and looked skyward beyond the tops of the pines. "A sign," he whispered, "tell me there is something more than myself ... a reason. Please."

Nothing. No voices from the sky, no spectral canines, no Gods, no bolts of lightning, just the wind singing its proverbial song. James looked again at the white pines that now seemed to be mocking him, laughing at his naïve belief that there could possibly be a reason for his experience beyond what he personally assigns. Silence was the validation, ostensibly proving beyond any reasonable doubt the utter senselessness of all creation. The realm of myth, this mortal world and James' individual journey all meant nothing.

So—I am alone. All that has taken place means nothing. Now, resigned to his fate, James hung his head, crushed and deflated. The anticipation was gone; the hope extinguished. He began to exit the grove.

At first, James thought the noise was mere imagination, a longing personified into an inner song. He almost continued walking until, as if waking from a dream, he realized what it was, and it was real. He turned and ran back into the middle of the grove where the white pines waited.

It was a mournful, yet joyous all the same, solitary howl coming from the night itself. Nature herself was answering James, and in an instant James turned from dejection to rapture. The revelation was imminent.

Unlike the night of his youth, it was but one voice. But it was out there lurking in the forest, speaking directly to James, perhaps not revealing its exact location for there was one final act in the journey. However, now James understood the language. He understood the song. It was all clear.

Overhead, the clouds broke, and the moonlight from the sliver of the sun's lesser partner bathed the grove in a cool light, casting a spotlight on the circular stage where James stood.

The epiphany hit him like a thunderbolt. He dropped to his knees in instant recognition. The final connections were drawn; the foggy memories cleared. What had been buried by the mundane details of existence seemed to come alive and seize James. His throat tightened and breathing became difficult. And through the woods on the wings of the wind, the stories returned. In his mind James was transported back to a time when he was but a weak adolescent lost and injured at Shawn's cabin. The old man's voice now floated through the darkened woods. Whether it was mere memory or actual voice no longer mattered.

"It is said that Original Man and Wolf walked the Earth at the beginning of time and came to know all of her. In this journey they became very close to each other. They became like brothers, and in their closeness they realized that they were all part of the same creation. Then one day the Creator said to Man and Wolf, 'You are to separate your paths.'"

James held his hands skyward as Shawn's voice continued.

"So Fenris was bound ... or so they thought. But all things must end, James, and it is told that in the final battle, Ragnorak, between the Gods and the forces of evil, Fenris will rise again. First will come a terrible winter called Fimbulvetr. Snow will drive from all quarters; the sun will be of no use. Great wars, floods and famines will ravage the land,

and brothers will kill each other for gain. The whole surface of the Earth will tremble and mountains will crash down. All fetters and bonds will be snapped and severed. Fenris will break free. He will advance on the home of the Gods with wide-open mouth, his upper jaw against the sky, his lower jaw on the earth. His mouth would gape even wider if there were more room, and his nostrils will blaze with fire. The Gods will be destroyed in this final battle while two other terrible wolves, Skoll and Hati, will swallow the sun and moon. Then the sky will turn black, and the Earth will sink into the sea. The bright stars will vanish from the heavens, steam will rise up from the conflagration and a high flame will play against heaven itself. But a new world will arise, James, from the ashes of the old. The new world will be fair, eternally green. The sun will have borne a daughter to take her place. Two humans will have survived to continue on the race of man. From out of the destruction, out of the disorder and chaos, new life will emerge."

James gazed toward the moon, which continued to shine on him as he knelt on the ground with his arms stretched wide. The lone howl echoed through the night air, merging with Shawn's voice.

"You can learn a lot from these stories, James, for they sleep in you, in me, in everyone. They just need to be reawakened ... "

"A new world will come about, James. The wolf will return as sure as day follows night and death begets new life. Man has grown separate from his creator and the timeless laws of nature that are His will at work, just as he was separated from his brother, the wolf. Man has fallen from God's garden and sought to recreate the world in his own image. In the process, the truth found in the great myths has been forgotten, replaced by strip malls and the garbage pit of television. This is the cause of the troubles we see today, the troubles that haunt the diseased mind of modern man. But one day man will return to the truth. From what man falls from, man is destined to return in the end."

"The new world will be brought about by a hero, the one man who sees the world as it is. Fate will force him to go on a journey where he will retreat from the sick society and die to his self, only to be reborn in spirit. Then he will receive a revelation that will bring man back into accordance with Nature's God. He will return to society with his message to recreate the world anew, and the old, corrupt world will be destroyed. And this experience of the hero will be but a metaphor for the struggle and potential of all."

"What I have told you, James, is a symbolic separating and return to the ultimate truth embodied in the natural law. One wolf at the beginning and one wolf at the end. And those stories, James, those stories rest in you ... live them ... "

One story from the beginning of time, one from the end, and from the two will come the foundation of a new universal worldview, a worldview at one with what is symbolized in both. And Nature is not mere physics and chemistry and economic units. She is God's will at work.

"Return," James said aloud in a mere whisper as Shawn's voice disappeared into the night. "Return and bring with you what you have learned. It is I. I am the one ... the hero. Return."

James fell prostrate on the forest floor as once again high, thin clouds obscured the moon. Complete darkness descended upon the womb. To the west the larger community waited. James Norris the individual had ceased to exist.

Chapter 18
The Return

Sunday morning, a new day at the start of the new week, holding the hope and promise of fresh beginnings. The day awoke warm. A dense, sleepy fog, brought on by the rapidly melting snow, clung to the streets and homes of the metropolis. The great river was swelling, raging and gathering momentum on its southward journey. Skeleton survivors stumbled amidst the deserted buildings while families held hands on once-green soccer fields. They were all waiting, anticipating, as they looked toward the horizon in the ominous, grave air.

Far to the north and east, the man arose from his soft pine needle bed. The sun had yet to rise, and the world was perfectly still. And so the man began to walk, bursting forth from the shroud of vapor that encased the mouth of the womb. He glided effortlessly, ghost-like across the adjoining clearing. His shirt was torn into rags, and his pants were ripped and covered in mud. An unkempt beard grew unchecked across his weathered, hard face. His eyes were sunken, and his entire appearance seemed otherworldly and distant, like a person returning from a voyage to a faraway, strange land.

His walk had purpose. The old feeling of longing was gone, and he was now sure of his destination. Soon a small frozen lake broke the surrounding forest. He squatted by its thawed edge and splashed the cold water onto his face. The water felt refreshing, and it helped to clean away some of his grime. Then his eyes fell across the lake to its south side and a neat stand of red pine. A weak wisp of smoke remained suspended over their tops. He set off in that direction.

Possessed by his purpose, he traversed the west shore of the lake and came to the spot where a creek forged a deep ravine. For a moment he stopped there to look at the decrepit jumble of boards built into a tree.

He left that special place and arrived at a field. The stand of red pine and the charred remains of a house lay beyond its eastern border. A black horse trotted silently up behind him. The man placed his hand on the horse's mane and patted his head. The horse was uneasy and excited. He too knew his role and his master's ultimate destination. The man looked at the horse and then toward the west, still dark, as the sun was just now rising to his back above the uppermost tops of the trees on the eastern shore of the lake.

He spoke. "All this time I believed that society constructed who I am. Nothing had meaning except for what I personally subscribed. By living this lie, I have separated myself from Nature and estranged myself from Him whose will works thru her laws. I have fallen, fallen from that union. But now I will return. For all this time I have been but living … I have been living the fall."

The man climbed onto the horse as the sun's first, premature rays shone over his shoulder. The animal started out in full gallop without being coaxed; he knew where they now must go. They rode toward the west and came out on a paved country road before turning south. The horses and cows loafing in the pasture only a mile down the road turned their eyes toward the rider. Some walked to the fence by the road to get a better view of the scene like spectators at a road race. Further on, they passed a tavern that was shielded by red pines on the tranquil lake where sleek reeds of grass broke through their icy prison.

The man rode through the empty town of Loretta and turned

west on US Highway 70. The horse charged ahead, its awesome heart-lung machine running at peak efficiency. The man kept his gaze forward, confident and purposeful, with not even a hint of hesitation. Nothing could stop him.

On and on the pair rode, past the lakes, past the small towns, never stopping. In fact, the man and horse were picking up speed the further they went, pushed onward by a force beyond themselves and out of their control. A critical mass was forming in the very air, and there would be no slowing down until the mission was done. The sun was now overhead in all its midday brilliance, and the air was stagnant yet filled with the sweet aroma of spring. Temperatures rose into the seventies.

He passed a church, its graveyard now free of snow and covered in white trillium flowers pushing through the dead leaves. Uphill and downhill he rode, across the gentle undulations of the countryside. At one point, giant maple trees on either side of the road grew together at their uppermost branches, creating the appearance of a tunnel. White, cotton candy-like wisps of dandelion seeds wafted through the air. Some fell en masse in front of the man before being swept up in the rush of air as he passed. They then fell softly once again down to Earth, consciously seeking that patch of ground to start life anew and fulfill the designs bestowed upon them from above.

The man and horse continued to grow in the strength that can only come from purpose. They rode past the flooded agricultural fields, hollow gas stations, abandoned lake homes, extinct main streets and empty-shelved stores, all tombstones of a dying age.

Sweat now ran down the man's face, dripping waterfall-like onto the horse's head and mane as the temperatures shot into the low eighties. The roads were empty. What once was the domain of the automobile now belonged to him and the flesh and blood of his steed. At this point, the man crossed a bridge with a hellish river underneath it foaming and writhing like an angry, tormented serpent. He then turned to the southwest and rode through the towns that bordered a chain of lakes and all seemed to grow together. The threat of being swallowed up by the ever-expanding metropolis to the south had passed, but so too had the life of the villages themselves. They sat vacant and quiet, and not a living soul greeted the man. Instead they ran. But they could not escape the message. So the man continued onward. He had left the forest and rode through the pastoral. The great cities were drawing near.

It was now late afternoon, the time of day in the spring when great, destructive storms flare up and do their necessary work of restoring order. The multitudes were all out now, embracing each other and looking skyward. They stood on once neatly manicured golf course-like lawns surrounded by their lifeless, impotent vehicles. A slight breeze was building in the north, growing stronger. Soon it would be a wind. It gently fanned the hair of those assembled, the surviving ambassadors of civilization, caught up in the drama of what had happened and what was about to happen. They looked to the north as their stoic faces awakened in recognition of the mammoth, monstrous thunderheads now assembling on the horizon.

The man was bearing down on the great metropolis, that once great shining abstraction from nature, riding past all the barren, soulless housing developments that once grew like a cancer upon the land. Soon he left the two-lane highway and set his direction due south. The horse was running with a mad, possessed desire, eager for its date with destiny.

Countryside was giving way bit by bit to the empty car lots, dead multiplexes, vacant strip-malls and doomed chain stores, all testaments to the fleeting and the ephemeral. Driven by forces beyond all comprehension, beyond the hubris of man and his desire to rework the truth, the man and horse veered off the roadside and onto a broad plain that ran adjacent to it. A small woodlot lay on its south side and beyond it was yet another field. They were cornfields at one point in time, right here on the edge of suburbia. Now they lay fallow, sandwiched between desolate housing developments, and a soft bed of flowering clover covered their expanse amidst the melting snow.

The man and beast charged across the first field heading due south and entered the wood lot. The man ducked the branches of the oaks and maples, which were intent on sending him to the ground, with great skill. And as he broke the threshold of the wood and exploded forward across the second field, one's eyes were lifted from the man to the sky above him. For here a vast, great black wall cloud was growing and gathering in power and significance, stretching from the eastern to the western horizon, engulfing the entire world. No man in history had witnessed such a gathering of storms in intensity and ferocity. Immense, grotesque in size, destructive in their intent, they moved swiftly to the south, driven by the stagnant humid air and formed of the very energy that some believed had dissipated and died. The great storms and horrible winter that had covered the Earth and paralyzed her great cities were but precursors to the greatest event of all. The destroyer of worlds had now arrived, incarnate in thunderhead and the man.

Colossal cyclones reached upwards of 80,000 feet in the atmosphere, and their awesome power and scope created powerful downdrafts that sucked down a great fury of super-cooled air. Terrible winds raged toward earth at speeds of 200 miles per hour, sweeping cascades of power, behind the advancing horseman. All the Earth had been subject to was but a prelude to this.

The wall cloud roared toward the metropolis, unstoppable. It filled the entire northern horizon with its angry, undulating thunderheads. Lightning cut swaths across the advancing front, which illuminated the sky in momentary flashes of intense light and showed to all the reach of the storm clouds into heaven itself. Eyes and gazes turned to face the advancing destroyer. Then as if all humanity were connected unconsciously, the screams began. Trapped out in the open, the multitudes were powerless against it, and the pride of man that sought to rework nature and her laws was now exposed as the lie it was. The tempest traveled at great speed and howled overhead, consuming the man-made skyline of the cities. There was no escape.

Then the winds hit, obliterating all in their path, shattering entire city blocks. Houses, buildings and all of man's creations were leveled and blown away as so many matchsticks in an inferno. Row after row of vinyl-sided cookie-cutter houses sitting in the once expanding suburbs were shattered in seconds. Skyscrapers fell as their multiple windows blasted out in thunderous applause at the return. The very Earth herself shook, bringing all mankind to its knees in terrified recognition. All would pass away.

Rains came swiftly, a deluge, at a rate of ten inches per hour, mixed with sleet and hail. The swelling waters of the great rivers reached a critical threshold. They could be held back no longer. A wall of water, tsunami of the Mississippi, bore down on the great cities. Bridges were snapped from their moorings and carried away in the torrent, along with a terrifying mass of man's creations. The noise was terrible and drowned out the screams of the multitudes. All this was in preparation for the return, the return of the hero and his message, which would bring about the union with that from which man had fallen.

The man rode toward the vortex of destruction illuminated before him by lightning strikes. He had arrived and fulfilled his mission, his individual self no longer distinguishable from the multitudes. Soon there would be no separation. And he disappeared into the whirlwind of doom, consumed by the power of nature, like all men.

Almost as soon as it started, the great thunderheads passed and continued their advance to the south with a call that rhythmically echoed against the horizon. The winds died to a mere whisper. Rain continued to fall, but gently now. It washed the concrete and rubble and cleansed what was left of the shattered world, pattering monotone upon the desolate streets as the great front thundered softly every so often in the distance. A silence fell over the earth. The sky grew as dark as night, yet no stars or moon broke the gloom. Temperatures fell as a dank cold settled across the land.

Chapter 19
The Fall Redeemed

Ash is the fundamental element upon which all new worlds must be built. The city shells still stood, but mere ghosts. From a God's-eye view, the expansion had stopped; no longer was the organism marching eastward or westward. The necessity of growth was not a necessity after all. There were no longer any computers to log on to, diversity meetings to sit through or crowded parking lots set amidst the soccer fields. The trivia was wiped away, and the slate was now clean. At least, that was the impression from the elevated view, and, this time, there was no ambiguity. The Twin Cities were no New York City, yet they shared its fate, as did all civilization. The results had been the same.

The sun had yet to rise, but a soft, inviting light was slowly revealing the skeleton buildings and shot-blasted hulks of office buildings. A gentle wind tossed the flotsam of a former age across the once wide, clean streets. Fog clung stubbornly to the land, enveloping the remains. Wide cracks split the surface of the blacktop and concrete as green life achieved its spiritual élan. In the quiet suburbs, where at one time peace and contentment ruled the day, Nature undid the Johnson's worldly monuments. Once neatly manicured lawns grew together with the hated weeds, and grasses reached waist-height. Greenery filled the joints of the sidewalks and crept over the foundations of the devastated homes. The scene had never been content, only in appearance.

The man appeared first at the site of the former mall. Now all that remained of the monument was its rusting steel frame, and its inner soul was now laid bare for all to see, revealing what was there all the time— nothing. The man walked through the silent corridors, and his footsteps echoed down the empty halls. The sanitized world of underwater was forced to live up to its lie, for now the corpses of its former occupants were rotting silently, their bodies returning to the Earth. The process had been hid from view in the former age, but now the truth had returned. He left this temple built in honor of the deceased God of consumption and walked toward the northeast.

He was silhouetted against the remains of a ragged skyline, and his body was naked to the elements, like a newborn babe. Yet his walk had intent, and his steely gaze was fixed ahead. He traveled the once traffic-choked artery into the capital city. He was now not so much a man as mankind, and all of creation looked down on this new dawn.

The façade of the capital was unkempt and crumbling down to the lawn below. Once grand statements inscribed on the walls no longer held significance, mere platitudes they were, ultimately subject to powers beyond weak words. Marble blocks were sunk into the soft grass, which grew unchecked and wild. This pillar was destroyed. From this point a long avenue led to a place of higher elevation in the west, a hill overlooking the shattered city. The man knew where he must go.

He turned toward the once-thriving pulse of commercial buildings. The economic pillar was no more. Their hollow shadow remains looked down on him as a slight breeze whistled through their empty bowls and told of a splendid reunion. Loose grimy papers blew across the darkened, empty streets. Hulks of cars lined the sidewalks, and city parks, those once-pathetic remnants of Nature's God, broke their boundaries and spilled out into the new day, devouring the former world's abstractions in the process with the sheer will of consciousness.

The great center of entertainment, now stripped of its exterior, was shown to be as fleeting as the events once housed in its confines. The man turned to look across the placid river. A bridge that once crossed its flow was gone, and the warehouses, graveyard smokestacks and power plants along its shore were forever silenced. Overhead a few geese honked joyously as they announced the return. The man smiled as he looked skyward toward his companions.

Upon circling the entertainment arena, he arrived at a grand street leading toward that highest of hills. Behind him the first rays of the sun were just beginning to pierce the veil of earth. But they were growing stronger by the minute. They illuminated the path in front of him, and he set his eyes on the splendid heights. And there it still stood. Above everything else, above the economic pillar, above the governmental pillar, it stood, a permanent reminder of man's ultimate destiny.

The cathedral was still there. Its windows were forever shattered and part of its great copper dome had crumbled to the earth. However, though it may have been bowed, it was far from broken. The sun was now reflecting off what was left of the dome and bathing the weathered, pockmarked granite of its exterior with inviting tones and textures. The man gazed toward its presence. What was once the scene of James Norris' greatest personal failure would now be the scene of man's ultimate triumph.

His eyes never wavered. Behind him the sun grew ever warmer and more powerful, and the entire Earth woke in hope and recognition. He followed the grand street past the parking lots and over the freeway beyond before coming to a steep hill of grass with a dirt path leading to the steps in front of the cathedral.

A chorus was building in the very air, more powerful than a thousand armies, hailing the man and filling the world with joyous sound. The voices were singing a welcoming refrain, once known so well, and now the sun was reflecting so brightly off the cathedral it appeared to be the source of light itself, shining like a second sun. The man had to squint in its brilliance. Closer and closer he drew to his final destination as the chorus echoed off the very heavens. Finally, he reached the crest of the hill.

Their eyes met instantly, locking in recognition, as the man took two steps toward the wolf and stopped. Its fur was radiant in the risen sun. It was the completion of a going and returning, a reconnection with what lay behind all reality, timeless and eternal. From chaos comes order, and as man strays from his creator, he inevitably returns to his creator.

So a new world was born out of the ashes of the old, encompassing the entire globe. From its various cultures, now sprang a unifying ethos. Man may forsake the natural law, but the natural law will not forsake man. Such is the ultimate journey and search of humanity, and the possibility of all individuals if they can discern the truth through the noise of modernity and lift themselves to a timeless truth beyond their egos, centering and rooting themselves in the process.

The man's eyes never left his brother, and joy swept over his being. From a God's eye-view, the sun spread her rays across the silent metropolis with an intensity never imagined. The man and the wolf held fast on the hill, alone in the once-humming abstraction, as the view fanned upwards and outwards to the awakening day. All of creation danced, for order had been restored. There was no more separation, and the fall was redeemed. Mankind had come full circle.